A FRIEND IN SPIRIT

AN ALICIA FRIEND INVESTIGATION

A. D. DAVIES

ISBN: 978-1999978112

NOVELS BY A. D. DAVIES

Adam Park Thrillers:

The Dead and the Missing

A Desperate Paradise

The Shadows of Empty men

Night at the George Washington Diner

Master the Flame

Alicia Friend Investigations:

His First His Second

In Black In White

With Courage With Fear

A Friend in Spirit

Standalone:

Three Years Dead

Rite to Justice

The Sublime Freedom

Co-Authored:

Project Return Fire — with Joe Dinicola

For my friends Jan and Bern for everything you have done and all you continue to do

CHAPTER ONE

NOTHING SAID *winter in England* quite like a dull evening and an impromptu sleet shower, soggy clumps of half-frozen water plopping out of the sky just when you least expect it. And no one expected it tonight. As soon as Karen Krasowski closed the minicab door and placed her hand in Jerzy's, they both hunched against the sudden downpour and jogged over the road to The Roundhay pub, the blackboard sign reading *"Demelza will look into your soul—give it a go! What do you have to lose?"*

Karen hadn't wanted to come, at least not to this slightly rundown destination, but she and Jerzy managed so few date nights, it wasn't worth a debate. When her dad offered to watch the kids and let the pair out for a two-weeks-late anniversary celebration, Jerzy suggested the place they met on that New Year's Eve so long ago, a pub frequented by a younger breed of drinkers, what some might deem "rough," but what the folk where Karen was from would consider "too posh." The fact there was a psychic performing appeared to animate Jerzy, the idea of a laugh to be had, fun to poke at the poor saps throwing their money at a con artist.

What have you got to lose?

Well, for one thing, Karen had lost a nice meal in a grownup restaurant. Yet she could not sniff at an evening with her husband, no matter how silly the setting. And now she was cold and damp, so simply making it inside a musty, warm pub made up for the inconvenience of sharing it with a person who, at best, would freak out the audience a little or, at worst, take advantage of the gullible and bereaved.

Maybe she was reading too much into it.

"First round's on me," Karen said. "Find a table. Somewhere quiet."

Her husband kissed her cheek and smiled. "Pint of Guinness, love."

The epitome of "tall, dark, and handsome," Jerzy smacked her on the bum before heading for a place by the window, pointing and giving her the thumbs up. His Polish accent rubbed shoulders with his adopted Yorkshire home, interspersing local terms even when speaking Polish. Karen once heard him on the phone to his mother, exchanging small talk like, "I'm fine, thanks. How are you?" which in his native tongue was, "Czukę się dobrze, dzięki. Jak się masz?" But he'd added the English word *love* to the end. In fact, he took to the word quite quickly, once he understood that in Yorkshire, "I'm fine, thanks, love," is not a misogynistic phrase liable to get a person fired if used in the workplace.

In *most* workplaces, anyway. Certainly not in the gym that employed Karen or Golden Start, the employment agency founded and run by her husband. Heck, even in the twenty-first century, "love" is often used in a non-gay way between men—something those outside the county find extremely weird; a cultural touchstone that those born within God's Own Country were keen to cling on to against a world addicted to political correctness.

The barmaid handed over the change, and Karen said, "Cheers, love," collected her gin and elderflower tonic and Jerzy's Guinness, then made her way through the mostly young crowd, larger groups preferring to stand than take a table. One area was cordoned off, a wide set of three stairs going up to a separate part of the pub, not officially a stage, but a place they put acts on even fifteen years ago when Karen was a regular.

Once seated with her husband, he gave her one of his smiles that sprung to life so enthusiastically that his hair flopped to one side and his eyes virtually sparkled.

"Remember that night?" he said. "You were drinking Blastaways."

"Blastaways." Karen didn't even try to stop the smile as she reminisced. What a nasty drink that was: Diamond White—the sort of high strength cider favoured by homeless winos—mixed with an orange alcoholic drink, the name of which evaded her at that moment. "I was drunk."

"A beautiful drunk princess." Jerzy's grin didn't falter. "And this place, it has changed. But did you feel it when we came in?"

"Feel what?"

"The energy. Like it remembered us."

Karen laughed and sipped her gin. It wasn't quite up to the standard of the bars she tended to frequent these days, but it was passable. "Are we eating here?"

"I do not think they serve much food tonight. Sandwiches, snacks. But wouldn't it be better to get a kebab on the way home? Or a greasy pizza?"

Karen placed her drink down and patted his hand, forcing a serious expression. "Jerzy, I love that you want to replay our *amazing* romance, but there are two things I am not doing

3

tonight. One is shagging you against the wall out back like we did on New Year's Eve—"

"Oh, yes, another wonderful night." His eyes took on a dreamy quality for a moment.

"And the other thing I will not do is put a disgusting slice of pizza, dripping with fat in my mouth."

"No kebab?"

"Even worse."

"Oh." His eyes switched to the ceiling then back to her. "Chinky?"

Meaning Chinese food. Considered a bit racist in some circles, but just a reference to food for Jerzy.

Karen said, "Maybe. But I'm not waiting until closing time. Two drinks here, then we go."

"Deal. Okay. Looks like it's starting."

"You really want to see this?"

He shrugged. "Might be fun. Come on."

They moved from their table, congregating in the audience consisting of three round tables near the front that seated four at each, with most people standing in a loose crescent behind them.

Although Jerzy pretended he was doing nothing more than having a laugh, he'd never outright declared any firm beliefs, beyond a casual acquaintance with Christianity. Karen had met his extended family, including mad aunts who saw the spirits of their dead husbands and mothers, and his grandma who "sensed truth" when it suited her. In other words, if she thought you were lying, she used her "powers" to prove it. According to Jerzy's mother, it worked a treat when she was a girl, but less so now. Jerzy never argued with his relatives about their sight or clair-voyance, but tonight was the first time that Karen confirmed he'd been sucked into it; her husband was a true believer. She thought it cute that he felt the need to hide it from her.

And yes, she *would* have taken the piss. Still might.

Following a flat, toneless intro by a scouser who appeared to be in charge, Demelza tottered out to ripples of applause, which grew as the people seated at the front whooped like they were Americans greeting Ellen or Oprah. It was only polite. The star of the show was in her fifties and wore a tight white dress, clinging to her curves, contrasting against her black hair and lipstick, thick mascara, and painted nails. Painted *black,* naturally. She sported no jewellery except an opal pendant around her neck, the size of an espresso saucer, and set in what looked like cheap white gold. Not an over-the-top Gypsy stereotype, but certainly a well thought out look.

"Good evening." It was her own deep voice that hushed the applause and cheers. No PA system necessary in a place so small. She sounded almost male, but no amount of surgery would grant someone born a man *that* figure. Bosoms and hips, but not fat or unhealthy. Body types were features Karen increasingly noticed since she shed her own weight and qualified as a personal trainer. And Demelza knew how to use her assets, swaying as she observed the crowd. "You are all here to witness something special, yes? Something … unbelievable?"

Murmurs commenced. The odd, "Yeah," and "Uh-huh."

"That doesn't sound especially energetic." Demelza expressed concern via closed eyes. "I'm sorry, but doorways to the next world require *life*. They demand those who wish to learn from souls who have passed on, who should be at peace, to give back a little of themselves. I need to *feel* your responses, not just hear them. Hit me with your best answer. Do you wish to witness proof of the next life?"

This time, the tables at the front led with affirmative replies, shouting, "yes," and, "woo," and other such enthusiasm. Karen guessed they were regular patrons of Demelza's and knew the routine, acted as cheerleaders to help gee up the energy. It didn't take long for it to work, as the volume rose considerably until Demelza appealed for quiet.

"Better," she said, spinning sharply, and striding away from the audience.

In a whisper, Karen said, "I wonder what she'd do if people didn't give it some like that. Walk off and say she can't open the door?"

Jerzy gave her another smile, but this one didn't sparkle, or move his hair, and he returned his gaze to the stage almost immediately.

"I would like a volunteer to start things off." Demelza swept her hand to the audience. No one volunteered. "Perhaps one of my friends at the front here?"

The table-bound patrons huddled together, giggling like teenage girls at a concert for one lip syncing boyband or another. Karen stood on tiptoes to get a proper look, finding two men and ten women of varying ages seemingly discussing the situation amongst themselves.

Demelza puffed out an exaggerated sigh. "When you're ready. Last orders is only four hours away."

Finally, a lady of around forty was persuaded to the stage to yet more cheers from the front, which transformed into light clapping from the others. Demelza held the lady's hand and asked her name. Before the woman could answer, Demelza turned to the audience and said, "Yes, yes, I should know her name, but the spirits like to make me look a fool sometimes."

A few laughs rose, but little more than that.

The woman was called Audrey, and Demelza explained to the room that she'd seen Audrey several times at her shows, while Audrey said she'd been to a few but never dared get read.

"Why?" Demelza asked her.

"Because I wasn't really a believer the first time I went," Audrey replied. "But I feel a bit braver now I know Demelza is the real deal."

"You still seem nervous."

"I'm just … a bit worried about what I might learn."

Demelza reassured her that her lost family would not invoke hurt or suffering and asked her to go with it. To trust in Demelza's powers. It sounded scripted, and badly so, but Karen figured that was par for the course with psychics.

It was a straightforward routine without bells and whistles. No smoke machine or fireworks, no spooky music. Demelza simply tuned in to the next world, located Audrey's dead husband, and described Audrey's current life, her fears for the future, and the advice her husband would like her to heed. The advice mostly involved living life to the fullest, moving on but not forgetting, and generally being happy.

Meanwhile, Karen had commenced a second gin and elderflower, and after Audrey retreated to applause and unenthusiastic cheering, she said to Jerzy, "That's the sort of generic crap you get from a horoscope."

Jerzy frowned at her as if not understanding. "But Demelza knew things she couldn't possibly—"

"It's a plant." Karen sensed the room go quiet and still, realizing too late that she'd spoken louder than she intended.

Demelza herself was staring right at her. "A plant?"

Karen's cheeks warmed. Given the chance she'd have folded herself up and crawled into her own shoe. "I … I just meant … I meant …" She looked to Jerzy for assistance.

He said, "My wife is not a believer. Maybe later, she believes."

"Maybe." Demelza raised a single eyebrow. "But the best way to believe is to experience, is it not?"

Karen shook her head. "Oh, no, really. I'm fine. We're grabbing a Chinese right after I finish this." She held up her drink as punctuation. "Nearly done. I'm sorry. Carry on."

But Demelza just watched Karen. "I think it is only fair you give me a chance to disprove your accusation."

"My ... no, it wasn't an accusation, not really." Except it was. "I just meant…"

"What? You see, these people are here not only for a show, but for hope. You wish to take that hope away?"

Karen fought the urge to leave, but Jerzy had nudged her twice. He would never *literally* push her up there, but he was certainly urging her to go.

"Is that what you want?" Demelza pressed the point.

Karen had one last card to play. "What if I come up and you get everything wrong?"

"If I am willing to take that chance, what have *you* got to lose? Except your scepticism?"

"It is a good point," Jerzy whispered in her ear.

Karen had no comeback. "Fine. But I'm not playing along if you screw it up."

The crowd parted, the cheers louder this time, more genuine, and it was only when she was on the upper level and Demelza said, "Yes, you may need a stiff drink shortly," that Karen noticed she'd brought her large gin with her. She smiled, blushing, and placed it on one of the tables. She caught Jerzy's grin as he filmed the show on his phone, and returned to Demelza.

"Now." The psychic took both Karen's hands and held herself stiffly in front of her. Chin up. Those thickly lined eyes wide. "Hmmm. A lot of resistance here. Why don't we loosen things up with your name?"

"You don't know it?" Karen said.

"As I mentioned before, the spirits don't always furnish me with a birth certificate."

"I'm Karen."

"Karen. And you are married."

"My wedding ring is a bit of a giveaway."

Demelza ignored the chuckles. "Married to someone from far away?"

"His accent is a *lot* of a giveaway."

A few laughs then, but Demelza continued. "Children. Three ... no, two children."

"The visions a bit blurry, are they?"

Unperturbed by more amused murmurs, Demelza closed her eyes a moment, before opening them with a smile. "You have a nice house, Karen."

"I'm wearing designer labels. It's a fair guess."

"Not like the house you grew up in, though."

Karen's face remained stone, a reaction that drew an "Ooh," or two.

Demelza said, "No, that wasn't an easy upbringing, was it? Not quite outright poverty, but you still struggled at school. Bullying. You were..." Her face looked strained. "You *were* the bully. In trouble a lot."

Karen tugged her hand lightly, now too uncomfortable to willingly continue, but too worried about looking idiotic if she fled. She just returned Demelza's stare.

"But you worked hard in the end," the woman said. "With help from your parents, you knuckled down. Eventually. Some hard, adult years too, but you finally settled down. Got serious. You pay your fair share of the bills for the house, but you are not extravagant. Like you did not grow up in poverty, nor are you outright rich now."

It was all true. Spot on, in fact.

"Your parents are a source of strength. Yes?"

"Yes," Karen said.

"Your father..." She studied Karen, closed her eyes again. When she opened them, there were tears. "He was devastated by the loss of your mother."

Karen's heart fluttered in her chest. She swallowed. "What about her?"

"She is at peace, but you've never really believed it."

"No..." Then Karen happened to glance at Jerzy.

He was still filming her, watching, a faint smile on his lips. Not sharing her emotions, her discomfort, but happy at what he was seeing.

"It's a setup," Karen said.

The audience emitted a series of "ooh"s, this time of anticipation rather than amusement.

"Jerzy," she said, glaring his way. "This is not funny."

Jerzy looked up from his phone, his mouth an "O", his eyes innocent and round. Still filming. "This is not me."

"Wait," Demelza said.

Karen yanked her arm away and focused on her husband. "You were *way* too insistent on coming here. I should've known something was up. What'd you do? Feed her my life story? For the entertainment of *these* pricks?" At the audience's intake of breath, she said, "No offence. I didn't mean anyone in particular." Back to Jerzy. "How *dare* you?"

"Karen, please," Demelza said.

"No." Karen rounded on the performer. "I came here for a nice evening with my husband. Our anniversary. But you con these people into thinking you have some sort of special power, and all the time you're conspiring with relatives for ... for what? A laugh?"

"Karen, please, listen."

"I will not listen. I'll—"

"It's your father."

Karen halted mid-rant. Her fingers and toes went cold, and she completely forgot about her husband. There was no crowd, no pub, no groupies. Just her and Demelza locked eye-to-eye. "What about him?"

"He's not here, is he." Demelza placed a hand on Karen's shoulder, firm and sure.

"He's looking after my boys tonight."

"He is hurt, Karen. Go. Go now. Right now."

Karen snapped back to the moment, not caring if people laughed at her. Not caring if it was all for nothing. Even if Jerzy confessed right now that it was all a joke, *a laugh*, she'd still need to check on her dad. She just ran from the makeshift stage, snatched her coat from Jerzy, and was outside in seconds, calling her dad's mobile.

No ringing. Just voicemail.

She was about to try the house phone, but this was stupid. There was no problem. No point in waking up the boys.

Still, now the idea was in her head…

Barely aware of the falling sleet, she waved at a minicab as it dropped someone off outside, dashed forward, and stopped the door from closing.

"Sorry, love," the driver said, "you have to phone up and book or you're not insured. Not allowed to just pick you up."

She flopped in the passenger seat, only now aware of tears streaming down her cheeks. As Jerzy caught up and opened the back door, she said, "Please help me. I need to get home. I think something awful has happened to my dad."

The driver took a moment to consider it, plainly weighing up the possibility that this was a council sting or a genuine emergency. It took a few seconds for his humanity to kick in properly, at which point he told her he'd take her home, but only as a *favour*, not a fare. He radioed in that he was off the clock for the next fifteen minutes, and took her home to the Shadwell area, where he accepted a £10 "tip" from Jerzy.

Karen ran up the drive of the simple detached house, small in comparison to many in the area but, as Demelza surmised, a vast improvement on her childhood home. She flung open the door, calling for her dad.

And that's when Karen's life imploded all around her.

CHAPTER TWO

ALICIA FRIEND COULD NOT BELIEVE it had only been a year since she first met Donald Murphy, and as he held three-month-old Stacey in the crook of his arm, singing *You Are My Sunshine* softly to her, she could no longer picture her life without him. In part, because he was good with the baby. His voice resonated deep but soft, which paused Stacey's screaming and appeared to be something she was demanding when not hungry or filthy in the nappy department. But more than that, Alicia hoped they'd be friends even without him getting all broody on her.

Perhaps it was their recent shared experiences. The way men and women were flung into romantic or even purely sexual relationships due to a surge of adrenaline and the ability to relate to an extreme situation the way no one else could. Not that there ever anything sexual between her and Murphy.

Eww, no. Just thinking about it made Alicia want to whip herself with a belt.

First, there was the age gap, Alicia in her early thirties, with Murphy well into his fifth decade. Not that that had stopped Alicia from falling for the older man who fathered her child, but Murphy *looked* and *acted* his age. His grey moustache. His deep-set eyes. But more than the age issue, was the height difference. Alicia barely scraped five feet, while Murphy towered at six-and-a-half; the physical side would be deeply impractical. Finally, he was often hard work. Although he accepted and appeared to like Alicia most of the time, there was still the odd occasion when she caught him sighing as her true self broke through, like whenever she called him "Donny."

"That's some singing voice, Uncle Donny," Alicia said.

Murphy paused in his final *You Are My Sunshine* verse to smile. He kept his gaze on Stacey's tiny face as he replied softly, "If you have to call me uncle, do you think you could manage to call me Donald?"

"No. It's Donny. I can't compromise to Donald. Makes you sound old. I can drop it as far as Don, but that's my final offer."

Murphy sniffed and tilted his head a little more, Stacey's eyes following the movement. "I can live with Don."

He returned to his song, and Alicia left him to it, backing out of the room and wondering how long to leave it before tapping him up to babysit for a full evening.

Murphy hadn't particularly liked her when they first met, especially her "true self," but Alicia saw through his grumpy demeanour and engaged him in what she thought of as *the five stages of Alicia*. First, he experienced disbelief, the notion that someone as perky and unrestrained as her could possibly be considered one of the best in the field of criminal psychology. He, like many police officers, was shocked at her upbeat personality, which led to the second stage: irritation. Detective Inspector Donald Murphy let his irritation at her shine through, but as her insights and forward momentum in the case of a kidnap-murderer increased, he started to see how great she was. From there it was a quick hop to stage three: acceptance of her ability and of the fact her brain came hand in hand with her perkiness. Stage four was reliance, where he found himself automatically seeking her input, and stage five was collaboration, where he actively wanted Alicia around.

It always went that way. Five stages. And that was how she liked it.

Now Murphy was a detective chief inspector, in part thanks to that first case, then his loan to the FBI in the spring, and the oddball serial killer back in Blighty over the summer, all of which Alicia lent a hand in. By all accounts he was doing well. He deserved it.

When Murphy emerged from the nursery, Alicia whisper-called him through to the kitchen down the hall. She still shared the place with Roberta, who had been as supportive as any friend could be, but recently had been spending more time out with people she worked with than she ever used to in the BS days.

BS meaning *Before Stacey*.

"Thank you," Alicia said, producing a wine bottle from the fridge. "Drink?"

"Driving." Murphy patted his pocket.

"You know, you're a better uncle than my actual brothers."

Murphy's moustache moved awkwardly, trying to deflect the compliment. "I'm sure they're very happy to be uncles."

"Oh, how very diplomatic. No, they've been by a few times. Not as often as my bloody mother, but they've met their niece."

"How is Dot?"

"I've told you before, Murphy, I'm not setting you up with my mum."

Murphy's mouth remained open a second. "I'm not—"

"I'm dicking with you. Relax."

He exhaled through his nose, nodding in relief. "I know. But look … she's helped you a lot. I'm happy to help too. When I can. But, you know…"

"Being a big bad detective chief inspector. I know. It's a lot of hours." She poured herself a small glass of pinot grigio. Normally, she was a red wine gal, but her taste buds had changed recently. "You sure I can't tempt you?"

"Can you drink that when you're breastfeeding?"

Alicia squeezed one boob, now a D-cup rather than the B she'd been before. "No, I'm pretty full at the moment. When she wakes up at one in the morning, I'll empty this into her. The wine will have been digested by then."

When Alicia glanced up, Murphy was staring at the open fridge.

She said, "For a guy who never had kids, you're pretty good with her."

"My ex-wife had nieces and nephews. Which means I had nieces and nephews."

"She's actually your ex now?" Alicia placed the wine bottle back in the fridge.

Murphy switched attention back to her as she closed the door. "Not officially. But if I think of her that way, it's easier."

Alicia tried to get Murphy to open up about him and Paula only once since he first explained what happened between them, but he always deflected. Now he was cornered, she figured she could try. "I can recommend someone, you know. If you didn't want it to be over."

Murphy reacted the way he usually did: a grateful smile, a sigh, and, "I've tried all that. She won't."

Alicia wanted to offer to speak with Paula herself, and might have bulldozed her way into things if it was not quite as personal a situation, but she promised never to do that.

And she'd keep that promise. Until Murphy changed his mind.

"Mind if I make a cuppa?" he asked.

"Of course not." Alicia moved around the small space, checked the kettle contained water, and turned it on.

Murphy opened the fridge and took out a bottle of milk. Pause. Plucked a ragged cabbage from a shelf. "That's a lot of cabbage." He must have spotted the other two as well. "Still getting some odd cravings? I thought they went away."

"No, that's not for eating." She pulled her loose T-shirt aside at the shoulder, flashing the top of her bra where a cabbage leaf poked out. A shrug as she snapped the neckline back in place. "My nipples are raw. Turns out some of granny's remedies actually do work better than modern creams or ointments."

Murphy stared at the cabbage in his hand as if it were a grenade and placed it carefully back on the shelf.

As the kettle boiled, and Alicia dropped a teabag in a mug, Murphy held still a long moment.

"Is this only a social call?" Alicia asked, deducing something from his stiff upper body. "Or is there something else?"

"I do have a couple of work things to discuss."

"Sure."

She made the tea and led him through to the living room, poking her head in on the sleeping Stacey as she went. She couldn't help but take in the sight of the creature that brought her equal amounts of happiness and crippling despair. They said it would be special. That the love a person feels for their child is all-consuming, without compromise. At times like this, Alicia felt it, for real. At others … less so.

She hadn't spoken about that with anyone, preferring to wait for that uncompromising, unfettered, pure love to kick in. Perhaps, after almost four months of motherhood swamping what she thought of as her "true self", it was time to speak her concerns aloud.

Not tonight, though.

She sat in the armchair, allowing Murphy the more spacious couch, and they nursed their respective drinks.

"Okay," Alicia said. "Go for it."

"Keeping-in-touch days." Murphy seemed happy to chat about that, checking his work phone which likely contained the notes emailed to him. "You're employed by the Serious Crime Agency out of Wakefield, but you applied to spend a week at Sheerton instead."

"I wanted to pick up where I left off. The SCA is more computer-based now, and Bobby Stevenson is doing a fantastic job filling in for me. Besides, I'd like to be involved in proper police work for a while."

"And you understand a keeping-in-touch phase means you'll definitely be returning to work sometime in the next six months?"

"I intend to come back by the spring. We're still mid-January, so I figured middle of the month gives me until the end of Feb or mid-March on maternity leave. I'll do another week at the beginning of March too."

Murphy flicked off his phone with a satisfied swipe and sat back to drink his tea.

Alicia sipped her wine. "What's the other thing?"

Murphy placed his cup on the coffee table. Reached in his jacket and retrieved a plastic bag containing four open envelopes. "The letters."

"Ah, yeah. The letters."

Murphy dropped the bag of correspondence beside his cup. "You can't send evidence in, asking for favours like that. It needs to be logged as an official complaint, and then we can do the analysis you requested."

"But that might mean an arrest."

"It might."

"And she needs help, not arresting."

"You're sure it's her?"

"About ninety percent sure, yes." Alicia sipped, but the wine now tasted sour. She put the glass down. "They're addressed as if they're from Richard. Not threats, just insisting he isn't a bad man, that I am so two-faced, hiding the baby from Katie."

"But no implicit threats."

"No."

"You just want a forensic analysis done. In the current system. Where everything gets a case file and no search on any database can be performed without logging it into evidence?"

Alicia didn't really know why she thought she'd get away with it. She'd managed to get stuff done on the quiet in the past, but recent years had seen police abuse of power fall under more scrutiny than ever before, so every little gesture and step was monitored.

"Sorry," she said. "I didn't get anyone in trouble, did I?"

Murphy's phone rang. He checked the number and said he had to answer. Alicia said it was fine and Murphy stepped out of the room. She eavesdropped of course, but then she was pretty sure Murphy knew she would.

"Right," Murphy said to whoever was calling. "Cordon off the scene if you haven't already. Get witness statements from the daughter and husband while it's still fresh. I'll notify Sheerton and have them allocate an FLO. You get Lemmy to call SOCOs down there ASAP, give them my name as authority."

It was acronym central tonight.

FLO—family liaison officer.

SOCOs—the scene of crime officers, or "forensics" to the layperson.

ASAP—well, that one's obvious.

"I'll be with you in thirty minutes. Any other witnesses need chasing up?" A pause. In his frowny voice, Murphy said, "Sorry, did you say a psychic?" Another pause. More listening. A sigh. "Fine. I'll assess it myself and allocate an SIO when I look at who's available."

He hung up and returned to Alicia. "We'll have to finish this later."

"Murder?" Alicia said.

"Yeah. Gruesome one too, by the sound of it."

"Did the psychic do it?"

"Witness. Or … something. Seems the psychic warned the victim's daughter her dad was in trouble. When the daughter got home, her dad's innards were all over the damn place, and his throat's cut. Two kids asleep upstairs."

"Yeah, that does sound gruesome." Alicia kept talking, but at the same time tried to picture the scene. "What's the psychic's name?"

"Look, let the letters thing drop or make an official complaint. And I'll get HR to contact you about the keeping-in-touch day."

As he left the flat, Alicia called after him, "Okay, thanks. And have fun tonight. Psychics are the *best* witnesses."

But as the door closed, and Stacey began to grumble next door, her brain dropped into a faster gear, and the last thing she wanted to do right now was give nourishment to a child.

CHAPTER THREE

WALKING out through the lobby of Alicia's small block of flats, Murphy put in a call to Sergeant Ball and got a gruff-sounding answer from someone who *wasn't* Sergeant Ball. Murphy asked who it was and got the reply, "PC Grogan. Call me Lemmy, though, everyone does."

Murphy hastened his pace and pushed out into the night, thankful the sleet and rain had eased. "Hello, *PC Grogan*. This is Detective Chief Inspector Murphy."

"Cool. What can I do for ya, sir?"

"First, you can remember you're talking to a detective chief inspector." Murphy bipped the alarm on his BMW 5-series. "Second, you can put Sergeant Ball on the phone."

"Ah, sorry ... sir. He's kind of tied up. Comforting a widow."

"Widow? I understood the victim was already a widower and was found at his daughter's home?"

"Oh, right. Just a sec." Although PC Grogan—Lemmy—must have placed his hand over the mouthpiece due to the smothered sound, Murphy still heard him call to Ball, asking who the woman was to the victim. He came back to the phone fully. "Yep. I mean, yes, sir. You're right. Daughter."

Murphy reached the car, opened the door, and dropped straight into his seat behind the wheel. "Can you tell me what happened? More than I got from the dispatcher?"

"Sure, I can!" He sounded excited.

"Out of earshot of any family members?"

"Right, right." Now PC Grogan's voice lowered to a stage whisper.

"You're a probationary constable, I assume?"

"Right. Yeah, two weeks in. Sergeant Ball is awesome."

Even a probationary constable should, by the time he graduates training, understand how to present a professional attitude. And after two weeks shadowing an experienced sergeant—heck, after a *day*—he should not be acting like an excitable fanboy meeting his favourite sci-fi actor. If Murphy didn't know how much drugs testing went on, he'd swear the lad was high. Murphy made a mental note to have a chat with Sergeant Ball about more than the case.

The background changed as Lemmy Grogan moved location, outside by the sound of it. "Okay, so, a woman gets a message from beyond the grave saying her dad's been killed. She goes home, finds her dad on the floor, guts all over, throat cut—"

"A message from beyond the grave." Murphy inhaled deeply and let it out slowly, focusing on facts rather than the probie's manner. "Is that what she said?"

"Yeah, she was at this psychic reading, and the medium, she says, 'You must get home! Your dad's been killed!' or something like that."

"'Something like that'?" Murphy said.

"Yeah, sorry, the sarge has the exact wording."

"What's the victim's name?"

"Bicklesthwaite. Dean Bicklesthwaite. Great Yorkie name, huh?"

"Wonderful. Very traditional." Murphy rubbed his temples with the thumb and forefinger of one hand. "Any actual witnesses?"

"Someone's down at the pub asking about the psychic witness, so just the son-in-law and daughter so far. But we're not getting much out of her. Mrs. Krasowski, that is. She's a Brit, but married a Pole, and—"

"Okay, thanks, I think I've got enough." Murphy nearly said, "I've had all I can bear," but figured knocking the probie's confidence wouldn't help his development. "I have the address. I'll be on scene in…" He checked his satnav as he typed. The address zoomed in and returned an approximate travel time. "Thirty-five minutes."

"Make it forty-five!" said a woman's voice from the back seat.

Murphy's heart shot into his throat and he dropped his phone. No need to turn around. It was Alicia, somehow having got in without him noticing, so he simply bent down, picked up the phone, and said to Lemmy Grogan, "Forty minutes."

He hung up.

Alicia said, "Haggling now. How very worldly."

Murphy turned his whole body. His long, unwieldy left leg bent at the knee to the side and his arm curled over the head-rest. "Oh, Jesus, do you have to?"

"What? It's perfectly natural."

Murphy looked away from the breastfeeding woman but maintained his body shape now he'd manoeuvred his way into it. "How did you get in?"

"I was sneaky. And I kept a fob from the last time you let

me drive. So, listen, about my keeping-in-touch days. I want them to start tonight."

"Tonight? I can't do that."

"Sure you can. You're the boss. I'll grab Stacey's car seat and—"

"I'm not the boss. Chief Superintendent Harris is the boss. Actually, he's *my* boss. *Your* boss is still Chief Super Paulson, and she doesn't like you very much."

"She likes me fine. I even had a card from her. And a onesie for Stacey."

Murphy didn't argue. As far as he could tell, Paulson had disliked Alicia intently, Alicia's perky attitude never making the positive impression it did on most people. That Alicia disagreed with her during their previous case together, and was proven right, seemed to thaw that dislike, but only partially. Paulson was also present at the birth of Alicia's daughter, the circumstances too complicated for Murphy to recall properly, but perhaps that had given Paulson access to one of the latter Stages of Alicia.

"Okay, fine," Alicia said. "But you can let me have a look at the scene. Sounds violent. And the psychic angle is too cute—*ow!*"

"Are you okay?"

"She's like a bloody vacuum cleaner some days." Alicia shifted Stacey a little, altering her angle and eliciting a slurp. "Oops. Might have got a bit of milk on your seat. You cool with that?"

Murphy groaned internally, almost wishing PC Grogan would call back. "I have wet wipes, thanks."

The suckling resumed, and Alicia said, "Right, so it's decided? My mum'll watch Stacey and—"

"It isn't a command issue. I *literally* can't get the paperwork through tonight."

With her free hand, Alicia fed several papers through the gap to him. "It's okay, I'd already completed most of it."

"I thought this was all online now."

"I completed it online but have to print it out. Just needs your signature. Probably the Chief too. Can you wake him up?"

Murphy accepted the papers but dropped them on the passenger seat. "Even with the signature, it needs HR to file it and rubber stamp it. No paperwork, no insurance. No insurance, no work. I'm sorry, but you must stay away from the scene tonight, or it could jeopardise a conviction in the future. Clear?"

No answer. Murphy turned to look at her and she appeared downcast but accepting.

"I want to do this first thing."

Murphy couldn't hide his smile at the thought of having Alicia on this case. "We'll rush it through. No one wants to deny a new mum the ability to return to work. Too afraid they'll sue."

Alicia affected a super-serious face. "And I will. I'll sue all of you scumbags violating my rights."

"*Tomorrow*, Alicia. Not before."

"Fine, I'll call off the Mom-bot. But I'll be in your office at ten. So, put your admin hat on first thing, okay?"

"Tomorrow's my day off."

"Not anymore." Alicia unlatched Stacey from her nipple and did herself up, then positioned the baby at her shoulder for a burp. "The Alicia express is back in town, and it gets to deal with a psychic. I've never dealt with a psychic before."

"Yeah," Murphy said, repositioning himself behind the wheel and starting the engine. "And I'm betting the psychic's never dealt with anything quite like you, either."

CHAPTER FOUR

THE KRASOWSKI FAMILY lived on a main road in the heart of a suburb called Shadwell. Murphy knew it well as an upper-middle-class place where the residents sometimes came across as full-on aristocracy. However, there were a couple of estates, safely ensconced across a dual carriageway, which brought the median income bracket down to slightly above average. The Krasowskis lived firmly in the more comfortable section, though. Not quite the Millionaires' Row a couple of minutes' drive away; the street was wide enough for four lanes but was only two, with grass verges and twenty-yard driveways instead of the fifty-yarders over the way. The house boasted five bedrooms, a double garage, a broad front lawn, and a door large enough to carry a sofa through without any awkward manoeuvring; a nice, expensive property, yet well-short of a mansion.

Murphy half expected to find Alicia already at the house when he rolled up to the kerb behind the white police van and the patrol car being used to block off the section of road immediately in front of the scene. He was immediately suspicious of a short, feminine-shaped, scene of crime officer in white paper-like coveralls and hood, overshoes in hand. But as the SOCO turned around Murphy was satisfied it was DC Fleming, a newer addition to the forensic team. Fleming, and her two taller colleagues, had not been admitted beyond the crime scene tape, as civilians were still present, hence they held their bootees rather than slipping them on over their shoes. It wouldn't be long before they ditched the coveralls and returned to the warmth of their van.

Between Murphy receiving the call and his arrival, a crime scene manager had been appointed and had set up the cordon at the most convenient point, which was from the property's border out to the middle of the road, then strung between the two police cars with their flashing blues.

But that's all Murphy approved of.

Detective Sergeant Bhancho was a British-Asian woman, only four or five inches shorter than Murphy's lanky frame, but she was bulky with it, a gym enthusiast and kick boxer. She was ordering two uniformed officers around, ensuring they kept half a dozen neighbours back, out rubbernecking in this wide, affluent street. He presented his ID even though they knew each other by sight, and signed her rubber housed iPad to confirm he was entering the crime scene.

"I assume I'm the highest rank at the moment?"

"Yes, sir," Bhancho said.

"Okay, then flag me as SIO until I appoint someone else."

She did something on her tablet computer, murmuring, "Senior Investigating Officer ... DCI Donald Murphy ... done!"

"Good. Now, I need this cordon extending the whole of the street. Nothing gets in or out. The killer could be a neighbour, could still be on scene watching, or might have parked a bit further away than directly outside. Clear?"

Bhancho stepped back, her mouth open but silent.

"I'll take that as a yes. The neighbours? I assume they know what's gone on? At least the highlights?"

"Umm, yes, sir."

"Push them back, get them inside their homes. They're obedient types. Tell them we're searching the street in case the perpetrators are still here. Use the word 'perp' if you like. People *love* American TV shows. Let them know we'll be by to take their statement and make them understand they're the most important person here. Even a sound they might have heard could crack the case. They'll love that even more. Once that's done, set the SOCOs to work on the outer part of the property, so the bereaved inside can see we're doing something." On a roll, Murphy allowed time for Bhancho to only nod. "And *please* tell me someone senior to Sergeant Ball is running things inside."

Bhancho paused. "Sergeant Ball is running things inside."

Murphy let out a sigh. Softened his frown into a neutral expression. "Apart from the points I mentioned, good job. Now crack on."

"Yes, sir." Bhancho spun away and activated her radio as Murphy tramped up the path.

In the drive were two cars, a plug-in hybrid Hyundai Ioniq and a Mitsubishi Outlander, another wired to a socket seemingly fitted bespoke for both vehicles. He paused at the door to don paper overshoes and plastic gloves, nodded to Detective Constable Lahore who lurked just inside, also with paper bootees and gloves, then entered.

Like many of these newer homes for the relatively wealthy, this had been designed for "flow." A wide hall with a cloakroom to the right, then stairs, then a smaller lounge to the left. The passage ran along the stairs to an office under the staircase, a kitchen up ahead, and a "best" lounge off to the left adjoining the smaller one. It was in the best lounge where the body lay.

Murphy passed this room without a glance.

In the wide, well-lit kitchen, a stocky, uniformed male officer with jet-black hair boiled a kettle on a kitchen island, four cups ready beside. He noticed Murphy enter and gave a salute.

"You only salute the senior brass, son," Murphy said.

"Oh." The lad dropped his arm.

"PC Grogan, I assume."

"Yeah, yeah, that's me. Lemmy." The young man rushed around the island and extended a hand. At least it was gloved.

Murphy shook it out of politeness. "The victim's family is still here?"

"Yes, sir. On the veranda."

Murphy took in the officer's appearance. His jet-black hair made his face seem pale, and the point of a tattoo poked out from his collar, and… "Is that eyeliner?"

"What?" The kid touched the skin below his eye. "Oh, yeah, my band did a gig just before I came on shift."

"Right." Murphy tried not to rue the slackening of the Police Service's standards, although he was pretty sure eyeliner was still not allowed. He'd look it up later. "Don't make any more tea. Don't touch anything else until the SOCOs give the all clear."

Murphy walked away without another glance, heading for a pair of sliding doors that gave way to a conservatory equipped with deep sofas and armchairs, a coffee table, and a 50" TV with a games console attached. Two crescent-shaped leather pods were stacked in one corner, which Murphy recognised as "gamer chairs", whatever they were. Glorified beanbags, he guessed.

Sergeant Ball was sat in an armchair, while the man

Murphy assumed was Jerzy Krasowski hugged a woman he assumed was Karen Krasowski, the victim's daughter, on the sofa. The two boys, aged seven and four, snuggled between them: the elder, Harry, in plain pyjamas, with Lincoln sporting something called Paw Patrol, puppies decked out in paramilitary equipment or something.

Murphy didn't linger. "Hello."

Everyone looked up.

Ball stood. "Sir." He'd shaved his beard and he looked a little slimmer than before.

"I'm Detective Chief Inspector Murphy. I am very sorry for your loss tonight."

The adults nodded sagely. They'd be hearing that a lot over the coming days and weeks.

"I will be in overall charge of the investigation, but I will be appointing a detective to take the lead. You will be allocated a family liaison officer, who is currently en route."

"Who's FLO on this?" Ball asked.

Murphy concentrated on the couple. "A lady called Jackie Osbourne will ensure you are kept up to speed with the investigation, and deal with any issues that are sure to arise. She'll manage the degree of press contact, which can be zero if you choose, as well as arranging bereavement councillors or legal advice."

"Legal advice?" Jerzy said. "Why we need a lawyer?"

"Not like that, sir. There will be matters like who is the executor of your father-in-law's remains, monetary concerns, property—"

"It's okay," Karen said. "Let him finish. I'd like to see Dad again." She gazed up with tear-streaked eyes. "Can I?"

Murphy glanced to Ball, who swiped the air with both hands—*no way.*

"I'm sorry, Mrs. Krasowski," Murphy said, "but we need to

preserve the crime scene. You'll be afforded some time with him when we've processed the room and moved him to a more … suitable place for viewing."

Karen nodded, sniffed, and laid her face on top of her eldest son's head. Both boys just stared.

Murphy raised his chin. "Sergeant Ball, a word?"

He stepped out into the kitchen where Lemmy tidied up the cups. "Do not wash up."

"No sir."

"Wait with the family, please."

Lemmy gave a half-salute before remembering it wasn't necessary and rushed to the adjoining room.

Murphy pulled the sliding door and ushered Ball out into the corridor, stopping by the room with the corpse. "Explain your night."

Sergeant Ball had been *Detective Sergeant* Ball until the summer just gone. He'd been stuck at the rank of detective sergeant for ten years, which meant he was required to spend a long spell back in uniform as a sergeant, a requirement known as tenure, intended to put the detective back in touch with grassroots policing. Although his actual rank never altered, it was considered a demotion by many. He would have to work hard to get back out of uniform, and for once, that's what he seemed to be doing.

"We got the call at 22:30," Ball said. "Blue lighted it here. Came straight in, found Mrs. Krasowski in tears in the kitchen with her husband holding her. We … made some noise, which I think woke the kids."

"Kids were asleep the whole time?"

Ball nodded. "Yes. The dad brought them into the kitchen, and once I checked on the body, I called in the murder and then we searched the house. Garden too. We found no intruders."

"But you kept the family on site."

"It was a choice between having them sit in a police car for an hour or keeping them where they requested to wait. I know, I know. I should have removed them ASAP, but ... they're crushed. Donald, you know me. I got years of experience here. Lemmy and me, we'd already been all over the place, so we weren't adding anything more for the SOCOs, and neighbours were already taking an interest. This wasn't the best call forensically, but for the family…"

Murphy didn't like it, but Ball was right. He'd have to find a sensible way of writing it up so no one got in trouble, but he'd done it before, and he'd be surprised if he never did it again.

"The body?"

"Sure." Ball opened the door but didn't enter. He wasn't wearing overshoes.

Murphy stepped inside, walking over deep, white carpet. The furniture was cream leather, a huge TV on the wall over a real fireplace, which looked neat but would take some getting used to, neck cricked up constantly. A wide bay window looked out over a garden about a quarter the size of a football pitch, currently floodlit.

"The halogens?" Murphy asked.

"Motion activated usually," Ball said. "I turned them on manually. For the search. And to put off anyone returning. Or, y'know, lookie-lous."

"Right." It was a good call. Murphy had known neighbours come right up to a window to get a glimpse of a body or the wreckage left by a burglary. "And the curtains?"

"Curtains?"

"Who opened them?"

Ball thought for a moment. "No one. They were already open."

"You're sure Motorhead Boy didn't touch them?"

"He never came in here. Only me. Didn't want anyone else in the room but needed to be sure the victim was deceased."

Murphy was again surprised. As a detective, Ball had been sloppy and complacent, relying on his instinct for a crime to drive him to the evidence. He had an odd, disarming way with people, too, which Murphy attributed to his slovenly appearance, making him non-threatening rather than slick, the effect being a lucky break rather than working hard on his manner. Still, despite the slack crime scene initially, Murphy saw the mistakes were more of a humanising quality than a lack of diligence.

That said, even from a distance, it seemed unlikely the victim could be anything other than deceased.

The body lay on its back, slashed through clothing, skin, fat, and muscle. A gaping wound in the man's abdomen had let intestines spill, and further deep cuts higher up suggested the killer attacked in a frenzy. Without moving the body, Murphy attempted to view the hands and forearms. Although both were coated in blood, there were clearly visible cuts where the blade had sliced across limbs as Dean Bicklesthwaite attempted to fight off his attacker.

There was little doubt the stomach wound was a fatal one, yet the neck had also been cut through, deeply, severing the windpipe as well as both carotids.

"Someone knows his way around a knife," Murphy said.

"Why beat him like that, too?" Ball asked, although it was obviously rhetorical.

Dean's face was a mess, his mouth a jumble of broken teeth, lying open in a final, silent scream. His eyes were swollen, one almost shut, and the nose was angled to one side. Like the body, it was difficult to see where the lion's share of blood originated, but nor did it seem to matter. It was a difficult death. Perhaps it was a blessing Alicia was finagling her way onto the case.

With his gut clenched against any emotional outburst, such as cursing the person or persons who committed such an act while children slept upstairs, Murphy stood and returned to the door. "Nasty."

"His daughter came in, saw the body, and ran. Called us. I asked the usual questions, *sensitively*, but she is certain enough to give a statement that this is Dean Bicklesthwaite, her father. We'll do DNA to be sure because … you know." He opened his hand and gestured at the corpse's face. "Lemmy's keen to learn that side of it, so I'll let him do it under supervision. Chain of evidence will be signed off."

Murphy didn't like the sound of it, but he'd ensure Fleming was the supervisor on that, not Ball. "Anything taken?"

"The safe was opened in the office under the stairs. The family is still too upset for a full inventory, but the son-in-law says it looks like a bit of jewellery, what he called a small amount of cash, but is about ten grand between you and me, and there were documents in there too, but he'll check fully later."

"Jewellery worth much?"

"About twenty."

"Grand?"

"Yes."

"Okay." Murphy again looked back at the body. "It's not a massive heist, but it's a lot of cash for people who've got nothing."

"Yeah, I'm thinking they broke in, maybe at random, or maybe waited until the owners were out. Roughed up the vic for the combination, and he spilled the digits. Then when they were getting away, he went all macho, and it became a fight."

Murphy observed the blood smears on the walls, the furniture, and a pattern over the carpet. "Some spatter. But looking at the wound on the neck, he must have almost bled out before they went there. With the carotid cut like that there'd be spray."

Ball nodded agreement.

"Not much had been wrecked." Murphy cast his gesture at the furniture.

"Room's so neat and sparse there isn't much *to* wreck," Ball said.

"Could be." Murphy observed some more, unable to add much at this stage.

Ball coughed to snatch Murphy's attention. "Listen, Donald, I'm thinking maybe I could run with this?"

Murphy eyed him sternly. "You?"

"I know I shouldn't be allowed, with this being a murder and everything, but I've made adjustments. I'm keeping up with the youngsters and the old hands who like uniform work. Look at me." Ball opened his jacket. "Seriously, put me in."

Murphy took him in, assessed him the way he did the corpse: definitely slimmer, at least a stone lighter than in the summer when Murphy last worked with him, maybe even twenty pounds; he looked well. Must've been laying off the booze, too, if not entirely then certainly a reduction. His hair was neat, clean, and … styled? That was new for a man Murphy first encountered with a ketchup stain on a section of shirt stretched over a beer gut.

"I'm sorry," Murphy said. "If we were really short, I'd consider it, but I have to justify taking a uniform off rota."

Ball stared at his feet.

"It's more to do with the shortfall on the street," Murphy said. "I'm sure you've done a great job in uniform, and I think you made the right calls here, even if some of them weren't technically protocol. But look, I'll make Cleaver my deputy SIO, and I'll make sure you and … whatsisname, Lemmy? You guys'll get first dibs on overtime, and I'll make sure any contributions go on your file. Fair?"

Ball nodded, accepting the decision. "Thanks, Don."

"And don't call me Don around your probie."

The pair shared a smile, Ball happy for the breadcrumb back toward the detective pool.

A newcomer interrupted and said "hi" to DCI Murphy, nodded to Ball, and introduced herself as Jackie Osbourne, the appointed FLO who would sort out the family's accommodation and other needs for the night and into the next day. Ball volunteered to show her to the bereaved family, leaving Murphy to take out his phone and thumb through his contacts for Detective Inspector Cleaver. The man answered after four rings, the fog of tiredness slurring his voice. He was on call, so it was only to be expected.

"Hi, sorry for waking you," Murphy said. "But I need you as my deputy on a murder. It's a bad one. Come on out, I'll get you up to speed, and we can get started at ten a.m."

"No problem," Cleaver said in a sleep-disturbed mumble.

"Oh, and bonus. Guess who's coming back to work for a few days on this?"

CHAPTER FIVE

THERE WERE many things Alicia liked about her reputation. One of them, which she learned through Murphy, was that people saw her as "bouncy." Because of her choice to be a happy, cheery copper rather than a ball-breaking, win-at-all-costs grumpy female sleuth like those women on TV police shows, it added certain micro-expressions and ticks that gave the impression of her bobbing along even when she was sitting still. It was the personality she held over from her student days, of carefree times, her "true self" that she wished to hold on to, fearful the darkness of her profession might consume her. At times, it was hard to beat back the bad stuff, but love is stronger than hate, so her true self won through.

Mostly.

One thing that threatened to unlock Grumpy-Bum-Alicia and inflict her upon the world was fatigue. When a case gnawed her down, or a physical threat pummelled her, or those times a cooing four-month-old infant decided the previous night was the time to metamorphose into an owl. A hooting, screeching owl whose propensity to store up its wind into a painful bubble was surpassed only by its ability to defecate just as it was nodding off. Then it would get hungry thirty minutes later, and the feeding would set in motion the wind cycle again.

In short, Alicia managed approximately two hours of sleep the previous night, and only one of those hours was continuous.

Worse, though, was her wonderful roommate, Robbie, who'd come home a little late and had to work today. They passed one another around 7:30 a.m. as they muddled through breakfast cereals and coffee, but even Robbie—the only person Alicia knew who was bouncier than herself—trudged about as if carrying a sack of wet clay on her back. They'd made a pact before Stacey came along that the baby would not interfere with their friendship; if it got too hard, Alicia would move out, even if it meant shacking up with the Dot-Bot for a couple of months.

Alicia's mum did not appreciate being called the Dot-Bot, especially considering the amount of support she'd given so far, meaning Alicia restrained herself around her. Particularly on days like today, when she was doing her such a huge favour at short notice. Once she dropped Stacey off, along with everything she'd need to survive an apocalyptic event, Alicia dragged herself to Sheerton station in the east end of Leeds, about thirty minutes out of the city centre.

It was the first time she'd left Stacey for a full day. Dot watched her many times for a couple of hours, and Robbie had stayed home when Alicia needed to go shopping or just take a breather. She'd expected more guilt leaving the baby for longer. Going out, working, neglecting her. But this was worse. Feeling little more than a flutter of concern generated a sense of emptiness in her, leaving her searching for an emotion —guilt—that she could not locate.

Was there something wrong with her?

Alicia signed in, and Murphy himself presented her with the hardcopy of the information HR emailed to her around 9:30 a.m., and she was granted a full pass, warrant card to serve as her police ID, and log on details for the databases and various systems employed by West Yorkshire Police. She wasn't allocated a laptop yet, but she could share.

Murphy had requisitioned a lockable room away from the open-plan squad room to serve as their base for this investigation, an office mothballed the previous month when its division merged with Leeds Central as part of a range of cutbacks. It was unusual for a single murder to result in the detectives being equipped with the luxury of their own space, but a strong suggestion had come down from the Police and Crime Commissioner himself, Graham Rhapshaw—a friend of Alicia's, and the first senior officer to really understand her brilliance. He was also a man so confident of winning the post of PCC, largely due to the incumbent's dreadful record, that he resigned his position as one of the top dogs in the West Yorkshire Police in order to run. Now in a civilian post, Graham had no real authority over the execution of an investigation, but the top brass were happy about his appointment and wanted to keep him sweet, so when he *strongly suggested* something, the suggestion tended to get followed.

Although Alicia genuinely respected the man, she—like Murphy—accepted the isolated room with a touch of suspicion. Perhaps Graham was now tainted in the officers' eyes by holding elected position rather than one attained through merit bestowed by his peers. Politics always crept in.

Still, it was an advantage. And it contained four large desks set up for laptops or desktop computers, along with whiteboards on which the freshly slimline Detective Inspector Cleaver was currently sticking gory photos of the crime and making notes by each one. The woman who, it seemed to

Alicia, was quickly becoming Cleaver's protégé, watched on, scribbling in a lined pad.

Detective Constable Rebecca Ndlove was an ambitious young woman in her late twenties, her skin even darker than Robbie's, and she rarely smiled. She'd done good work in the summer, and Alicia was keen to see what she might bring now.

Cleaver beamed to see Alicia and wandered over for a hug. His smart new beard tickled her ear as they disengaged. He made small talk about the baby and Alicia deflected with congratulations about his promotion from DS, earned largely off the back of their previous case together. He'd been a bit of a knob when they met last year, jokey and somewhat sexist in his humour, but he had cleaned up his act and was now in a relationship with Murphy's computer-expert niece, which Alicia also enquired about.

"Things are good," Cleaver said, and left it at that before returning to his post.

Ndlove settled for a nod and a, "Ma'am."

It was here that Murphy brought Alicia fully up to speed with all they'd gathered so far, issuing her an iPad where she could read the statements as Murphy talked through them. She could also access the West Yorkshire Police intranet on the device. Murphy kept it brief, telling her to catch the details as soon as they had them. Updates were coming in regularly.

"Dean *Bicklesthwaite*?" Alicia said at the point she learned the victim's name. "Could he be any more Yorkshire?"

Murphy sighed and broke off his commentary. "And before you ask, no he was not wearing a flat cap, nor did he own a whippet."

"Why, DCI Murphy, I would never make light of a murder like that."

"Never?"

"Almost never. Not in this case." She didn't add that she was too knackered. "Carry on."

Murphy did so, and as he started on details of the wound, Sergeant Ball entered alongside a constable Alicia had never seen before with coffees for everyone. Ball, who'd lost even more weight than Cleaver, introduced his probationary charge as Lemmy Grogan.

"Alright, love," the new youngster said. "They told me a new girl was here and might need this."

"How sweet." Alicia accepted the coffee. With a lovely smile, she added, "And I adore the 'girl' line too. You'll go far in this business, young man."

"Nice." He winked, clicked his tongue, and flicked a finger-gun Alicia's way before taking Ndlove her coffee too. No wink for her.

Ball explained they'd just come off shift but were hanging around to make sure the detectives had everything they needed. Which didn't sound like something Ball would do at all.

What's happening to the world?

Was it too egotistical to think Alicia might have been a catalyst for the pair's change in attitude? It wouldn't be the first time, but she'd not been around for a while.

"Let's hear the rest," she said.

Murphy completed his recital of the official steps to date, and as if on cue another pair entered the room. What had seemed spacious at first was soon filling up. This time it was Graham Rhapshaw with a familiar-looking, grey-haired woman in a pantsuit carrying a handbag by Chanel.

All stood and uttered various greetings around the word "Sir." Except Alicia who beamed and waved and said, "Oh, hi, Graham."

In his dress uniform, which was unnecessary for his

current role, but he liked to wear it anyway, Graham nodded to her. "DS Friend. Good to see you back in the thick of it."

"Only for a week," Murphy said. "She'll be back properly in the spring."

Graham dodged straight to referring to his companion. "For those of you who don't know her, please say hello to Marissa Poole, MP."

Alicia recognised the name, and now connected it to the face.

Poole was elected as the member of parliament for Leeds North at the last election, relieving the incumbent of his seat. A former judge, she'd spent more time in London than York-shire, and was currently battling accusations of inconsistent sentencing while serving on the bench. The press had decided it was a good story, and were raking over many of her cases, starting with her handing down more severe sentences for black youths than white. With a wider examination the accu-sation expanded into social cleansing rather than racist profil-ing. In other words, those criminals from a poorer background —and black youths were predominantly less affluent—got harsher sentences than those with good jobs or whose parents had money, despite the crimes being comparable in nature. It wasn't anything illegal, but since she was plainly pitching for a government cabinet role in the future, her character needed to survive such scrutiny.

"This was a grisly murder that happened in Marissa's constituency," Graham said. "I would like to keep her in the loop as much as possible."

"I promise I won't be a burden," Poole said. "Just nudge me out of the way if I hinder you too much."

All very pleasant.

"Have you briefed Mrs. Poole?" Murphy asked.

"Everything you sent me first thing," Graham said. "I'd like to see where you're taking this."

Murphy did a great job of not looking like a guy who wanted to slap the big boss man. "I'm SIO, but I need to stay across a number of ongoing cases. DI Cleaver is my deputy and will be running things on the ground."

Graham Rhapshaw faced Cleaver but did not need to say anything to convey what he wanted.

Cleaver used the photo board to highlight his own corner of the case. Since Graham knew everything Alicia did, they moved on to the actual investigation. "Victim was identified on scene by his daughter, Karen. Due to the violence and damage inflicted we'll also do a DNA swab to confirm."

"It would be cruel to put her through it again," Marissa Poole commented.

"You're welcome," Lemmy said, a proud expression suggesting it was a big deal that he'd been allowed to take the swab.

"Once the lab guys get to it, we'll confirm it in the file," Cleaver went on smoothly, referencing a photo taken from the DVLA database. "This is Jerzy Krasowski, Karen's husband, and the victim's son-in-law. I met him before coming in today, introduced myself through Jackie—the FLO assigned to them. We got them in a Premier Inn, but once we've done with Dean Bicklesthwaite's own house, Jerzy is hiring a van to move them temporarily into that home."

"We need to treat Dean's house as a crime scene too?" Lemmy asked, yawning.

Ndlove shifted from her chair to stand beside Cleaver. "We need to see if anything was disturbed there. Any sign of a break in. Any threats. We'll take his electronic equipment too, PCs and the like."

"Why, though? If—"

"Young man," Poole said. "I don't know what kind of briefings you are used to, but when someone senior to you is talking, you listen."

Silence.

Alicia broke it. "It's not a bad thing to ask questions. He's still learning."

Lemmy shot Alicia another wink and smiled his appreciation. "Right."

Poole's mouth pinched, and Murphy stepped in. "It's to see if the victim himself was targeted, or if it was the Krasowskis' property. Robbery seems to be the motive, but the attack itself looks personal. DS Friend?"

"There's insurance, isn't there?" Alicia said.

"Two million," Cleaver said. "Nice amount, life changing, but not a stupid windfall."

"Enough to be a motive. It might be personal." Alicia thought for a moment. "But it could be panic. Looks a bit frenzied. I can be more thorough when I get a full report and see the body myself."

"There's more," Cleaver said, speaking directly to Murphy.

"More since I went to pick up Alicia?"

"Yes, sir. DC Ndlove contacted the OC unit in the SCA—"

Poole raised a hand, frowning.

Graham translated for her. "The OC is Organised Crime. SCA is—"

"Serious Crime Agency, I know that one," Poole said. "I thought they'd shut down."

"Scaling back," Alicia said. "Some merging with other agencies."

"OC will devolve to us locals soon," Ndlove added, "so they're happy to cooperate. In this case, Dean Bicklesthwaite owed a few grand to a bookie they've been keeping an eye on. Ernest Borek."

"Borek," Alicia said. "That's Polish. Like Krasowski."

Ndlove consulted her notebook. "Yes. They know each other socially. We spoke to Jerzy and he confirms a friendship with Mr. Borek. They worked together before branching off to run their own businesses."

"Mr. Krasowski insists Ernest and Dean were friends," Cleaver said. "We will have to dig some more on that, but it'd be an odd combination for a bookie to be in league with a psychic."

"You're assuming the killer and the psychic must have had contact?" Graham asked.

"Yes. For now. Until we learn otherwise, we're treating the psychic as a suspect too. Couple of uniforms are picking her up."

"I doubt it," Alicia said.

Everyone looked to her. Poole adopted that pinched expression again, as if Alicia's comment annoyed her.

"It would be dumb." Alicia made it sound casual, no big deal. "We have to treat her as a co-conspirator, but I'd bet on her being told it was a wind up, having someone slip her a couple of quid, and then she performs her routine. Otherwise, she's advertising she knew about a crime."

Lemmy raised a finger to interject. "*Psychically*."

Now everyone shifted their attention from Alicia to him.

"Just saying." He retracted the finger. "If she's the real deal, she could've seen what she says she did."

After a moment, Murphy said, "Thank you, Constable Grogan. But I think we need to assume there's been collusion ahead of time, even if … what was her name?"

"Demelza," Ndlove said. "Demelza Shine. Which, bizarrely, is her real name, from birth, not a stage name."

"If Demelza wasn't in on the murder," Murphy said, "she's a witness, which means she could be in danger. Either way, she's coming in."

"Do we have the footage from the reading?" Alicia asked. "Jerzy's statement said she got a lot right. Spooked them both. And that he filmed it."

"Is that necessary?" Graham frowned her way, puffing his chest up a little as Marissa Poole appeared to nod in agreement with him.

"I think so." Alicia tilted her head toward Ball and Lemmy. "This pair think it's real, so we need to explore that."

Ball raised a hand. "I never said it was real."

"No, but you do, don't you?"

"No…?" He didn't sound convinced, and Alicia had called his bluff successfully. It was why he was here; curiosity piqued by an oddity. He said, "But, you know, we have to explore every avenue, don't we?"

"We do." Alicia smiled again, hoping she sounded serious. "Fire it up, someone."

Cleaver collected his own iPad and hit some links, and the big TV at the head of the room lit up with an image of the pub. Shaky, and filmed portrait instead of landscape—one of Alicia's pet peeves—but the sound was good, and the picture was easy to follow. They sat—or stood—through the minutes of Demelza's routine opposite Karen Krasowski, through the bullying revelations and culminating in the warning that Karen should rush home immediately because something terrible had happened. When Karen ran off and Jerzy remembered to cease recording, Cleaver killed the video and the TV switched into standby.

Eventually, Ball said, "What sort of name is Demelza?"

"Scottish?" Lemmy suggested.

"Cornish," Alicia said.

"Whatever, it's pretty impressive, right? No way could she know those things."

Alicia turned to Lemmy. "Look, Lemmy, I like you. You're sweet. I know that. And I do have my own powers, you know?"

"*You* have powers?"

"Oh, great," Murphy said, almost under his breath but loud enough for the room. It was probably what they were all thinking.

"Oh no," Graham Rhapshaw said. "I'd like to see these powers at work."

"Thank you." Alicia stood in front of a wide-eyed Lemmy. "You really are a nice man, aren't you? I sense that. And … I see driving … yes, you are an excellent driver. Very skilled."

Lemmy nodded along.

"And friendship is important…"

His eyes narrowed, neck straighter.

"Because you're very selective. You only have a close circle of friends, but … you're open to making it wider."

Lemmy relaxed a little, but his eyes remained slits.

"You don't trust easily, but you are extremely loyal. When someone betrays you, you take it personally, and it takes time to build that back up. And your close friends … you support them to the ends of the earth. You stick by them and stick up for them."

He was nodding now, eyes back to normal, a glance at Sergeant Ball, satisfied.

"How did I do?" Alicia asked.

"Good." Lemmy threw her a thumbs up. "If you're the real thing, how come Demelza can't be?"

"Because I'm not the real thing."

His thumb went down.

Alicia said, "It's called 'cold reading'. I'm not great at it, but that was the most basic level. Works well on people who want to believe, but even better on a sceptic. Which is what Karen was. As soon as you tell a person something about themselves that you can't possibly know, they either lap it up happily—like you, Lemmy—or start to accept the possibility —like Karen." She addressed the others now, pacing. "With Lemmy, I took something that is true for almost every func-tioning human being, that friendship is important and read his reaction. There are generally two reactions to that: happy acceptance or suspicion that the psychic is going the wrong way. In Lemmy it was the latter. I saw it was true, but I *guessed* there'd be caveats. The most common caveat is that friendship is important but the person being read doesn't have a *lot* of friends. In that case, it's usually because you are either socially inept, which I know you aren't from our brief interaction earlier, or because you find it hard to let people close. That means friends are a premium, and you cut people off who you feel are not suitable. The last bits are easy. When it comes to loyalty, everyone considers themselves loyal and willing to stand by a true friend."

"What about the driving?" Lemmy asked.

"Easy. Almost every person who holds a driving licence thinks they're at least an above average driver. I could have said that about anyone else in the room and it'd be true." A few shuffles of the feet told her she was right again, whereas, in reality, only Murphy was likely to be significantly better than anyone else, and that was down to his advanced driving courses with the police. "And since over ninety-five percent of all police officers hold a driving licence, I knew you could drive. You're a bit cocky—in a nice, loveable way—so I knew you'd fall into the category of people who rate their skills behind the wheel higher than they really are."

"So, guesswork," Ndlove said.

"Not entirely. It's reading one of two reactions. Positive or negative. Say something that could be rephrased with a 'yes' or 'no' answer, but don't *ask* it. Like, 'Do you have a lot of friends?' would give us a yes or a no, but the way I phrased it, I'm looking for a *reaction* from the subject. All a fake psychic needs to do is keep going with questions about how the person perceives themselves then move on to more specific items. The top psychics deduce a lot, and they're much better than me at it, because it's their job. In the performance with Karen, the mention of kids and how many she had would be worked out through her reactions to the number spoken, the family stuff is simple, but the bullying thing is interesting. That's professional level stuff. Cleaver, can you pull it back up?"

They all watched the screen as it switched back on and Cleaver lined up the footage, skipping seconds at a time. They watched it back again.

On the screen, Demelza said, "No, that wasn't an easy upbringing, was it? Not quite outright poverty, but you still struggled at school. Bullying. You were … You *were* the bully. In trouble a lot."

"Pause," Alicia said. Once frozen, she pointed out Karen. "Her expression has changed markedly. 'Not an easy upbring-ing' is easy, since, again, many people think of their upbringing as difficult, no matter how wealthy, for at least part of their childhood. She more than likely could read something about her that says she wasn't born wealthy but is now, so she'd have had to experience hardship. When Demelza brings up bullying, Karen instantly looks suspicious. Holds her breath, in fact. It's another fifty-fifty, yes-or-no answer, and it's a bit of a gamble. Most people experience bullying in some way, whether it's witnessing it, being a victim, or dishing it out—"

"That's three answers," Poole said.

"Victim and witness are the same here. One reaction,

usually shame or regret, which she would drill into when she sees it, but the other response is guarded. That pause, when she says, 'You were...' it's Demelza waiting to read what Karen is hiding. Guilt about not intervening, or guilt of something else, something she doesn't want anyone else to know. Her face gave away what she needed."

"Or..." Ndlove started, but her voice faded.

Alicia faced her. "Or what?"

"Nothing."

"No, go on. We're probably on the same page here."

Ndlove stared at the screen. "If we are assuming the killer is either in cahoots with Demelza or told her to send Karen home, couldn't the killer have known all this about Karen?"

Alicia beamed at the room. "My big reservation too, thank you, Rebecca!" She spun in what would have been a graceful pirouette a year ago, but she stumbled a little. She held up a hand to Ndlove for a high five, which the detective constable met limply. "I think we're in agreement. Rather than putting spooks and spirits in the official investigation, we go with actual police work for now. What do you say?"

Ndlove looked past Alicia. "DCI Murphy is in charge. Whatever he says, we'll go with."

Alicia continued as if she hadn't been ignored. "I'm just happy to point out the bullshittery of the profession. Bullshittery, by the way, is my word. Trademark Alicia Friend! Thank you. Which leaves two possibilities in this scenario: first, she was a willing participant, be it through bribery or collusion in the murder; second, it's pure coincidence, and she performed a cold reading and wanted the sceptic gone from her show, so made up the crisis brewing at home before Karen figured out her methods."

Murphy took her cue and said, "We'll keep an open mind, but I think it's more likely she's in with the killer."

It was met with murmurs of agreement all round, including Alicia. The only additional factor was Marissa Poole's lingering gaze on Alicia, which switched back to Graham Rhapshaw a second later.

Murphy summed up, "We need to find out *if* someone paid the psychic to pull Karen out of the crowd, and more importantly, who it was. DI Cleaver is in charge while I'm out. Treat Ms. Shine as a witness at first, but remember, if you can link the 'who' to a 'why', that's our killer."

The meeting broke up, and everyone but Cleaver and Ndlove prepared to leave: Ball and Lemmy to head home to their beds, Alicia and Murphy were to hit the morgue to view Dean Bicklesthwaite's corpse, and Graham would escort Marissa Poole to whatever important matters of state awaited her. Unfortunately, Cleaver's phone rang and as soon as he raised it to his ear, he called them all to a halt. Listened a moment longer, then thanked the caller.

"That was the bobby I sent to pick up Demelza Shine," he said. "She's not home, her car is outside, but her neighbours don't think she came home last night. We'll check some more, but right now, our most important witness is missing."

CHAPTER SIX

THE BIGWIGS—THAT'S Graham Rhapshaw and Marissa Poole—asked for a word with DCI Murphy in private, and almost as an afterthought in the doorway, Graham asked for Alicia to join them. Mrs. Poole, MP, twisted away from him ever so briefly, before resuming her poise with a smile that might have been smelted in iron.

Gender politics.

Alicia seemed to wind up women like her, and she knew why. Nothing to do with feminism, either, at least not the brand to which Alicia subscribed, or how she understood the point of it. Women like Poole resented that Alicia was able to remain as sweet and jolly as she was, while many career women were forced to alter their personalities to fit in with a male environment. They didn't enjoy that. And, to Alicia, it was the least feminist thing about a woman making it in a man's world. Seeing Alicia act perky and bouncy and still be considered one of the best in her field just made them jealous.

And yes, there's a footnote: occasionally, she would annoy a woman the same way she annoyed the men upon first meeting them, the same way she annoyed Murphy, but it took a lot more for the women to wade through the Five Stages of Alicia than it did most guys. Her cuteness seemed to break the ice faster in the male half of the species.

In Murphy's corner office off the main CID squad room, it was just Alicia, Graham, Poole, and Murphy. It wasn't a huge space, enough room for a decent desk, Murphy's high-backed chair, and what used to be two chairs opposite, and two walls of filing cabinets. He had done away with the storage now, replaced by a low table, a hard-looking couch, and three thinly padded chairs.

"Murphy, is that a meeting snug?" Alicia asked.

"It's a conference area," Murphy said.

"It's a snug, Murphy. I never had you down as a snug person."

Murphy glanced at Rhapshaw, who returned an eyebrow bob, as if to say, *Not my problem.*

Murphy said, "Files are all computerised. I was the only DCI with manual copies in his office. The chief super suggested I … upgrade."

Alicia sat on the couch, legs up without her shoes touching the fabric. "Well, I like it." She took in Graham and Poole as they sat, Poole with her gaze averted. Murphy sat in the third chair and Alicia said, "So what's with the top-secret meeting?"

"It's not a top-secret meeting," Graham said. "It's an informal chat."

Murphy held still, only his face tilting Graham's way. "Informal?"

Marissa Poole then sighed, crossed her legs, and placed both hands in her lap. "What is your best guess?"

Murphy switched to her, again only his head moving. "It's not about guesswork. We collate facts. We don't even have forensic analysis in yet."

"Come now. We all know how police work works. You get

a gut for these things."

"We have to keep an open mind. I won't allow my people to make assumptions, then find facts that only back up those assumptions."

"Off the record," Graham said.

Murphy stared at Alicia, then the floor. He inhaled so slowly, he might have been stalling or more likely he was keeping his annoyance in check. "Graham, you've only been off the job six months. Even though you are still dressing in that uniform, commissioner is an *elected civilian position*, as we can see from the company you keep." Another glance at Poole. "But you control *budgets* and *policy*. You don't have a rank to hold over me. You can't order me to make guesses that could bias an investigation. And I won't make such guesses."

The pair of politicians held their gazes on Murphy. Alicia listened to a clock tick somewhere but couldn't locate it. She swung her legs off the couch and planted her feet on the floor, put her fists on her hips, and frowned. "Right, that's you two told good and proper."

The three turned to her.

She wagged a finger at Graham, which she regretted as the breast on her left side wobbled painfully. She ignored it but ceased wagging. "Naughty commissioner asking the boss to break the rules. Don't you know if we arrest the wrong man it'll be blamed on the police? Next time you have to ask the public to vote for you, even though you don't really give the orders anymore, they might bring this up."

Graham coughed gently. "Mrs. Poole just wants to be sure we have a line of enquiry."

"We do," Murphy said. "Get all the witness statements, background everyone involved, and start breaking alibis. Then we'll have a suspect for you."

"By the end of the day?" Poole asked.

"When the information is available, that's when it'll be here. But it's the highest priority, ma'am, so rest assured we can let you know as soon as we can legally release the names of any persons of interest."

Alicia was starting to like this officious Robo-Murphy. She reverted to her regular demeanour. "Which means we need to get cracking. If you don't mind?"

Her sweet smile appeared to do its job, namely inviting the pair to leave. All stood, and after some stern handshakes that made her right breast hurt as much as her left, and plenty of thanking the officers for their time, Alicia and Murphy were alone.

He closed the door. Faced Alicia with his hands in his pockets. "Right then, what *is* your best guess?"

Alicia was never one for shying away from a guess, but she played the loyal underling to Murphy because she knew he had a point. Making sure Graham understood boundaries would ensure he didn't start insinuating himself too deeply in a police matter.

"The husband, Jerzy," Alicia answered. "Personal connection, and there's money at stake. If we find his company … what's that called again?"

"Golden Start. Employment agency for low paid workforce."

"Right. If that's in trouble financially, it's the perfect motive."

"Thing is, he was at the pub."

"He hangs with an unlicensed bookie," Alicia said. "That means he has a past with criminals, which means he has access to people who can carry out a murder that looks like a burglary gone wrong."

"But it looks angry too. Could be personal."

"I'd go with thorough. Panic, maybe. Dean was a big guy, despite his age. Could have fought back. We could get lucky with DNA. But the biggest reason of all for it being Jerzy is the psychic."

"The one who told them to go home?"

"Correctamundo!" Alicia paced to the window and leaned her back against it. Cold. She turned and touched her sore boobs to the glass. "Ohh, that's better."

"What are you doing?"

"I need to express some human juice for the little human at home. Do you have a place I can use?"

"There's a parent and baby room by the canteen."

"Cool." She pulled away, sensing she was less than two minutes from staining the front of her nice professional-looking blouse.

Murphy followed her out as she collected her larger-than-usual handbag. In the corridor, he said, "Come on, you know you want to tell me your reasoning."

"You want me to bias your thinking?"

Murphy's long legs easily kept up as she trotted on. "As long as you don't go blurting it out everywhere."

"Are you talking about my theory or my breast milk?"

Murphy pulled a face like she'd squirted in his eye already. "You know how we work."

"You don't usually mind me blurting stuff out."

Murphy scanned his pass to let them out of the double doors into an area accessible by both police officers and members of the public who had business within the building. "You're a copper, but we normally use you as a profiler when we don't have a suspect pool. We didn't know where to start with the kidnappings last winter, and the attacks we averted in the summer were so twisted up in weird logic,

I'm still not looking forward to the court case on that one—"

"Don't worry, I'll dazzle the judge with my delivery."

They reached the canteen's first entrance, the other a few yards away, and Alicia's stomach simultaneously demanded food and threatened to expel what little coffee was in there.

She said, "The psychic."

"Right."

"What's your take on her? Why set up Karen to be sent home?"

Murphy nodded as he walked. "They wanted the body found."

"But why then? Why not after the pair have finished their night out?"

"I guess…"

"No guessing. There's only one explanation. What was Dean Bicklesthwaite doing at the Krasowski house?"

Murphy halted on the far side of the canteen after the second door, beside what used to be a disabled loo, now labelled *Parent and Baby Facilities.*

He said, "Watching Jerzy and Karen's kids."

"How old?"

"Four and seven."

"If you were a burglar so desperate for a hit that you'd kill a resident while robbing the place, would you care about the kids finding their dead granddad on the floor?"

"No."

"What if you were a son-in-law or friend of the family?"

"I wouldn't want the kids to find the body."

"Let's say Jerzy is doing something unsavoury like committing fraud. Karen's father finds out. Jerzy has the man killed. Seems from what I read this morning, Jerzy believes in psychics, so he makes the mistake of thinking others will just believe it too. Draws attention to the body via Demelza to get his wife home ASAP, *and* he spares his children the risk of popping downstairs to find their grandad dismembered."

"Simplest explanation. Family members."

"Right." Alicia opened the door to find a warm, empty room with a bench seat, a toilet stall, and two changing tables. She paused. "Stick with the most obvious, even though he has an alibi. But don't write off the gambling either. Follow the husband. Background the bookie."

"Okay, I'll get the surveillance set up."

"Great. And Murphy?"

"Yep?"

"I need to close this door before my tits explode."

Murphy backed away sharply and Alicia stepped inside for some much-needed relief, already planning when she'd need to do this again in around six hours. Organisation was key. She had a feeling it was going to be a busy day.

CHAPTER SEVEN

MURPHY WENT BACK up the corridor, trying to get the image of whatever Alicia was doing out of his head. He had no idea what contraption she'd use—a manual pump, something electric, or if she'd just milk herself like a … he didn't want to think the word "cow", but it popped up too quickly for him to swat it down. Guiltily, he swiped his way back into CID territory.

Managing a squad of detectives investigating various cases meant a DCI might fall in as SIO on a single investigation, but only if seniority was absolutely required, and only if it was a major inquiry. Dean Bicklesthwaite wasn't one of those, at least not yet. It might even be considered straightforward; a thorough gathering of evidence, whittling away the suspects until the right one was left. Either a burglary gone wrong or a family member or friend who messed up by bringing a psychic into the plan. For the former, it'd mean the psychic had to be the real deal or she made a damn lucky guess, or she would turn up dead—a loose end snipped off to prevent testimony. Were Demelza Shine found murdered, though, it would add a new series of clues, more evidence, and they'd be led to the killer through her as well as Dean, cementing the conviction rather than hampering them. It didn't strike Murphy as a particularly organised crime, and any plan that involved Demelza had so many holes they might even joke about the incompetence in the weeks after the brutality of the act wore off.

Murphy now considered taking on the role of senior investigating officer himself to be a mistake. He should have allocated it to Cleaver, his first big case since making DI, then stood back to let him run the whole thing. Now Murphy was tied to it, and with four other active cases under him, he hoped Alicia would not cause too many waves with the MP. Cleaver didn't rein her in the way Murphy did. Perhaps he would not have taken on the responsibility if it hadn't been for her.

A keeping-in-touch week.

Used to be a day.

But the world was changing, and although Murphy might have resented that a few years ago, experience taught him resenting such progress was useless, and embracing it was the only way to get through any difficulties. Ensuring women can return to work on their terms without taxing budgets and the goodwill of fellow officers was a balancing act no one could pull off flawlessly, so Murphy would have to juggle the problems that might crop up as and when they did.

When Murphy first started on the force—and it was known as the Police *Force* then, not a *service*—Alicia would have been shown the door as soon as she started faffing about with her working hours. Not giving an exact return date before her maternity leave would have been unheard of too. Oddly, the males on the job seemed more willing to tolerate things like skipping out to cover for an ill child minder or to express milk than the childless women, who made the harshest remarks about their colleagues when they needed to slack off occasionally for family reasons. It was another thing Murphy had to juggle. He wouldn't comment on it and tried not to have an opinion unless it spilled over into outright bullying, but the biggest reason he went with the flow was simple: things were better now.

For all the crowing about political correctness or "pandering to the femi-Nazis", Murphy had seen women, and indeed the men who took their full paternity rights, evolve into committed and, mostly, excellent officers. That little bit of tolerance during their children's formative years seemed to imbue a degree of loyalty and commitment, and even though there was always a small minority of people who would take advantage of such goodwill, the positives far outweighed the negatives.

So why was he not entirely at ease with Alicia being here?

Perhaps it was because he was beginning to understand that she had a single mindedness bordering on the psychotic. He wasn't convinced that her happy-all-the-time act was actually her, but it gave her the confidence and clarity needed to compute the variables of a crime. She called her brain a mini-computer, and that wasn't far off. But after the case last winter, she traipsed off to America searching for a suitable conclusion, for "closure" as he supposed the psychologists would call it, where she was ruffling so many nests it was a wonder no one tried to silence her. More concerning was her recent sojourn into a potential killer's property whilst heavily pregnant. No matter that she was right. She shouldn't have placed herself in such danger.

Murphy wondered sometimes if she belonged on some sort of spectrum and what would happen if the happy veneer ever wore away. That need to explore her thoughts, to hold on with an iron grip to the chirpy personality which she believed defined her. She'd been to therapy, and seemed to take it seriously, but it was possible she hadn't addressed the demons plaguing her.

The father of her child, for example. Richard Hague. A killer, now brain dead as far as Murphy knew, and although he was technically alive he would never be able to answer the questions Alicia must have for him. There was none of that damn *closure* to be had. Alicia even named her child Stacey, after one of Richard's victims; the wife of Alfie Rhee, a private detective still tracking down others slain by what was now dubbed the "Century Killer."

All that swirling around Alicia's computerlike brain could not be healthy. And the perky personality could simply be a cork preventing all that crap from spilling out and crippling her. Murphy wasn't sure if he wanted to be a long way away when that happened, or to be on hand to catch her when the cork popped.

Whatever the issues, the situation at present was simple: with Cleaver handling things in the field, and Alicia seemingly pursuing a logical straightforward path, Murphy could step back for a couple of hours. Give others some face time, which was what he set about doing as he stepped back into the squad room. Yet, with Dean Bicklesthwaite, or more relevantly, Alicia Friend, playing on his mind, he would be back in that private office in a very short while.

In the meantime, now he'd signed off on the overtime, they all had their assignments.

Lemmy Grogan wasn't one for turning down money, but he was dog tired, and a bit pissed at Stevie Ball for accepting the four hours overtime without asking him. As soon as DI Cleaver offered them the task of tailing the family, and specifically Jerzy if he separated from the others, the sarge slapped Lemmy on the back and said, "Sure, we'd love to." Ten minutes later, they were back in civvie clothing and Ball was signing out a plain vehicle for them to use.

Sod's law kicked in, as usual, and rather than waiting around and allowing Lemmy to recline the seat and snooze, Jerzy Krasowski emerged early from his hotel with no wife or kids in tow. Jackie Osbourne logged that he "needed to nip to the office to take care of a few things." It was his company, so it was understandable he'd need to set things up in order to take time off, but Jerzy's route did not swing close to his Golden Start recruitment agency.

The coffee wasn't enough. Lemmy wished he could stop off for some poppers or a quick dose of speed. There were rules preventing them being on shift for any longer than the additional four hours, but Lemmy was pretty sure his mentor would have gone for extra if he could. Ball had already offered one of his caffeine pills, but Lemmy was so hopped up on coffee and Monster energy drinks that he half expected his heart to burst out of his ribcage any moment. He was at the headache stage of caffeine overdosing, so he sipped water instead.

Leading them from Shadwell to Chapel Allerton, Jerzy's car was one of those hybrids that Lemmy's girlfriend was always on about. Neither of them could afford something like that, though, so they made do with his beat-up Ford Ka for the time being. If Lemmy kept his head down, worked hard at this job, and progressed the way his sergeant told him, he'd soon be on the fast track to a place he could pick up whatever mid-range car he chose.

On the other hand, if his band got signed, it'd be Ferraris and Range Rovers all the way.

Of course, that scenario was looking increasingly unlikely.

They'd gone through two drummers in the past year and lost their first-choice vocalist to a cruise ship, so with Lemmy on bass and his best mate Dave on rhythm guitar both signing up to regular jobs, it seemed like the end was nigh. Both Lemmy's police gig and Dave's stint as a parking enforcement officer—or traffic warden—paid far more than their Motorhead tribute gigs and the occasional pub gig that let them play their own songs.

It was time to consider that maybe, just maybe, the band was never going to be his main income. He argued with his girlfriend about it, but at twenty-six, he had begun to accept she was probably right. Time to grow up. Forge a career in the real world.

He just hoped he hadn't made a huge mistake that morning.

"Okay, here we go," Ball said, pulling into a street near a church.

Lemmy focused. Sipped his water. "Who's this?"

In the northern part of an area called Chapeltown, Jerzy parked on a residential street of terraced houses, the whole row cladded to make them appear constructed from large sandstone blocks rather than the red bricks more common to the area. There was no garden, the front door opening directly onto the pavement via a deep step. Ball pulled in seven houses away. After Jerzy went through three bouts of knocking, the door opened to a woman in a nightgown who looked like she'd just woken up.

Lemmy checked the time: nine a.m. "Late night?"

"Looks like Jerzy's got himself a bird," Ball said.

"They look happy to you?"

Indeed, they didn't. Jerzy placed a foot on the step, but the woman pushed him back. He squared his shoulders and spoke animatedly, but not yelling as Lemmy heard nothing come this way. She replied with much pointing and gesticulating, and Jerzy opened his hands in a pleading manner. Ball raised a camera with a long lens to his eye and zoomed in, making a *hmmm* noise that sounded to Lemmy to be a little excited.

The woman folded her arms and huffed, and Jerzy spoke for at least a minute, until she melted a little and held both his hands in hers, her face close to his. From this distance, it was hard to interpret her expression, but once he'd taken several pictures Ball passed Lemmy the camera to get a better view.

Lemmy had heard some bad things about Stevie Ball, not least that he hated being called Stevie rather than Steve, but he'd been a good mentor. Experienced. A little eager to get out of uniform like this morning, but generous with time and advice. Handing over the camera wasn't unusual.

Through the eyepiece, Lemmy focused, observing as the woman did indeed show sympathy to Jerzy, who was clearly was in distress. She walked backward, holding his hands, and as he followed her in, Lemmy snapped more photos. Including as the door closed.

Ball was already on the phone to DI Cleaver. He explained what they saw and suggested they go in immediately to interview them while the pair were clearly acting hastily. The reply was plainly not what he wanted to hear, as his face creased momentarily.

He said, "Understood, we'll wait," and hung up. He paused, then told Lemmy, "Needs to be a detective who interviews them. We have to hold off until someone arrives."

"Who are they sending?"

"Who do you think?"

CHAPTER EIGHT

ALICIA WAS happy for DC Ndlove to drive them to Chapel-town, although conversation was stilted. Ndlove spoke on the hands-free to Ball, asking for more details as they progressed. He and Lemmy had passed by the house and heard raised voices inside. Ball offered to intervene, but as he conceded that nothing suggested violence was imminent, Ndlove advised him to stand by. "We'll be in Chapel Allerton in fifteen minutes."

"I think it's more Chapel*town* than Chapel Allerton," Ball said.

"Ooh," Alicia replied, "when did you get so pedantic?"

"See you in fifteen." Ball hung up.

Alicia grew up in Leeds before moving, like many average-income Leedsites—or "Loiners" to give them their proper designation—to the cheaper town of Wakefield a short drive down the M621. That Wakefield was also the location of her main place of work, the Serious Crime Agency, was just a happy coincidence. Her expertise was in demand for several years, so much so that she was loaned out whenever a psycho-logical makeup was required. From serial killers to kidnappers, pet thieves to hostage situations, she was happy to participate. Even Europol tried to poach her from the SCA, the Europewide law agency with whom she worked on several occasions, most notable being the capture of a German serial killer who'd struck in Britain only twice, but all over the continent dozens of times. It was a job offer she was now reconsidering, and wondered if she should call her supervisor from that case and see first if he remembered her (*of course he would*) and second enquire if there was a vacancy.

The SCA was now merging much of its knowhow and facilities with MI5 and Counter Terrorism Command, such was the focus of the intelligence community on Islamic and far-right extremists, and Alicia had already been informed by the detective backfilling for her that he'd wasted a whole month backgrounding and profiling a group of Egyptian students who'd turned out to be planning a mixed disco aimed at raising money for charity; the secrecy was due to their ultra-conservative families back home believing dancing was a sin, and mingling with the opposite sex doubly so.

Another alternative was transferring to a different station. She kind-of fancied working directly under Murphy rather than dropping in occasionally, but that would mean tackling bog standard crime. It was a snobbish attitude, one she was fully aware of having, but when a person has been handed the plum cases for several years, it'd be hard to go back into standard rotation, investigating the occasional GBH or mugging which had little chance of being solved.

That might finish her as a copper.

Yet, Leeds was her stomping ground, a place she knew and loved. As a child she played in streets on her bike, as a tween she dossed around Gledhow Valley Woods, and as an older teen she hung about various parks with her mates, sampling extra strength cider, experimenting in various ways, not all of them sensible, and generally having a laugh. As a young woman, one of those experiments resulted in pregnancy, one her parents all but forced her to terminate, which didn't bother her much, not for many years, but when she finally grew up and got a proper job—as a police officer—she took stock of her life. Whenever she saw a child the age hers would have been, a dull spike drove into her gut, and the only thing that could ease the pain was blaming her mum and dad and fighting to show the world she could make it better. And make it better she did. Every day. With her smile and her attitude.

Being a native, she knew about the two northern suburbs that Sergeant Ball couldn't separate. She'd made fun of him a little, but there was a good reason for that.

Chapeltown was closer to the city centre and became Chapel Allerton immediately after, merging into Moortown a couple of miles farther north, then Shadwell as you travel onward. The difference was Chapeltown and Chapel Allerton shared the same postcode prefix—LS7—and so were technically the same area, whereas Moortown and Shadwell boasted different postcodes. Alicia long assumed it to be something of a snobby attitude, an historical hangover from when Chapeltown was home to a predominantly black community and Chapel Allerton mostly white. No prizes for guessing which half the poor side was, and which was more affluent.

As they drove past the upscale bars and eateries of Chapel Allerton, she considered her own snobbishness, her distaste for "regular" police work now she'd had a taste of the worst humanity could offer. Perhaps taking a break from the extreme end of things was a wise move.

They pulled up behind Ball and Lemmy, on a street Alicia would most certainly have deemed Chapeltown in the past, but which had now done away with the dirty fried chicken place on the main road, closed the laundrette, and opened a tiny but overpriced bar alongside an Indian takeaway, branded so it looked like a restaurant. Did the gentrification of one area allow it to be renamed another?

Did it even matter?

Alicia and Ndlove sat in the back of Ball's car and listened as Ball filled them in on the resident, one Brenda Williams.

"Brenda?" Alicia said. "We're really scraping the barrel with names on this."

"You have photographs?" Ndlove asked.

"Oh yeah." Lemmy tapped several buttons on the camera and Ndlove's phone beeped.

She paired with the camera via Bluetooth for a larger screen and the ability to zoom, and showed Alicia the photos as they filtered through.

It didn't take a degree to infer the pair knew each other, that they were more than simple acquaintances or friends. Lovers? Ball and Lemmy appeared to have already decided there was hanky-panky at play, but Alicia wouldn't offer a conclusion just yet.

Both Alicia and Ndlove thanked the pair and got out, then walked toward the house.

For Alicia, it was worth the risk of exposing the surveillance and insulting a potentially innocent man; if he were guilty, he could be getting ready to run. He might also be attempting to dispose of evidence, so they could not take the risk of waiting.

"Have you known DI Cleaver long?" Alicia asked.

"Eight months," Ndlove said.

Despite Ndlove being a head taller than Alicia, their footsteps fell into sync. Ball and Lemmy remained ten feet back, as planned. No telling what was waiting the other side of the door.

"You're young," Alicia said. "Been out of uniform long?"

Ndlove paused in her stride, resuming out of sync. "Eight months."

"First job. You like it?"

This time Ndlove stopped completely. "I'm eight months into a detective constable role, DS Friend. Before that, I spent two years in uniform. I am married with one child, who is eight years old. Yes, I had him when I was very young, but the father and I are still together, so please—no stereotyping. I'm fit, I work out, and I work hard. I like kayaking. Is there anything else you wish to know?"

Alicia wasn't sure if this was efficiency or aggression. Best not push it right now. "I think that's brought me up to speed, thank you, Detective Constable. Would you care to lead the interview?"

"You're senior, ma'am."

"I'm not a ma'am. I'm Alicia. And I do much better observing. If you're comfortable leading, I'll chip in from time to time. Does that sound like a plan?"

"I can do that." Ndlove covered the rest of the distance and knocked on the door.

Alicia caught up, stood beside Ndlove. Ball and Lemmy waited by Brenda's neighbour's house.

Ndlove knocked again. "Will you be doing your … thing?"

"My thing?"

"The skippy, perky thing, ma'am. I assume it sets people at ease or distracts them or something."

"It's just me."

"I'm just thinking, ma'am, and it's your call of course but…" Ndlove flexed onto tiptoes. Swallowed. Eyes on the door.

"You think I should be all serious and boring when chatting to people?"

"In … some cases. Perhaps it's more appropriate."

Alicia stared at Ndlove, waiting to see if she would look back. It wasn't easy for her to ask her this, and Alicia was about to tell her she respected her honesty, but then Ndlove hammered on the door with the base of her fist and shouted, "Police! Open up!"

Alicia faced the door. Serious expression.

Footsteps. A muffled voice. "What do you want?"

"What we really, really want?" Alicia said.

Ndlove said, "Ma'am, we'd like a word, please."

Alicia bent over and flipped open the letter box. "And we'd really, *really* like it if Jerzy doesn't run out the back. That'll just make him look guiltier, and we'll have a ton of fun breaking him."

She let the letterbox flap back down and stood upright. "And yes, I'm going to be doing my thing. Hey, you could be Wise to my Morecambe."

Ndlove exhaled through her nose. "I know that's a reference to an old comedy act, but I can't say I've ever seen them. I assume I'll be the straight man."

"Unless you want to do the 'thing'. I mean, you can do my thing and I'll do yours if you prefer—"

"No. Thank you. Let's—"

The door opened. Brenda Williams stood tall, her jaw forward and shoulders back. Attractive face, even sleep-fuzzy and makeup free, and she was plainly lithe and long-legged, despite a frumpy gown built for comfort rather than eroticism. Jerzy lingered in the background, leaning on a wall. He offered a little wave, his manner screaming *casual*.

Alicia stepped in, Ndlove following.

"Hi," Jerzy said. "You are looking for me?"

"Following you, actually," Alicia said. "Can we sit down?"

"Why not stand?"

"It's better if we sit," Ndlove said.

Jerzy looked to Brenda.

Brenda said, "Kettle's on."

Alicia and Ndlove stood aside, allowing Brenda room to move ahead of the detectives. Not easy. The outer hall was too narrow for two people to stand shoulder to shoulder, and the living room to the right was tiny, way too small for the massive television. Magazines were stacked beside the cream leather sofa, overflowing from a rack. The kitchen waited straight ahead, where Jerzy had already entered.

Brenda went ahead, as protocol demanded—never turn your back on a suspect in an enclosed space—and the two detectives arrived last. Like the living room, it was small, but made better use of the space with fitted worktops and a linoleum floor. Enough room for a tall table with two stools to serve as a dining table. Very clean, though. Not cluttered like the other room. Two doors stood closed, one to the garden and the other to what Alicia assumed was a utility room off the side.

Brenda pulled her gown tighter. "What's this about?"

"Did you say the kettle was on?" Alicia asked.

"It wasn't an invitation. Not yet, anyway."

Jerzy leaned on one of the stools, feet still on the ground. A subconscious tick that prepared him for flight as his overly casual body language faltered. He also kept his lips sealed tight.

"It's like this," Alicia said. "I'd really like to know—"

Ndlove interrupted. "Ma'am. Their caution?"

"What?"

Ndlove produced her phone and set an app to record. "Brenda Williams, Jerzy Krasowski, you are not under arrest and we can stop talking at any time. But I must caution you that this conversation will be recorded. You do not have to say anything. But it may harm your defence if you do not mention when questioned something which you later rely on in court. Anything you do say may be given in evidence. Do you understand?"

Brenda folded her arms. "Sounds like I haven't got to talk to you."

"That's right," Alicia said. "Thing is, our next stop is Karen Krasowski. All I have to do is call her up and say, 'Hey, just wondering if you know Brenda Williams. No? Because your husband seems to—"

"Okay." Jerzy stood.

Brenda tutted and spun away, leaned on the worktop with the kettle on it, her back to the cops. "For crying out loud, Jerzy…"

"They will find out eventually. Call records, spending. I should not have come here." He wasn't scruffy, exactly, but it was clear he'd barely slept. A lapse in judgement, perhaps. "They have to turn every stone, yes?"

"Indeed, sir," Ndlove said.

Alicia remained silent. It was sometimes better.

Jerzy said, "Brenda and I are … we were together until recently. With police looking into the family, I thought … thought I should warn her. If … if you find out. And you have."

Her head down, Brenda responded in a low tone, anger barely concealed under the surface. "They found out because you led them here, you moron."

Jerzy looked to the two detectives.

Alicia said, "It's true. We were following you."

"Why?"

"Because you're a suspect in the murder of your father in law."

"Me?" His eyes boggled. "But I was with my *wife*. The psychic, she said we must go home. How—"

"An accomplice, dickhead." Brenda again turned to the three people in her kitchen. "If you're having an affair, it's not so farfetched your slutty lover might be in on it."

Ndlove remained straight-faced. "Ma'am, can you confirm your whereabouts yesterday evening between the hours of—"

Brenda half-sighed, half-snorted. "From seven until just after ten I was driving from Middlesbrough after meeting clients. There was an accident on the A1, which slowed me right down. When I got home, I went straight to bed. You can ping my phone. Check traffic cameras, can't you?"

The body was found just after nine, so assuming the phone, traffic cameras and anything else they could check panned out, she was in the clear.

"We can check," Alicia said. "Thank you." She lasered in on Jerzy. "Which leaves the matter of who knew about this relationship."

Jerzy shook his head. "No one. No one knew. I swear."

A common claim among the unfaithful. They thought it was impossible for anyone to know, yet the longer an affair lasted the more careless the participants became. They got comfortable. Blasé.

"It's very casual." Brenda's comment was almost inaudible because her chin now pointed at her chest.

"I'm sorry, Ms. Williams." Ndlove held the phone closer. "Would you mind repeating that, so we can be sure to hear it on the recording?"

Brenda set her head high and regal, a woman with nothing to be ashamed of. "It was very casual. Indoors all the time. No dinner dates. No holding hands watching the sunset. Casual. As in *sex* and nothing more."

Shyly, Jerzy added, "Karen is not too interested in sex.

Twice a month, maybe, if I am lucky. I buy her favourite wine, candles, make real effort. But it always feels like she is rewarding me. Not that she wants to be with me. In sex."

Oh, so it's her fault, Alicia thought but managed to restrain the words from flowing from her. Maybe if they weren't recording. Then she realised she was holding her true self back for the sake of police work and said aloud, "Do you consider this affair your wife's fault?"

Combative questioning of a witness under caution. She'd be due a frowny face from the policy wonks if it made it to them.

Jerzy's mouth cracked open, but Brenda cut him off. "No, it's mine. I sought him out."

"You *knew* he was married?" Ndlove asked, carrying the frowny baton nicely.

"I targeted him at a small entrepreneur conference *because* he was married. I want no ties. I'm far too busy for that. It's better if he sticks with the wife, otherwise men can get too clingy."

"Is correct," Jerzy said. "She even said she wanted my anniversary dinner to go well."

"Right. And just so you know, since this affair is nothing to do with Jerzy's father-in-law's death, I will sue the police if this gets out and reflects badly on my business."

"And what business is that?"

"I mostly provide telecoms solutions to small businesses. But other services too. Basically, whatever a business needs, we can provide it."

"Ooh, vague," Alicia said. "We coppers love vague."

"It's all on my website."

"Your website doesn't speak into a phone. Sorry." Alicia offered a super-sad face.

Brenda sighed again. "We do staffing, logistics, IT support, and security, both for buildings and individuals if required. But mostly we're a comms specialist. If a company needs internet cabling, phone lines, bespoke mobile phone contracts, hands-free kits for their cars, we assess, quote them for our services. Physical installations, and we negotiate deals with ISPs and the like, then they either take us on or they don't. Most don't. The few that do don't regret it. The higher price is money well spent. I'm currently trying to upscale. My trip to Middlesbrough was to an NHS trust who wants to revamp all their IT and comms infrastructure to something more efficient and cost effective. I'll write their names down, so you can verify my presence."

"Thank you," Ndlove said.

"So, you'll be discreet?"

Ndlove looked to Alicia. As the senior officer in the room, it was her call.

"Interview terminated," Alicia said. When Ndlove switched off the recording, it would state the time automatically. No need to recite it the way they used to. Without an official record, Alicia said, "We'll check out the alibi. We'll do some other background. If it proves to have zero to do with our case, we'll be as discreet as we can. No promises, though." Alicia placed a hand on Jerzy's forearm, a gesture she could get in trouble for, but by the time she realised, it was too late to take it back. "These things have a way of coming out. I can't tell you to confess all, since Karen needs you to be strong right now. It's better if you're honest with her, but it's your choice as to when."

"You can't guarantee privacy?" Jerzy said.

Alicia took back her hand and stepped back next to Ndlove. "It's your choice, Mr. Krasowski."

CHAPTER NINE

CHECKING ALIBIS ISN'T as sexy as it sounds. It's not striding into bars, demanding CCTV footage, threatening to smash the place up because *I don't need a goddamn warrant*, then requisitioning the tapes. It's boring. Ndlove took Alicia through the process of getting a warrant to access traffic cameras while Cleaver signed off on an application to trace Brenda's movements via her mobile phone. He handled contacting the Middlesbrough NHS trust—a part-privatised initiative called Corn Acre—and confirmed their interest in Brenda Williams's services. It all takes time and painstaking thoroughness. And it pushed Alicia closer to the idea of leaving the SCA for Europol.

Sometimes she hated her lack of interest in paperwork. It made her feel so up her own arse, the kind of person she found objectionable to say the least.

I'm too good for this sort of work.

No, love, you really aren't.

Great, now she was having conversations in her head with Sergeant Ball.

Ball and Lemmy had to go home for some union-mandated sleep and much to Ball's annoyance they'd be back on uniform rotation by the evening. Murphy had to call a couple of people off a spate of non-lethal stabbings to sit on Brenda Williams and another to watch Jerzy Krasowski in case he did a runner. They waited on the SCA's Organised Crime Unit's report on Ernest Borek, Alicia pushing a note to Robert Stevenson—her backfill Bobby—asking if he'd be a darling and hurry it up. DNA was also a slow process, but they got the familial match back early, connecting Karen Krasowski with the dead man she already identified as her father.

Long story short, they left the family liaison stuff to the family liaison officer, spent the whole afternoon at desks, and made little headway on other aspects of the investigation, beyond ruling out Brenda as someone who could physically have committed the crime, but someone would go deeper on her finances to be sure she couldn't have funded a hit.

Dotting I's and crossing T's.

Scutwork.

But important scutwork. Scutwork which, if performed badly, offered a glimmer of doubt to some slimy lawyer in the courtroom. Alicia was fried by the end of the day.

The end of her *working* day at least.

When she departed Sheerton Station at five-thirty p.m. on the dot, Ndlove, Cleaver, and a DS called Humphrey-some-thing were still ploughing through the data. Murphy had allowed her to hang on to an iPad, so she'd be able to stay abreast of the progress, but she still couldn't shake the lump in her throat at bailing on them. Her mum's goodwill would only stretch so far, though, so she had to be home by seven as promised if she was to continue tapping that well of free child-care. She almost forgot to collect her breastmilk from the fridge, and amused herself with the image of a night shift bobby accidentally using it in his cuppa, before she retrieved it and headed home.

The Dot-Bot had kindly popped to the flat with Stacey, who was lying on her back fascinated by a mirror hanging from an arch over her play mat when Alicia came in. She threw one of her biggest smiles at her mum, then lay silently beside Stacey. Just watching her face. Didn't want to pick her up.

It wasn't often this little girl looked so content whilst awake or detached from Alicia's nipple. Her chubby little face swelled in the cheeks, her mouth parted and eyes wide. Thankfully, she'd inherited Alicia's eyes and a hint of the dimples were there too. Once Stacey started crawling and working off those fat reserves, they'd see for sure. There was little of Richard in there, but Alicia could not help but see the nose was thinner than her own buttonlike appendage, her cheekbones higher. A stranger would not place Stacey as Richard Hague's daughter, but if someone who knew him decided to look closely they'd find the resemblance they needed.

Alicia just hoped it didn't last.

Stacey turned her head, latched her gaze on Alicia, and the smile deepened. Warmth spread through Alicia, tugging her own mouth wider, and tears brimmed in her eyes. "You missed your mummy?"

Stacey's arms and legs set off like a train, kicking and grappling with the air. Alicia sat up, plucked Stacey from the mat, and the baby lay her head on her mother's bosom and hung there in her arms, still, for a long moment.

"Thanks, mum," Alicia said. "Do you want to stay for dinner?"

"That'd be lovely." Dot gazed down at the pair, hands in her lap. "What do you have in?"

"I have several frozen meals and a stack of takeaway menus."

Dot slapped her thighs and stood. "Chinese it is, then. Is the Lotus still open?"

Alicia texted Robbie to ask if she wanted anything ordering, and Robbie asked for a chicken foo yung and fried rice. She was due back in twenty minutes. In a fog of relief, Alicia used an app to order, paid via her phone, and was glad to be alive in an age of such convenience.

The relief was largely due to her worry that their friendship was straining under the weight of Stacey's refusal to sleep through the night and Alicia's fast acceptance any time Robbie offered to take Stacey off her for a couple of hours. Four months in, those offers were coming less often, which added more evidence in Alicia's mind that Robbie was growing less enamoured with their living arrangements.

She'd broach the subject once her keeping-in-touch week was over.

Stacey remained placid and happy and gurgling, over-flowing with the sort of cuteness that caused Alicia to be almost grateful for meeting Richard Hague. She carried the tot in her arms, kissing her head, jiggling her to make her laugh, whilst alternately pulling plates and crockery out of the cupboards ready for their dinner and stacking her expressed milk in date order in the freezer.

Super Mum and a perfect hostess.

Dot was on wine duty and Alicia asked only for a small one, the allure of her bed beckoning as the lack of sleep the previous night weighed behind her eyes. Plus, she needed to feed Stacey soon. A second session in the parent and baby room had not been forthcoming, and it was coming up to that time.

Robbie breezed in, as big and beautiful as ever, a hint of wine on her breath. She beamed to see Stacey, who grew almost as excited as when she spied Alicia. Robbie changed into her pyjamas and Alicia did likewise, laying Stacey on the bed to coo and try to roll over as Alicia got comfy. Her mum frowned at the casual attire but said nothing. The food arrived, and Dot served up, no hint of disapproval at using trays to eat in the living room instead of the kitchen table, perhaps knowing Alicia preferred to lay Stacey on her mat while they dined.

However, as soon as Alicia let go of her, Stacey's bright eyes darkened, and the grin faded.

"Oh, not now," Alicia said. "Please, not now. Don't—"

But Stacey simply opened her mouth, her face reddened, and she let out a howl of indignation. At least, it sounded like indignation. The howl morphed into a hick-hick-hick tantrum of tears. The way she kicked and swiped on her back was almost identical to the way she did when Alicia first came home, but the screaming grated through Alicia like lemon on a paper cut.

"Would you like me to take her?" Dot asked.

Alicia had been staring at the baby too long. "No, I have her."

She scooped Stacey up, but that didn't stop the crying. The baby arched her back, pushing away from Alicia, or so it seemed, but Alicia had read this wasn't a rejection, just a physical reaction to being in such emotional distress. She needed a physical outlet.

Dot and Robbie were seated. Trays on laps, waiting to tuck in.

"Start without me," Alicia said. "I'll take care of this."

She wandered the flat, hushing and jigging Stacey, whispering sweet sounding noises, checking her for smells and dampness, but finding nothing. She sat on the couch and opened her pyjama top. Stacey latched on and suckled immediately.

Okay, she's occupied. Maybe laying her down reminded her she was hungry.

Alicia gestured to her tray on the floor and Dot moved her own to pass Alicia's to her, the pork and chicken chow mein still warm. Alicia managed to wedge the tray on her lap under Stacey, who paused in her suckling at the intrusion, but resumed soon after. She attempted the process of forking noodles, then scooping them into her mouth. She speared individual chunks of meat and vegetable, but Stacey kept wriggling. She twice spilled a lukewarm noodle onto the onesie, and eventually gave up the manoeuvre, surrendering instead to the girl feeding in her arms.

She stared ahead, seeing nothing, aware of little else but the tug, tug, tug on her boob, until Dot said, "Should we put the telly on?"

It had been fifteen minutes.

Losing time wasn't something that had happened a lot, but it was a factor during these times of exhaustion. Alicia was still figuring out the business of keeping Stacey alive and happy, and the fact she hadn't given any thought to the case worried her. That her brain just zoned out instead of taking the downtime to focus on the important things meant, perhaps, she was losing more than just time; perhaps facets of herself were falling away too.

"I'm fine," Alicia said. "Put the telly on. I think there's a good Death in Paradise on tonight."

As the older woman surfed to the Alibi channel for a rerun of a series they watched together on occasion, despite having seen them all first time round on BBC One, Alicia checked on Stacey and switched sides, hoping to equalise the volume. It was more likely she was lopsided now and she expected she'd need a bit of a squeeze out of the full one before she could sleep. However, Stacey kept on going while the credits rolled on the fictional tropical island.

Police don't tend to watch many crime shows on TV, but *Death in Paradise* and *Life on Mars* were two that people in the profession tended to like. *Mars* because of the outrageous practices, and *Paradise* because, well, who wouldn't love a posting to a place like that?

Stacey finished up, falling asleep in ten minutes into the second boob without a burp. Alicia couldn't leave the girl like that, so she mounted her on one shoulder and went through the soothing process of winding her. A tiny belch emerged, but that was never enough, so she carried on. She scooped noodles into her mouth, now stone cold, and when a deep, throaty burp echoed forth, drawing shocked looks from Dot and Roberta, Alicia figured her job was done.

She shifted, checked Stacey was sleeping, and carried her to the bedroom, using only the light from the hall to see. Although there was a nursery ready for her, Alicia kept Stacey close by in a temporary cot. Easier to soothe her in the night. She checked the nappy, then lay the girl down and swaddled her in a blanket featuring Peppa Pig, and watched for a long moment, wondering why she was so filled with utter dread. Something wasn't right, and Alicia couldn't put her finger on what, exactly.

Then Stacey provided the answer by turning her head to the side and puking a white slurry all over her bedding, onesie, and blanket. She grumbled, then turned her head the other way, which both revealed the state of her face and spread the spillage.

Alicia just stared. She heard a noise emanate from inside her, a squeak or a groan or something approximating a cry for help. An indeterminate time later—seconds, maybe a minute —her mum appeared behind her.

"Oh dear, what happened?"

"Shh," Alicia said. "She's asleep."

"But, honey…"

Dot stepped toward the cot, but Alicia blocked the way, her vision blurring. Tears. She blinked them away and picked Stacey up and, predictably, she murmured, opened her eyes, and vomited more milk onto Alicia. Then she unleashed her lungs.

Alicia moved the wailing child to the changing mat with the high borders which she kept set up on her chest of drawers. There was no urge to scream herself or punch anything and even the tears abated. She harboured a secret desire to throw Stacey against the wall just to see if that shut her up but, like the tears, this urge dissipated, replaced by simple resignation that she'd known, somehow, that this was going to happen, and dropped into autopilot.

Instead she reassured herself she must be getting better at this motherhood business. A sixth sense that her daughter, although asleep, can't quite have been ready for bed. Advice from other mums she'd connected with for coffee mornings or walks around various parks had their own theories. She would start to try Maria's routine, of bathing Stacey just before Alicia wanted to put her down for the night. Maria said it gave the baby notice, a routine that helped when it came to sleeping through the night which, according to everyone she spoke to, was just around the corner.

With Stacey clean, and still screaming, Alicia picked the girl up and held her on her shoulder, where the distress eased somewhat, the volume reducing in increments. Alicia wondered, exactly, when life would get easier, and if returning to work sooner might help restore her sanity.

When the noise stopped, and Stacey curled up on her shoulder, Alicia was ready to lay her on the bed while she changed the cot but found the Dot-Bot had already done that for her. It both pleased Alicia and pissed her off immeasurably. She decided the scale tipped more toward pleased, so wouldn't chew her mum out for interfering, and placed Stacey back in the cot. She was about to swaddle her, when the baby's eyes fluttered open.

No screaming. Just a look of pure concentration.

"Just great." Alicia left her there, returned to the changing table, and prepared nappies and wet wipes, and listened as Stacey emptied her bowels at a truly impressive volume.

Alicia's mum was gone when she finally got Stacey down, and Robbie had already armed the microwave, zapping the noodles, and filling her glass.

"Hey." Robbie offered the wine. "She okay?"

"Yep." Alicia perched on her breakfast bar.

"You?"

"Nope." And Alicia felt her face crease. Pressure welled behind her eyes , then burst forth.

Robbie rushed around to her, pulled her in to a huge hug, and Alicia leaned on her, shaking, and racking with sobs.

She was tired. Only a few hours' sleep the night before, followed by a day's work, her first day away from Stacey. A day, though, during which she only really thought about the girl whilst relieving the pressure in her breasts. The rest was all business.

She hadn't missed her daughter until she returned home.

The ping of the microwave snapped Alicia back to herself

and she pulled away, laughing at herself. "Sorry, Robbie, I'm just exhausted." She wiped her eyes with the back of her hand and hopped down to grab her meal.

"Alicia, that's not like you."

Alicia opened the microwave and stirred the noodles, satisfied with the billowing steam. "I know, but once I get this greasy mess inside me, I'll be fine." She licked her fork as she sat back at the breakfast bar. "Yum."

Just like that, she felt better. Honestly, she did.

"Have you thought about …" Robbie twirled her hand in the air. "You know … talking to someone?"

"I'm talking to you." Alicia scooped a forkful that was a tad large for her mouth, but she managed to shovel it in and chew. She was starving.

"You know what I mean."

Alicia worked her jaw, unable to answer with her mouth stuffed. She poked at a pile of envelopes. Today's post. Swallowed. "I had a bad moment is all. It's over."

"It's nothing to be ashamed of, Alicia. Lots of women go through—"

"I don't have postnatal depression, Robbie. There's a world of difference between that and baby blues. Full on depression is crippling. You cry all day, refuse to go out, you don't take care of yourself. You can barely cope. I'm just new at this. I'm adjusting. Some days are harder than others. Tonight, everything went wrong that could and—"

"I've heard you crying."

That stopped Alicia's flow. "When?"

"Three or four nights last week. I can't remember the week before."

Alicia loaded her fork faster, with a smaller portion. Ate it. "I'm exhausted. That's all. I'll get it together. I promise."

"You just need to ask, girl, if you need anything from me. Tell me you got that."

"I got that."

Robbie sipped her wine and joined her at the breakfast bar, pulling one envelope toward her with a single finger. "This another from your secret admirer?"

Alicia sampled her own wine. It was *good*. "Katie, yeah."

"You going to do something about it?"

"I don't know yet. I think I'd like to talk to her first."

"How you gonna do that?"

"Haven't a clue."

"How you think she found out about Stacey?"

Alicia finished another mouthful. "Not sure yet. When I work it out, I'll let you know."

Once she'd finished her dinner and Robbie left her alone, Alicia opened the envelope. The latest note read:

Do you have any idea of the hurt you've caused, you poisonous bitch?

That was it. Short, sharp, almost cute.

Alicia had examined several malicious messages in her time, both academically and professionally, and this spoke of trying way too hard. First, it was grammatically correct, with even a comma in the right place, making it appear that a clear-thinking mind composed it. Second, it was phrased as a question but was clearly rhetoric.

Previous notes started out with cryptic phrasing such as, *Why do you keep your baby's daddy a secret?* which Alicia attributed to a news interview she was forced into whilst in America, a crank winding her up.

After three missives along similar lines, when Alicia was ready to lodge a formal complaint with the police, a fourth such note mentioned Katie:

You haven't told Katie what you were carrying in your filthy woman's sack. She will find out sooner or later.

Alicia realised it was Katie herself sending them. She'd found out about Stacey somehow, maybe overhearing Alicia at some point, or by adding up the dates. Only Robbie, Murphy, and Alicia knew for sure, but with Katie in the mix now, Alicia couldn't make it formal.

Since her father's crimes came out, Katie struggled mentally, and one of Alicia's fellow psychology students, Dr. Rasmus, took her on. Katie experienced alcohol problems, stress, and undoubtedly depression. With the powerful combination of those revelations, and the PTSD brought on by her kidnapping and what she endured whilst being held against her will, medication was necessary to regulate her actions.

Were the letters a pressure valve being released?

Alicia thought so. But she wasn't entirely sure what to do. The correct thing was to send the letters to Dr. Rasmus, but he wouldn't be able to discuss them with her, or even if Katie was still a patient. It was unlikely, since Alicia had trawled social media in search of her, locating her with relative ease at first via Facebook and Instagram. A student of sports science at a university in Wolverhampton.

The Midlands. Far enough from Yorkshire for a fresh start, close enough to pop back for a weekend.

Alicia reached out to Katie, asking simply to meet, but the troubled young woman then dropped off the internet completely, and all Alicia heard from her were the letters.

Some with a Wolverhampton postmark, others from Leeds. Meaning she was still actively moving around on occasion.

Without social media, Alicia was left with little choice but to phone around, which she attempted a couple of days earlier. The uni wouldn't give any info except to say Katie had not attended class for a while. The hospital housing her comatose father were happy to share that Katie had not visited for months, but the trust set up by the wealthy estate partly responsible for Katie's ordeal kept paying the bills, so they kept Richard going.

This rhetoric was a step up though.

You poisonous bitch.

Although it wouldn't stand up in court, Alicia was certain Katie was the one sending the letters, but … that one seemed much harsher. Angrier than the others.

Why?

And what would Alicia need to do to prove it?

She logged onto her personal laptop, checked all the social media channels she could think of, then dropped an email to the university expressing concern for the safety of one of their students. They were bound by law to investigate. It might not yield an answer, but it might intervene if Katie was in distress.

Just as she was moving herself to go to bed, Alicia spotted her bag. It contained her West Yorkshire Police iPad. With full access to the resources that her clearance allowed, which was a lot, she could plug Katie's details into the system, pull out a last known address, any vehicles she owned, check on—

She stopped that line of thinking. Any abuse of the police network for personal gain was not only a disciplinary matter, but a criminal one. Data protection, misuse of police assets, invasion of privacy…

No, Alicia would have to do this the hard way.

She poured half a glass of wine back in the bottle, switched off the kitchen light, and was about to turn in when a call came through. It was Murphy.

"Interesting development," he said. "We just picked up Karen Krasowski assaulting someone in the street."

"Please tell me she hasn't gone after Brenda," Alicia said.

"Not quite. And you won't believe what she used as a weapon."

CHAPTER TEN

THE WORST WEEK of Karen Krasowski's life just got worse. And lying in her father's spare bed, listening to the rain fall on the conservatory roof and occasionally patter against her window, she ruled out taking a pill. Not that she was fundamentally against a chemical assist, but she feared she wouldn't hear Harry or Lincoln if they needed her. Which left her ruminating on how life had spun upside down in a matter of hours.

Barely a day earlier, she found her father butchered on the floor of her living room, murdered while the boys slept upstairs. The image of his blood-soaked body was etched onto her brain, seared there as if branded by a hot iron. She swung between revulsion of the image and practicalities like whether any mortician would be skilled enough to patch him up for an open casket. Unlikely. A closed casket would be required. She'd barely recognised him herself. Each time she closed her eyes, she saw it, and each time she did she thanked God her boys hadn't woken up.

Would the killer have taken them from her too?

Was her dad a target?

She'd been truly proud of the man who raised her alone. Alone after cancer defeated her mother. He conducted a little shady business, but nothing major. Certainly nothing to warrant that level of brutality. He gambled a bit, and he had friends who'd been inside, but in their neighbourhood who didn't? In their neighbourhood, most people had family who served time for one thing or another.

She even met Jerzy through a friend of her dad's. The guy who organised the poker games and days out at the horses— Ernest, a sweet, bald chap with the personality of a teddy bear. Or maybe that was the youthful Karen remembering him that way.

After much wooing and false starts, she married that poker pal of her dad's, with Dean's blessing too. Jerzy was a great guy, and after several lean years he was on the up. As soon as they could afford the big house in Shadwell Karen figured she'd "made it" and popped out a baby boy, Harry. After three years as a stay-at-home mum, getting in shape and thinking about setting up a business of her own, she fell pregnant with Lincoln. A blessing, truly. And although it took her longer this time, when she attained her former weight she kept on going, until she sculpted herself into better shape than before her first son. She loved the exercise so much, she enrolled on a course, tapped up some friends that would train under her for free, and obtained enough testimonials to get a job at the local gym. She was technically self-employed, as the gym didn't pay her anything. *She* paid *them*, like a hairdresser renting space.

All the hard times were behind them. Years behind them. No way was she going back.

After last night, though, she could not shake the feeling that it wasn't gone. Petty thieves and crooks hold grudges. She told the police this, and they seemed interested. She insisted Ernest would have nothing to do with it, more likely a blast from the past—if indeed her dad was an intentional target—but they would need to eliminate the bookie from their inquiries.

That would have been a bad enough week. A dead father, her house stained forever with his blood, and now moved into her father's home with her two boys.

It was better than a hotel.

The police took what they needed, and Jerzy was moving suitcases inside along with box files of their personal documents, which was when Karen told him they had to sell the house. She could not live there another moment. Jerzy agreed to call the estate agent as soon as they caught whoever did it, but Karen blew up at him, accusing him of fobbing her off. She didn't believe he would sell it without a good, hard shove, and that was when he said it.

"I'm sorry, Brenda, I promise I'll do it."

"Brenda?" Karen said. "Brenda?"

"I am sorry, I mean Karen. Brenda … Brenda is someone from work. New applicant."

"Right. I'll just call in and confirm that." Karen whipped out her phone. "Okay with you? Shall I speak to Katrin? Ask her about someone called Brenda?"

They say a wife knows, but she'd always thought that nonsense. Who would put up with it if they knew? Yet, now, Karen understood. It wasn't that they consciously knew, not always; it was after, when they had confirmation. She'd gotten a whiff of Jerzy's possible infidelity before, consisting mainly of late nights, of jumping straight in the shower after returning from a trip away for work, of him locking his phone on many occasions as Karen entered a room to find him texting.

It was pure soap opera. Little signs she now felt stupid for not having added together, especially after he promised it'd never happen again. Once was a mistake. Twice was desperate.

Three times was an embarrassment too far, and Karen could not forgive him this time.

He confessed it all. Brenda was on his mind because the police caught him with her when he was supposed to be shoring things up at the office, warning the bitch about the murder. He was going to tell Karen, he said, he *swore,* but wanted to support her first. Didn't want to add to her problems.

And boy, had he added to her problems. Now she was without a father *and* she'd kicked her husband out. Double whammy. No family left but a couple of cousins who only entered her thinking at Christmas and when a birthday reminder popped up on her phone or Facebook. Her friends all texted or WhatsApped or Facebook Messaged her to say they'd do anything to help. Anything at all.

It was ten p.m., a little late to call on her school run friends, and those people online she hardly knew wouldn't take a call from her. Not willingly, anyway. Once the police eliminated Ernest from their inquiries, she would call him. Not for comfort. Just for someone to speak to who knew her dad well. Someone she could reminisce with, someone—

The tinkle of breaking glass froze Karen in her bed.

It was one of two spare rooms. Harry and Lincoln were sharing the other, bunk beds set up for sleepovers by her dad. Naturally, she couldn't bring herself to occupy her dad's bed, which was a good thing since the glass noise came from there.

A door opened.

Soft footfalls made floorboards creak.

Another door opened.

Karen scanned around for a weapon, finding only a clock the size of a brick. It wasn't anywhere near as heavy as a brick, but it'd do. A corner of plastic slammed into a cheek bone would hurt plenty.

She placed one foot on the floor, the clock in hand, ready should her own bedroom door open.

The floorboard directly outside creaked.

A pause.

Footfalls crept away.

Karen left the bed, glad she'd opted for sensible pyjamas instead of a short nightie, and pressed herself against the wall. Listening.

If he went near her boys' room, she'd be out there in a flash.

The next sound was of the top stair squeaking, then the next one. The third didn't make a sound, but the fourth did.

He was heading downstairs.

Karen moved to the bedside table, snatched up her phone, and dialled 9-9-9. The operator picked up and asked which service Karen required when another noise made her arms cold and her neck stiffen. She prowled back to the door, the operator asking if the caller was in distress or needed help. Could she tap on the phone if she was unable to communicate verbally?

Karen let the phone fall by her side and cracked her door. She could see the stairs.

And Harry's head was disappearing down there. "Mum?"

"No."

She rushed out, but the noise must have startled Harry, as he now hurried onward, down the stairs, calling for his mum. He must have been disturbed, concluded it was Karen moving around below, and now some spectre was chasing him.

Karen got halfway down the staircase when she saw the man, all in black, including a balaclava with three holes—both eyes and mouth. Harry had bumped into him and now retreated without taking his eyes off the intruder.

"Harry," Karen said, "keep going. This way."

"Shit," the intruder said.

"Get out. Just go. Now."

"Okay, lady. Take it easy."

Harry, shivering now, sat on the bottom stair at his mother's feet. The burglar sidestepped past them, a black bag in his hand the size and shape of a child's rucksack, his other hand open, as if to say he was no threat. He kept Karen and Harry in sight as he felt behind himself for the door. He spun briefly to unlatch the Yale lock, then turned the mortice. Facing them again, he fumbled the door open.

There was a small front garden beyond, a dozen feet to the wall bordering the street, a nice enough area, silent at that time of night. Only the rain could be heard.

The man paused in the doorway. "You were not in danger."

"Get out."

"Mummy?" came a voice from up the stairs.

"Back in your room," Karen snapped, no need to turn to Lincoln, now roused by the noise.

"You have a nice family," the intruder said. "They are safe too. Try not to worry—"

But this man, this person violating her father's home, could have been a killer. He could have smothered them all, and the fact he was here, just one day after the murder, was too much of a coincidence. Now, him uttering mention of her family, her boys, was too much for Karen. A howl of anger escaped her, and she pitched forward, the clock in her hand ready to strike.

The man ran.

He fiddled the gate open while Karen sprinted for him. He slipped once but didn't fall as he frantically tried to get away.

On some violent instinct, she tossed the clock and snatched up a twelve-inch-tall garden gnome, one stood on a toadstool with his hand in the air like a man making a speech. The stone ornament was heavier than she expected, but her rage drove her on, vaulting the wall instead of opening the gate. She didn't even feel the rain.

With the intruder heading for a battered old Vauxhall Corsa, Karen closed the distance easily, swung the gnome, and caught his trailing leg. He swan-dived front first onto the asphalt, and rolled, clearly waiting for a follow up attack.

An attack Karen was willing and able to provide.

She kicked him in the balls first, then as he sat bolt upright she brought the gnome down in an arc, swiping it across his face. Blood splashed and he grunted. She reached the end of the arc and brought it back, this time catching him flush with the full force of her makeshift club.

The gnome's arm broke off at the shoulder, the noise against the intruder's skull like a paving slab dropped on damp grass.

Even as the man fell sideways, she scrambled for the larger remaining piece, lifted it, and returned for another go at this guy, bleeding on the slick, wet road. But before she could inflict more damage, the night flashed blue and a sharp *whoop* halted her in her tracks.

The police car had been parked outside for reassurance, something Karen forgot all about, and now out jumped male and female coppers. The male, she thought, might've been a community support officer, a PCSO, or "plastic policeman" as folk round her way called them back in the day. The female gave the orders, first for Karen to drop the gnome, then to place her hands on her head.

As the cuffs went on, a moment of clarity caused Karen to inform them there were two minors in the house, unattended. She then gave the name Jackie Osbourne, her family liaison officer, then added DCI Murphy as the man in charge.

"You're Mrs. Krasowski," the male said.

The female said, "Oh, shit. *We're* the ones supposed to be protecting *you*."

"No kidding." Karen now felt the full wetness of the rain upon her. Soaked through to the bone.

And the guy she smashed on the head wasn't moving. Something the male noticed as he crouched beside the man and radioed for an ambulance.

"Sorry, ma'am," the woman said, "but we're going to have to place you under arrest."

Karen's week from hell had just got marginally worse.

CHAPTER ELEVEN

AFTER A NIGHT with a full six hours sleep—coming in the form of two hours at the beginning of the night then four solid hours to take her to seven a.m.—Alicia didn't need to force the skip into her step. Such a luxurious night was as close to bliss as she'd known in weeks, so she used it as fuel to keep going. She even added a little hope as pudding: perhaps sleeping through the night *was* closer than ever.

She dropped Stacey at the Dot-Bot's again and made it to Sheerton by eight-thirty. Cleaver and Ndlove were already there, with Ball and Lemmy hanging around. They'd been chasing down informants and people who'd worked for Ernest Borek through the night without much success, but their report had to wait as the man who broke into Dean Bicklesthwaite's house, now named as Tomaz Gortze, had been released from hospital and declared fit for questioning.

Karen was in the station along with her kids, having been released last night but ordered to show up first thing to conclude the questioning. After the injury she inflicted on a man *fleeing* her home, she shouldn't have been set free, but having convinced the chief super it wouldn't play well,

Murphy got permission to release her and her kids to a hotel nearby; the house was now being processed as a crime scene. Again.

Karen was treated as a witness in this second incident too. She would be seen by the public, the press, and most police officers as a victim twice over—first bereaved, then burgled. It was doubtful the CPS would prosecute either, although their guidelines do state a person should be in immediate physical danger to justify knocking someone unconscious with a garden gnome.

Okay, it might not mention gnomes *specifically*.

For now, Murphy and Alicia prepared to observe. The old fashioned two-way mirrors were less common these days, and although Sheerton did have a couple of those, restrictions on space meant the observation suites now doubled as storage, so detectives and other officers were left observing on TV in their inquiry room. She preferred the up-close windows, which made it easier to spot deception indicators and other give-aways, but now they'd started using 4k resolution, it was nearly as good.

A uniform led Tomaz Gortze, his head bandaged, into the room along with a duty brief to serve as counsel, where they conferred with their faces averted from the camera. No sound. Cleaver and Ndlove soon entered, Cleaver with a plastic box the size of a milk crate, and after a brief exchange, the sound came to life and Cleaver said, "I need to make it clear we are now recording both sound and vision. You have been detained under section 9 of the theft act 1968 and will be interviewed under caution." He then recited Tomaz's rights.

"I understand," Tomaz said. He spoke like a local and gave off the slack body language of a youth pretending he didn't care what was happening to him. Bulletproof.

"Please state your name," Cleaver said.

"Tomaz Gortze."

They went through various ID questions, establishing he was nineteen years old, unemployed, and lived about twelve miles from Dean Bicklesthwaite's home.

"Long way to come for a random burglary," Cleaver said.

"No comment."

"Your name. That's Polish?"

"I'm British."

"You mother? Father?"

"Mum. Dad buggered off before I was born. Never knew him."

Alicia was far from hard-hearted, but these sob stories stopped having any effect on her years ago. She didn't quite roll her eyes the way Murphy did, nor did she rub her thumb and forefinger together to represent the world's smallest violin like Ball did now the sarge had joined them. But since she knew with a 100-percent certainty that single mothers brought up good kids all the time, she never allowed an absentee father as the sole excuse for a crappy life.

Cleaver went through several establishing questions, detail after detail. Confirming Tomaz was present at the home, that he broke in, then got into the minutiae.

Which window.

The main bedroom at the back, standing on the conservatory room.

A good three minutes discussing the tool he used to gain access.

Plastic tape on the window, a small hammer.

The brand of tape and hammer escaped Tomaz, so Cleaver hit him with how many other homes he'd turned over that night.

None, it was his first.

"First?" Cleaver said, jumping on the phrasing. "You were planning others?"

"No. No others."

"Why this one?"

The young man sucked his teeth, slumped deeper in his chair. "Heard the owner got iced. Figured it'd be empty."

"How?"

"How what? He's dead, single. Why'd there be some slag there with her kids?"

"I mean, how did you know he was dead?"

"News."

"But how did you find the address?"

Tomaz frowned.

Some unseen nudge or signal spurred Ndlove to speak. "What DI Cleaver is alluding to is that although the name of the dead man had been released in time for the six o'clock news bulletins, his address was not. In fact, we specifically asked the press to withhold even the area he was living in, since we'd already arranged for his daughter to spend the night there. You don't strike us as having much access to DVLA—"

"Right, right, I get ya. How did I learn his address when I'm just some pleb? That what you wanna know?"

"Correct, Tomaz."

"In that case, no comment."

"It'll help you," Cleaver said.

"Yeah, how?"

Cleaver dipped into the plastic box and pulled out four items in transparent evidence bags, labelled and sealed. He slid the first to the centre of the table. "This is crown evidence TG-0412-A, a watch engraved with the words 'Love ya, dad - Karen.' Did you take this from the property on Linkfield Avenue, where you were arrested?"

Tomaz made a show of looking at the watch. "Yep. That looks like it."

Another bag, this one containing a small firearm, a pistol, heavier than a toy by the look of it. "Item TG-0412-B, a replica Walther PPK."

"Replica? Damn, I thought that was real."

Alicia leaned over to Murphy. "Dean was a James Bond fan?"

Bag number three. "TG-0412-C is a passport. Is this your passport, Tomaz?"

Tomaz didn't even look this time. "Nah, found it in the house."

"No, officers have examined it and found it actually belongs to Jerzy Krasowski, son-in-law of the deceased owner of the house."

Tomaz shrugged.

Ndlove stepped in. "The only reason someone takes a passport is to sell it on. That means you know people involved in identity theft, which carries an additional sentence on top of the burglary."

"Bollocks it does."

The duty solicitor placed a hand on Tomaz's arm and whispered in his ear.

"Is that what we'll get out of this?" Ball asked behind Alicia. "Some fake ID scam? Ain't getting us to the killer."

"You never were the best in interviews," Murphy said. "Watch and learn. The details are key."

Ball bristled, crossed his arms the way Tomaz had done until now.

"You're bloody useless anyway." Tomaz yanked his arm away from his brief's hand. "Why aren't you objecting and shit? How come I have to answer all these questions when I've been GBH'd?" He pointed at his head, addressing Cleaver.

"How come you're not asking me about the bitch who did this?"

The duty brief shifted his chair a couple of inches away.

Cleaver edged the final evidence bag toward Tomaz, a bulkier item that rattled. "Item TG-0412-D. A Tupperware box containing twenty-one pairs of cufflinks. Some of them valuable."

"Hobby?" Alicia asked.

"Some people like watches, some people like bangles," Murphy said. "Guess Dean liked cufflinks."

Cleaver said, "This moves you up a notch. From what we understand, some of these cufflinks contain real diamonds, which puts you in a jail with the big boys."

Tomaz frowned. "Yeah. Cool."

"You want jail?" Ndlove said.

Tomaz shrugged again, arms folding back over his chest. "I can take it."

A pause.

Cleaver consulted notes on an A4 pad, then said, "How did you locate Dean Bicklesthwaite's address?"

"No comment."

"You had a passport in your possession. Who were you planning on selling it to?"

"No comment."

"Who's your buyer for the cufflinks? Who would you sell them to?"

"eBay."

"How did you know about the conservatory?"

"What?" Now Tomaz sat up straight, froze as he appeared to realise his body language was speaking a bit too loudly. "No comment."

Alicia again thanked Stacey for giving her an easier night. Usually, this method of interrogation went on too long before gleaning results. The British police didn't go for the FBI style of breaking someone down—accuse, accuse, present evidence, offer them a way to mitigate their crime—instead painstakingly going through the incident bit by bit, step by step, then rephrasing any areas they needed to elaborate on or catch the suspect in a lie. Give them the rope. Allow them to hang themselves. When they had nowhere to go, they usually incriminated themselves, or got them backed into a corner from where they were forced to drop a bigger fish in the police's lap. Be it a fence for stolen property—the person who Cleaver plainly thought had located Dean's address—or someone converting real documents into fakes for illegal immigrants and people who want to travel anonymously.

"Uh oh, I'm having a moment," Alicia said.

Murphy turned his body to her. "What sort of a moment? Are you okay?"

"I am." Flashes of light passed through her computer-brain. She slowed them down. Snagged one. Examined it. Threw it back. "Too small."

"Pardon?"

Cleaver was moving on to something else. Another aspect of the burglary: how he knew where the safe was, and how he went about cracking the combination. Tomaz was smiling, commenting on how he owned the manufacturer details of around thirty models, the most common ones in homes, how he could break into most with a small drill and a screwdriver.

As Alicia happened on a flash that was shaped in a rectangle, Cleaver brought out the evidence bags containing Tomaz's tools, one for each; the more evidence numbers to present to a jury, the more damning it appeared.

Alicia stood and headed for the door.

"Hey, Alicia, are you okay?" Ball asked.

"In a sec," she said. "Which room is Karen in?"

In the presence of Jackie Osbourne who was taking care of breakfast and refreshments, Alicia spoke to the bereaved woman directly for the first time. She performed the usual business of putting Karen at ease, asking about her background, her job, and although they segued a little too long onto children, onto Karen's post-natal depression, and to meeting Jerzy on New Year's Eve then marrying him on New Year's Day three years later, they finally got around to Alicia's suspicion of Tomaz's motives.

With the answers she needed, she then headed straight for the interview room where Cleaver made a good show of being pleased to see her. Ndlove's reaction wasn't quite as convincing, but Cleaver's relaxed attitude prevented the detective constable from speaking. He said, "Detective Sergeant Alicia Friend has entered the room. With new information."

"Hello," Alicia said, pleased with his smooth assumption. "Yes, Detective Inspector. May I join in?"

"Please." Cleaver indicated a plastic backed chair against the wall, which Alicia pulled up to the table on Cleaver and Ndlove's side.

Tomaz looked at his solicitor. "You gonna allow this?"

The brief looked tired as he answered. "They can add a detective as long it doesn't become intimidating."

Alicia put her hands flat on the table. "And I'm the least intimidating detective in the world. Look at me. I can barely see over the table."

Tomaz frowned again. "Is this some trick?"

"No," the brief said. "It isn't some trick."

He must have come across Alicia before, but Alicia didn't remember him. She said, "The safe. You knew it was there."

"My client has already answered that," the brief said.

"I wasn't here. Can he say it again, please?"

Tomaz swallowed, eyes narrow. "This *is* a trick."

"I promise it isn't." Alicia held up her little finger. "Pinkie swear. Although I am about to drop a bombshell that I don't think you're going to like. I just need to know if you told us how you knew about the safe or you did that silly 'no comment' thing that harms your defence in court."

She waited.

Tomaz said, "It was behind a picture just the right size. I always check the pictures, even though most of them don't have safes. People think they're being clever, but…" he shrugged. "No harm in checking."

"And you broke in with your special drill?"

Tomaz smiled proudly. "Adapted it myself, yeah. Insulating tape, soft lining. Silent running as long as I get it right first time."

"And you got the safe open and took the posh watch, the cufflinks, and … what else?"

"The gun and some guy's passport."

"Right, the passport. See, I just got back from speaking to the lady staying at the house. She brought a whole bunch of documents with her in case they were needed for things like death certificates, insurance claims, mortgage issues with her dad's place. You know, all those things where people need identities confirming before they can speak to you."

"Sure."

"You said you don't have a buyer lined up for the passport."

Tomaz opened his mouth but the solicitor stepped in. "What he actually said was 'no comment'."

"Yeah," Tomaz said. "No comment."

"We'll assume you *did* have someone lined up."

"No comment."

Alicia waited. Then she nudged Ndlove with her elbow.

Ndlove, remembering her role, said, "We, and the court, will assume you did have a buyer for this, and chose not to share the information with us. That means you'll take the full brunt of the identity theft angle as well as the burglary."

Tomaz snorted a laugh.

"That's up to five years," Alicia said. "On top of the two you'll do for breaking and entering, theft of goods valuing several thousand pounds, which is one year for every—"

Tomaz sat upright, face twisted in annoyance. "Several grand? What?"

"The cufflinks are valuable, at least a hundred each, and since they're in a box, that's another year on your sentence. The watch is a Swiss thing worth five grand, which is another year. The gun was used on a James Bond film in 1975, making it a collector's item which we'll have to get valued—but they go for thousands too—and of course the passport which rewards you with a lovely five-year sentence."

She counted silently on her fingers, moving to her other hand, unit she got to ten.

"Ten years, Tomaz. Two or three, you're still twenty-two years old and your mates still think you're the dog's bollocks for doing the time. You come out, people are buying you drinks. You don't snitch on anyone 'cause you're such a tough guy. It's all such a laugh. But ten years, Tomaz. You're nineteen now. That's almost *thirty*. Tomaz, can you imagine being *thirty* years old?"

Tomaz's expression turned to stone for the first time.

"Think anyone'll remember you after ten years? Or if they do, might they have grown up and figured you for a knob, and want nothing to do with you since they're now probably working at a warehouse somewhere having changed their ways?"

Still no reaction.

Alicia softened "So come on, Tomaz. The passport. Who were you selling it to?"

"No one." He stared at the table.

"No one?" Cleaver said.

"No one. I just grabbed it. Figured I'd sell it on later if I could find someone. I don't…" His voice cracked. Although technically an adult, nineteen is still young, still immature, still carrying a chip on the shoulder against society. He and his mates would still be of the ilk who thought crime was a laugh and getting a job was dumb.

Acting tough, pretending you're a big man, showing everyone how you just don't give a toss about society's rules; essential armour for a kid growing up in a tough neighbourhood. The difference between two years in prison and ten was enough to penetrate the defences of all but the dumbest of these little big men.

"I don't know anyone in that line of work," Tomaz said. "Okay? Is that what you want to hear?"

"Yes." Alicia nodded. A glance up at the camera. She resisted a wink in case it came to be shown in court. Back to Tomaz. "But you also worked for Jerzy himself for a time."

"What?"

"You were on the books of his recruitment agency, Golden Start. But he dumped you after you failed to show up at not one but two jobs they found for you."

"I was with an agency for a bit, but I don't know any Jerzy. Them jobs were bogus. Dumb immigrant jobs. I'm not doing that crap."

"Then I want to know why you only took this one." She picked up the bag with the passport.

A twitch of Tomaz's head meant a bigger surprise than

Alicia's discovery and reveal that he worked with Jerzy. "What?"

"Why only this one? We have people at the scene now. Everything was left in situ. Nothing touched after Mrs. Krasowski was arrested."

"My head hurts."

"We're checking the safe, Tomaz. According to the only other witness in that house, she placed all four passports, along with birth certificates and wills inside her father's safe."

"Owww…"

The duty brief took his cue. "My client is clearly in physical pain. I insist we terminate the interview and find a doctor."

Cleaver immediately complied. "Interview suspended to allow Mr. Gortze to seek medical advice."

Cleaver and Ndlove stood, but Alicia remained seated. "Why only take Jerzy's passport, Tomaz? Did Jerzy pay you to steal it?"

Tomaz's pause was fleeting, less than a second, but it was enough for Alicia to confirm he was faking the pain. He continued to moan, to hold his head, but Alicia had what she came for.

Like most murders, this really was a simple solution.

CHAPTER TWELVE

BY MIDDAY, Ball and Lemmy had been sent packing again, and it was beginning to vex Murphy that they were hanging around so much. It was partly his own fault, having thrown them a bone in the form of backgrounding Ernest Borek. The man's alibi got confirmed by both friends he'd been with and CCTV of the Oarsman pub on the night Dean Bicklesthwaite died, but the shady connections and rumours of illegal poker parties persisted. An organised crime connection was not out of the question. Getting Ball to ask around, given his extensive network of confidential informants from his CID days, seemed wise at the time, but now Murphy had received an unofficial complaint from Ball's boss that Murphy was utilising boots-on-the-ground patrol officers as his personal gophers. Ball and Lemmy gave their statements, provided all the evidence accumulated, and handed over the murder to CID.

He felt a little sorry for Ball, given his upsurge in attitude since shifting back to uniform, but Murphy's hands were tied unless he made an official approach. Occasionally, he ran cases around the clock, especially when there was imminent threat or some form of time constraint.

The murder of Dean Bicklesthwaite was neither of those.

"With forensics returning no unexplained fibres or DNA, no fingerprints, and no CCTV taken from neighbours, this is now about building a case against Jerzy Krasowski." Murphy stood at the head of the room, with Alicia, Cleaver, Ndlove, and—as invited to keep him sweet and off their backs—Graham Rhapshaw. Marissa Poole received no invitation, and Rhapshaw saying she was on her way did nothing to persuade Murphy from postponing the briefing. "A contracted killer is the likely explanation, but don't rule out someone returning a favour or having a mutually compatible motive."

"No motive yet?" Rhapshaw asked.

"Not a solid one, sir. But it's not necessary in securing a conviction."

"I know that, DCI Murphy, but I like to have one when we go to court."

Murphy tensed, making sure to address the group. It was important to include everyone in the conversation, even when two people were dominating the discussion. At least, according to one of the many courses he'd been on. Frankly, Murphy would prefer to dismiss the detectives and thrash out some boundaries with Rhapshaw. "Right now, we have several possibilities. The prevailing theory is that Dean found out about Jerzy's affair with Brenda Williams and he used someone to murder him while he established an alibi. Or, given the two million pounds Karen will get from Dean's insurance, plus his house, there's a financial motive. Whatever the reason, he needed an excuse to return home quickly, and paid someone performing as a psychic to send them on their way so his children did not have to witness the dead body."

"Hmm." It was Alicia.

She'd agreed to let Murphy talk, and now Rhapshaw

picked up on the disagreement. "Alicia? You'd like to add something?"

"Me? No, not me. Thanks for asking, though, Graham."

Rhapshaw addressed Murphy again. "Any clue on the actual killer?"

"This Tomaz Gortze maybe?" Ndlove said.

"Possibly," Alicia said, "but I doubt it. Contract killers are often shipped around the country to carry out crimes, since local plod aren't as connected to one another as they should be. Even though—technically—we are absolutely wired in with each other. But coppers still rely on instinct as much as computers. It's instinct—recognition of human relationships and methods—that says me and Murphy don't like Tomaz for the killing."

"Why is that?" Rhapshaw asked.

"He's a sap," Murphy said. "He knows Jerzy from Golden Start. At least, Jerzy would have his details. We're working on if they'd ever physically met through work. It's a direct connection, putting Jerzy in the hole for at least the burglary. If he needed his passport, I'd say he was going to run before we made him a suspect."

Murphy waited.

"Alicia?" Rhapshaw said.

Alicia looked at Murphy, eyes big and innocent like a cat's.

"Go ahead," Murphy said. "We'll need to address it sooner or later. May as well be now."

"Thank you." Alicia turned and stood beside Murphy. "Why the psychic?"

"Demelza?" Ndlove said. "What about her?"

"Why use *her* as the excuse to go home and find Dean before the boys did?"

"They were at a pub with a psychic."

"But they didn't plan to go there. At least, Karen didn't.

What if she put her foot down and said no? Even if Jerzy planned it that way all along, why did he need to go that route? Why not just claim he was sick?"

Cleaver and Ndlove exchanged a glance.

Cleaver said, "Because ... he's stupid?"

"He's not stupid, though. He came over from Poland over a decade ago, barely able to speak English. Worked in fields, coffee shops, warehouses, while probably supplementing his income with some dodgy cash in hand jobs. He worked out the employment culture. Saved. Set up a business supplying low paid workers to various industries. And he's been a *success* at that. He's not dumb."

Ndlove again glanced at her mentor, who urged her to speak up. She said, "Plenty of intelligent people believe in things we cannot explain. How many Christians run multibillion pound businesses? How many Muslims? Jews? All religions have their super rich, extremely successful people. Belief in more than we are doesn't make a person dumb."

Murphy watched Alicia as her mind ticked over. She said, "True. But would a Muslim or Christian presume to use their god popping down and giving them a message as a way of supplying an alibi?"

Everyone absorbed Alicia's problem with the scenario.

Murphy hadn't wanted it to come out just yet, but it didn't hurt to discuss it ahead of bringing Jerzy in.

"It's a thread we can't tie off yet," Murphy said. "But right now, everything points at him being the culprit. Snatching his passport, the affair, and the belief in psychics. They're enough for us to concentrate on him. If nothing else, we learn a lot more about him, and the people around the family. Will anyone have a problem going along with this?"

All shook their heads, including Alicia, although Murphy

wasn't sure if she was copying the others in a bit of a mocking way. Only Rhapshaw remained still.

"Good work," the commissioner said. "I'll update Mrs. Poole when she arrives."

With that, Rhapshaw departed and Murphy announced it was time to dig in.

As Cleaver and Alicia moved away, Ndlove spoke in a near whisper. "Sir, I have the other information."

Murphy ensured his tone stayed neutral "What other information?"

"It came in shortly before the commissioner arrived. Ernest Borek. We have his background. And how strong his connections are to Dean Bicklesthwaite and Jerzy Krasowski."

Like Jerzy, Ernest came over with the first wave of migrants when the EU opened its borders to Poland. Both worked hard in fields, in recycling plants, in factories. They learned how to get by in the UK, and since they owned businesses back home, they knew how to run a company. They saved, they set up on their own, and Jerzy now owned a legitimate recruitment agency that supplied hundreds of companies with minimum wage labour. Ernest moved into the wholesaler cash and carry trade, with a little book-making and "informal casino sessions" on the side. Nothing to worry about too much, but the OC unit kept him under minimal surveillance in case one day he led them to a serious player.

Illegal, but harming no one. Hardly worth the effort but the SCA passed on their intel to the police station responsible for that district. Thankfully, it wasn't Sheerton.

As for Dean Bicklesthwaite, he was barely a blip on the SCA's radar, having been a low-level enforcer at one time and so fell under the purview of local police. He only came to their interest late on, and then only as a peripheral character. His main task, prior to his association with Borek, was ensuring the pubs in a dedicated area only rented fruit machines from a single supplier, namely Dean's mate Harvey Cooper. When Cooper went down for extortion unrelated to fruit machines, Dean fell in with Ernest's people.

Starting out as a bouncer at the card games, he soon progressed to helping plan them, then as his talent for arranging meets, events, and organising employees became clear, he started earning much better money as a logistics manager for Ernest's legitimate firm. Essentially the same thing: planning how best to move goods around the city and supply those who contracted with them. He moved into acquisitions soon after, and eventually became a partner.

For the first time, or so it seemed from his biography, Dean was fully legitimate, with no need to supplement his income with bulk and strength.

He attended card games as a friend and sometimes made money, sometimes lost. It was here, Ndlove posited, that he met Jerzy Krasowski. Through Dean, Jerzy would have met Karen, as her own statement confirmed, and the rest was history.

"So, a guy from the arse end of the tracks reinvents himself," Cleaver said. "How does this tie in with the murder?"

"I'm not sure if it does." Ndlove switched off the laptop, killing the TV on which she had presented the files sent over by the SCA.

"Background," Alicia said. "Useful. Does it tie Tomaz to any of them?"

"There's the Polish connection."

Murphy stroked his moustache thoughtfully. "Dean and Karen aren't."

"But Ernest and Jerzy are. They go way back. Jerzy built

his agency by signing up new arrivals from the EU. Not only Poland, but he started out using his connections from those communities, and advertising back home. He's expanded now, but the fact remains, the lowest paid workers in the UK are foreign. Leeds, and the wider area is no exception. Tomaz has a Polish mother, so it stands to reason, maybe there's something there."

"We should be careful," Murphy said. "Profiling like that."

"It'll be fine," Alicia said. "Criminals stick with people they trust. They trust people from their communities. If the ringleaders are Polish, it doesn't hurt to focus on that a while. As long as we don't *only* focus on that. Personally, I think the connection is less firm."

"How so?" Cleaver asked.

"If he used a guy like Tomaz, maybe he used someone else he knew was trouble."

"From his agency."

"Right. If Jerzy ordered the hit on Dean, or someone close to him did, that person might have access to guys who'd been through the agency, got blacklisted the way Tomaz did, and so knew they'd be shady."

Murphy shifted, stretching his back so he seemed even taller. "A ready supply of failures looking for a big score."

Alicia paced now. "I'm still bothered by their use of Demelza Shine, but maybe it isn't something we should put too much emphasis on. I don't want to jinx this, and I defo don't want to make light of it, but if we don't locate her, she's more than likely been killed to keep her quiet. If we can find her—and I assume we have people looking..."

"I put out a nationwide flag," Ndlove said.

"Good. If we can find her, she'll be able to tell us exactly what went on. Until then, we can only speculate."

Cleaver and Ndlove nodded in agreement.

Murphy said, "For now, we make the case against Jerzy. Alicia, Cleaver, look at Tomaz's friends, and specifically friends who were with him at the agency. Ndlove, I want you to redouble efforts into locating Demelza Shine."

All said, "Sir," and went about their assignments. Alicia needed to pay a quick visit to the parent and baby room on her way out.

CHAPTER THIRTEEN

TOMAZ'S local boozer was a run-down affair, the type people used to call "traditional" but now just looked old and in need of a hug. Most pubs this large had grown unmanageable through breweries forever squeezing their landlords for higher rent and more profit, and the majority around the country had been sold off to become Chinese or Indian restaurants rather than remain open as hostelries. The Oarsman consisted of a main, carpeted lounge with threadbare sofas and chairs, a basic bar with a wooden floor and uncomfortable seats, a sports room for watching live TV, and a pool and snooker section. The almost empty car park would easily hold thirty vehicles, but at two in the afternoon, only four were present. Cleaver's made five.

Alicia and Cleaver had visited the homes of Greg Thornton and Nathan Parker, to be told in both cases the twenty- and twenty-two-year-olds were down the job centre. Alicia picked this pair because both were formerly on the books of Jerzy's agency, whose files had been quickly requisitioned, and they were both friends with Tomaz on three social media platforms. The "job centre" was of course not an actual job centre—no one spends all day in such places anymore—but a place where they might pick up some work if they were lucky.

Inside, the odour of age and stale beer wafted over Alicia, and she took in the room, memories of another life flooded back to her. She and a group of friends occasionally went "diving" which meant visiting the worst pubs they could find, a change from their usual wine bars and nightclubs. These days, she was annoyed at her attitude and privilege that afforded her such a choice. The people in the Oarsmen were not wealthy, didn't seem particularly happy, and certainly didn't have the choice to abandon this establishment and head off to a place serving pink gin. It wasn't that they were some other species, as her mother might view them, but they lived a very different life to Alicia.

Four over-forty men at the bar drank pints, not interacting with each other. One dabbed away at a small smartphone, two stared into space, and the final one chatted to the barman whilst stabbing his finger at a newspaper laid flat between them. In a corner, a man and woman aged around sixty occupied a table, unspeaking, the man with a pint and whisky chaser and the woman with a half, two dogs lying at their feet. That was all.

Cleaver approached the bar, and the occupants all stared his way. He showed his police warrant card to the barman. "Any kids in today, mate?"

"I get ID from everyone who looks under twenty-five," the barman said. He was younger than Alicia expected, early thirties maybe.

"Relax, this isn't a check-up. Just need to know if you've seen a couple of guys. Greg Thornton, Nathan Parker. Know them?"

"I check photos and birthdates, not names."

"Hi," Alicia said. "Listen, I know you have to be all, like, *grrrrr*, with the police around here. But we really do just want a word with them."

The barman laughed once. Just once. "I mean it. I don't get their names. Some baby faces playing pool right now, but I ID'd 'em last time they were in."

"You remembered them then?"

"Faces. Birthdays. Not names."

"Thanks," Cleaver said.

The pair progressed through the pub to a door that led down a stinking corridor containing both male, female, and disabled loos, and out into a wide room with two pool tables and a snooker table. The lights overhead only worked on the snooker table, which is where Greg Thornton and Nathan Parker knocked balls around with two similarly scruffy, skinny youths looking on.

"Think they'll run?" Alicia asked.

"Let's find out." Cleaver approached the group, ID in hand. "Hey, police."

All four looked his way, then returned to the game.

"I need to ask you guys about a pal of yours. Tomaz Gortze."

The kid about to take a shot, Nathan, retracted his cue, placed it on the floor butt-first, and stood upright. He dead-eyed the pair of detectives. "He was with us all night."

"Nice try, Mr. Parker, but he was arrested last night."

Greg Thornton spoke up. "Yeah, well, we were all together. Nate must've been mistaken. He's usually with us. But yeah, I think maybe Tomaz was missing for some reason."

"Sorry we can't help," Nathan said.

"Oh, I think you can." Alicia scooted forward. Conscious of not flirting too heavily with the younger men, and deeply conscious she wasn't quite in the shape that helped men swoon around her, she played it coy instead. "You like your friend, and want what's best for him, don't you?"

"Sure." Greg shared furtive glances with his three friends.

"And if he was in super-big trouble because he was keeping his mouth shut, you'd back him up, wouldn't you?"

"Of course, yeah. It's his choice."

"But what if his actions were so bad, and the people he's protecting are much, much worse than whatever you boys are up to?"

"We ain't up to nothing."

"Even them?"

The pair who hadn't spoken shrugged.

Nathan said, "He's a sound guy, Tomaz is. If he's done something wrong, he had a good reason."

Cleaver strode past Alicia and stood behind Nathan. "If we search the four of you, which one will serve the most time?"

Greg's grip tightened on his cue. As Nathan caught his friend's eye, his fingers also curled more securely. The pair with no voice ceased leaning and now stood firm.

"Right." Alicia clapped her hands together hard. "This macho nonsense is loads of fun, but I'm just a wee girl who's getting all frightened by the muscles and testosterone, so if anyone is going to do anything violent, please direct it at Detective Inspector Cleaver, and not me."

"Hey," Cleaver said.

"Well, I'm sorry, but you're the one provoking these lads, and they're doing nothing more than playing a bit of snooker, having a pint, and dealing a little weed."

"Right," one of the unspeaking pair said.

"Nice one, knobhead," Greg said.

The guy who spoke frowned, then got what he'd just said. "Ah, no, I mean, yeah, we're playing snooker and having a pint, but—"

"Tomaz Gortze," Alicia said. "You boys aren't the sort to get muddled up in a murder, are you?"

"Murder?" Greg backed off, his fingers loosening on his cue. "We haven't done anything like that."

"And you don't want your friend going down for it, either."

"It's not us." Nathan held still and gave his friends a sharp look that suggested they stand their ground too. "You can't pin anything like that on us."

"And we don't want to," Alicia said. "I just want to know about Tomaz's other friends."

Pause. Glance. Swallow. Greg said, "They don't come in here."

"*Greg*," Nathan said in warning.

"Forget it, they'll never know it was us. Just want these pricks out of here."

"Love you too," Alicia said.

"The Gable House."

Cleaver turned to Alicia. "Around the corner from where Dean used to live."

"Rough?"

"Makes this place look like it deserves a Michelin star."

As it happened, the Gable House was no longer the pit Cleaver spoke about. Alicia hadn't recognised the name but when she saw the Gable House's location she instantly recalled that she and her giggly friends had also patronised what was a poky spit-and-sawdust place in her youth, but it appeared to have undergone something of a makeover since. As they entered through a doorway that blew hot air at them, Alicia considered maybe she'd had a drink in here at the same time as

Dean back when he was muscling fruit machines through the doors of unwilling landlords.

The suburb of Seacroft was undergoing a similar gentrification as Chapeltown, although it was slower going. The Tesco had popped up years ago, and as house prices in the nearby Moortown and Shadwell skyrocketed, it drove out those residents who'd grown up there and could not afford to remain.

The street in which Karen grew up, raised mostly alone by Dean Bicklesthwaite, now boasted house prices more akin to Chapel Allerton, while only five minutes' walk away the back-to-back terraces continued to fall in value. The refurbishment of the Gable House was clearly in reaction to the new breed of resident.

Cleaver ducked under a low beam as they made their way down three stone steps to a thick carpet, past a sign inviting them to wait to be seated, and over to the bar. The place was, literally, empty of diners or drinkers. A blonde woman of maybe eighteen wore a nose stud and a pretty smile that dropped away as soon as Alicia and Cleaver presented their credentials.

"Is everything okay?" she asked in a rush.

"Just need a chat with anyone who works here regularly," Cleaver said.

"I'm in three days a week. I can get James. He's the manager."

"Get James please."

She got James.

James wasn't pleased at being separated from his paperwork. He was a larger bald man in late middle age and his gut really knew it. Smudged tattoos ran down his arms, old green things he must have commissioned decades ago. He introduced himself as James Harper and his voice was deep and broken, his accent thick Yorkshire.

Alicia said, "I know you, James."

The big man looked down at her. "Not sure we've met."

"No, no. When I was a youngster. Like, nineteen, twenty."

"Not much older now, are you, love?"

"Aw, cute." She shoved him gently in the shoulder. "I mean, when I was a carefree girl, out for a good time. I'm sure you were here when we popped in a couple of times."

"Aye." James dabbed his hand over his smooth head. "Owned the place since the 80s. I went by 'Big Jim' back then. Going broke was the old place, so I, ehh, *upscaled* I think they call it."

Alicia took out her phone. On the way over from the Oarsman, she'd installed photos of all the principle suspects, one of which she showed to James. "You know him?"

"I know the face," he said of Ernest Borek. "Polish fella."

"Him?" She swiped to Tomaz Gortze.

"Maybe. Recently. But he's not part of the first fella's bunch of friends."

"Oh, the first fella's friends. Hey, let's sit down."

The detectives kindly declined a drink and James led them to a corner near a real fire that hadn't been lit yet where he explained he had a silent partner invest in the pub, someone who grew up around here and made it big. When they heard the place was closing they wanted to save it. "Ah, I didn't want to sell, and I knew the pub trade's in the toilet, but this guy, he was happy just to invest. This was my idea. All the fancy Dans moving in. Paid off too. You wanna know the weird thing?"

"What's the weird thing?" Alicia asked.

"Folk still come in. The old regulars. Not all of 'em of course. Beer's gone up by almost double. But guys like this." He pointed at Alicia's phone. "They always had cash. Still do. I'm just glad they're not like they used to be."

"And how's that?"

"Loud. Swearing. Oasis on the jukebox. Not shy of a fight if something cropped up."

"Place was a hole," Cleaver said. "I was in uniform back then, what, ten years ago?"

James nodded. "Yeah, bit rough."

"A bit. Couple of times a week?"

James chuckled. "Yeah, we had some coppers in here more than the regulars." He adopted a nostalgic expression, looking off into a different corner of the pub. "Wouldn't've let my daughter behind the bar back then, I can tell you. Even though there were always women around."

"Women? Rough ones?"

"Yeah, some. Weird, kooky types. Figured most were Eastern Europeans. But some locals. There were a couple who kept coming back. One in particular, I think she kept 'em in line. Local lass, took no crap, y'know. Weird girl, weird nickname, like she's trying to fit in with the Polish fellas."

"What was the nickname?" Alicia asked.

"No clue now, love, sorry. But she wasn't nice. Like I said, wouldn't have wanted my little girl hanging with 'em."

"No." Cleaver eyed the girl with her attention on an iPhone. "Do you miss it?"

"Sometimes." James returned his focus to Alicia's screen, which had locked itself. "Those guys cleaned up their acts about the same time the brewery put their prices up. Financial crash changed everything. Suddenly, it was like me making a profit was a sin or something. They wanted everything I had, then to pay me some pittance of a salary. Said it was the only way to keep going. We're freehold now, thanks to Benny."

"Benny?"

"My partner."

"Right."

"*Business* partner. I'm still married. To a woman."

"Okay." Alicia unlocked her phone screen and showed a photo of Dean. "Remember him?"

"Yeah, yeah, he was part of the group. Not in here so much now."

"He moved away."

"Then someone killed him," Cleaver said.

James's forehead crinkled a little but not outright concern. More caution. "And you think these lads might've had something to do with it?"

"Or one of their clients. What can you tell me about them?"

"Got any more pics?"

Alicia swiped to Jerzy, then Karen, then back to Tomaz.

"The guy, yeah. Not the young one. There's a bunch come in from time to time. The youngster, I don't think so. The woman doesn't ring a bell, but the other fellas know each other. That guy…" He was referring to Jerzy. "He didn't join 'em until later, though. Not part of things when it was rough in here. But yeah, he's one of the lads. Quiet these days, thank God."

He'd put Jerzy, Dean, and Ernest in the same group of friends.

"Who else?" Alicia asked. "I don't have pictures, but if you know any names, it'd be helpful."

"I don't really get names these days. Especially now they're low key. No trouble from them."

"What sort of trouble did they cause before?" Cleaver asked.

"Nothing big, not in here. There was some loan business. Fruities. Protection stuff. Gambling. Before it all dropped off a bit."

"A protection racket?"

"Yeah. I benefited without paying up simply 'cause they

drank here, but a few cafes and pubs gave in. Took the fruities, gave over a share of the profits. Not a good bunch, but more honest than the damn breweries. Nothing like being a freehold. We have a chef now and everything."

"You said they dropped away," Alicia said. "The naughty businesses. I'm guessing this is just before they got proper jobs."

"That's what I heard. But I don't hear much. I'm not interested really. But yeah, seemed they got a lot quieter after Bobby got put inside."

"Bobby?"

"Bobby Carr. He was their leader. Savage bugger. Him and his pal Louis. Got in more fights than the others combined. He was in charge of selling a bit of stuff under the table."

"Stuff?"

James chuckled, again in that nostalgic way. "They made out like it were stolen gear. Off the back of a lorry, you know? But it weren't. Just cheap knock-off stuff. Punters are more willing to buy real stuff when it's nicked. Better than fakes."

"What'd Bobby Carr go down for?" Cleaver asked.

James sighed, stared at the table for a moment. "Manslaughter. He killed a guy with his bare hands. Not here. Over Skipton way, I think. You'll have the details on file somewhere, I'm sure."

Alicia wanted to know more, but Cleaver said it was time to go, so Alicia thanked James very much, and they returned to the car.

Driving, Cleaver explained he didn't need anything else from James Harper, and nor did he need to review the file on Bobby Carr, even though Alicia knew he would. The man was thorough.

"It looks like the Krasowski family and the bookie are associated with Bobby Carr."

"I know I should know the answer to this, but I also know you're just itching to tell me. Who is Bobby Carr?"

"He's a hitman, Alicia. Just like we've been looking for. Responsible for at least twelve underground murders. He's no ghost, no spook, no special training. Just a guy willing to kill without mercy. Served five years for manslaughter, got out, reformed himself. Allegedly. Last spotted enjoying a walking holiday in Cumbria. A changed man. Again, *allegedly*."

"So, there's definitely an organised crime angle to work here." Alicia thought about it. "If there's a grudge going back, maybe it isn't Jerzy's affair we should be concentrating on."

Cleaver was about to speak, but the phone rang, echoing around the car with the Bluetooth connection. DC Ndlove's name flashed up on the satnav display. Cleaver answered. "DI Cleaver. I'm driving. Also present is Alicia."

"Sir," Ndlove said, "I found Demelza Shine."

"Dead?"

"No, sir, she's fine. She wasn't hiding. She'd just been busy. She's on tour in Blackpool."

CHAPTER FOURTEEN

REBECCA NDLOVE GREETED MURPHY, Cleaver, and Alicia as they bustled into the inquiry room, thinking she'd done a good job yet hoping no one would patronise her by making a big deal out of it. First, she explained the situation.

"I started calling the missing persons divisions to make sure they had all our intel, and to be sure they understood she was a material witness in a murder, which placed her in danger. I went wider and called a DC I know who transferred over the Pennines to Manchester, and she threw her net wide too. Got a hit from Blackpool."

"Bloody dive," Cleaver said.

"But so glittery." Alicia sat and put her feet up on the desk. "Since she's performing in a garish, over-hyped seaside town, do we get a day out at the beach, or are they bringing her to us?"

"She's doing a show under the name Talitha," Ndlove went on, annoyed at the interruption. "I asked, and it doesn't mean anything. Just mysterious."

"I prefer Demelza Shine."

"Yes, well, she got the knock from local police and they put her on the phone to me. Shocked at the murder, but she wouldn't answer any questions."

"Lawyer?" Murphy asked.

"No, sir. She just says she wants to, quote, 'do things right.' She said she's going to speak to her publicist before commenting further."

Cleaver rubbed the bridge of his nose, one hand across his stomach. Not impressed. "Can we not forget this woman is a suspect, not just a witness?"

Murphy stared at Ndlove for an answer.

She said, "Sorry, sir, I didn't push it. I mean, we think the OC angle is more likely, isn't it?"

"And if she's doing a runner right now?"

"She's on stage in half an hour, sir. And Blackpool have agreed to put a couple of uniforms on her. Protection, and … I'll make sure they know she isn't to leave the country. If she heads for an airport, we'll pick her up."

"Good."

"We'll get a bill, but I thought you'd rather we did it that way."

"It's okay, Detective Constable. What do you think she meant by 'doing it right'?"

Ndlove wet her lips, reluctant to screw up any more than she already had. "She's in show business. She wants to speak to a publicist before a lawyer. I think when she shows up to give her statement there'll be cameras around."

"I agree," Alicia said. "Now she knows she was duped, she knows there was a murder, so she knows exactly who the killer is. She'll milk it for all it's worth."

Ndlove detected a hint of annoyance behind Alicia's words. She'd heard the perky, happy-go-lucky lady superstar was a bit shy around cameras, partly because she found it hard to act like a professional, and partly because she simply didn't trust them. Ndlove didn't have much experience, but she'd learned not to treat reporters as the enemy by default. Alicia's weakness could allow Ndlove a little publicity of her own. Get her face seen by the higher-ups.

She wasn't ready for a promotion, but it couldn't hurt to get noticed.

"I'll be in touch with Blackpool," Murphy said. "DC Ndlove, can you forward me the contacts you have over there? I'll be sure to show plenty of gratitude before I ask them to pick her up and transport her over here."

"Get ready for the big bill!" Alicia said, standing.

"Anyone for the pub?" Cleaver asked the other three.

"Baby," Alicia said.

"Sorry," Ndlove said. "Childcare and a husband."

Cleaver shrugged. "Maybe I'll tap up Sergeant Ball before he comes on shift."

He left, and Murphy followed, bidding all a good night.

"Just us girls," Alicia said.

"Not for long." Ndlove packed away her iPad, logged out of her laptop, and gathered her bag and phone.

"Do I upset you?"

Ndlove paused. "Ma'am?"

"No 'ma'am', no ranks. Just two women." Alicia gave her a wide, bright smile, but it looked forced. "You need to smile more, Rebecca."

"I'm sorry, ma'am?"

"Smile. You need to smile more. Nobody like a misery guts."

"I'm not trying to make friends. I just want to do my job and get the results we need."

"But I'm such a good friend. So much fun! Even my name says so. And look." She pushed her fingers into the corners of her mouth, widening the smile into a clownlike grin. "When you smile on the outside, even if you're a super-serious type, you end up smiling on the inside. Try it."

Ndlove plonked her bag on a chair and sighed. "Ma'am, you say you want to do away with rank for a moment?"

Alicia dropped her hands, clasped them in front of her, and stood straight. "Yep. Just two cool girls chatting."

"Why do you want to be friends with me?"

"I want to be friends with everyone. I like having friends."

"White people like you…" Ndlove checked her tone. She didn't want to come across as combative. Just matter-of-fact. "You're often over-friendly to me. My husband says it's because white liberals want as many FOCs as possible—"

"FOCs?"

"Friends of colour. I'm not sure that's you, though. You seem to be like that with everyone. Overcompensating. Like if someone doesn't smile around you, you've failed. But you also don't strike me as particularly liberal."

"I don't?"

"The thing about Poles and other communities earlier today. It's accurate, but people like you are usually hand-wringing guilt trippers. Plus, criminals tend to die around you. The kidnapper last year … the psycho in a coma … the guy in America … that mad politics-inspired killer. There are probably more, since you get loaned out around Europol when convenient, and—"

"Okay," Alicia said. "I get it. And I'm sorry if I came across as anything but friendly." Her smile faded some but lingered as she picked up her coat and bag. At the door, Alicia said, "See you tomorrow, Detective Constable."

"Goodnight, ma'am."

And as Alicia exited, Ndlove wondered if she'd been too hard on her, or not hard enough. Perhaps next time Alicia asked, Ndlove would tell her the real reason she had a problem with her.

CHAPTER FIFTEEN

DID DC NDLOVE really accuse Alicia of *racism*? Was being *too friendly* a social malady now? Or was Ndlove's comment racist in itself?

White people like you.

Imagine Alicia making that comment back at her.

Black people like you.

No matter how she finished that sentence she'd be run out of town ahead of a mob with flaming torches and pitchforks. Normally, Alicia would agree with them.

Black people like you need to stop generalising about white people like me.

Fairly neutral, almost factual, since a true racist would be triggered by Ndlove's words and make that person even more racist. Even though she perceived Alicia's efforts as the brand of cringeworthy overcompensation practiced by the wet lettuce variety of liberal, did she really have a right to accuse Alicia that way?

Black people like you enjoy ice cream.

See, even though it was (probably) true that Ndlove enjoyed ice cream, it'd still feel wrong coming from Alicia.

And she *got* that there was always a power dynamic at work, that a white person making an assumption based on race—be it negative, positive, or neutral—was always diminishing in some way. She didn't like it, but she understood it.

Wow, race. How did it all get so messed up? What happened to everyone just doing their jobs, forgetting about skin colour or religion or country of origin? It was how Alicia treated school and university and the academy. She'd lived her life that way, and never once had anyone accused of anything stronger than being an annoying, unprofessional weirdo—but that opinion usually changed once they went through the Five Stages of Alicia.

Perhaps Ndlove just wasn't there yet.

That said, since everyone's point of view is coloured by their experiences, if Alicia was annoying to a person who had fought against a system seemingly designed to keep people like her from breaking out, it was natural for that person to view Alicia as a patronising liberal wonk trying too hard to show off her liberal credentials. While nowhere near as problematic as outright racism, it still put a divide between "them" and "us", even if it wasn't a hostile one. It showed society still had a way to go.

Alicia decided to quit her introspection and just get on with her evening. She'd arrived at the Dot-Bot's to collect Stacey and needed to concentrate.

Stacey was awake, as requested, and Dot had fed her half an hour earlier. The car journey back to Alicia's seemed to relax the girl and even resulted in excited kicks and giggles as Alicia carried the car seat inside, her bag over the other shoulder. Up to the first floor used to be a breeze on the stairs, but with Stacey in hand, Alicia resorted to the lift. Inside, Robbie was laid on the couch with a skinny Caucasian man on top of her, kissing. With tongues. Thankfully, both were clothed.

The guy ceased the kissing and sat up sharply. "Oh, hey."

"Good evening," Alicia replied in a voice she realised too late sounded like a mum discovering her daughter in the same position.

Robbie sat up too and shoved the guy onto the floor. Giggled. "Hey, Alicia, this is Tim."

"Tim, the art teacher, Tim?"

Tim the art teacher tucked his formal shirt back into his jeans. "Hi, yes, you must be Alicia."

"Sorry for interrupting. I'll be out of your way in a second." Alicia released Stacey from her car seat and she immediately zeroed in on Tim, a startled expression springing to life.

"No, really, I have to be going." Tim scrambled to his feet.

"Honestly." Alicia jiggled Stacey, who relaxed into her shoulder. "I just have to bath this one and then I'll be in my room all night."

Roberta gave Alicia a coy smile. "Chill, girl. It's all good."

Alicia now clocked onto what they were getting at. "Oh, you already … you're already…"

Robbie and Tim stood, both shy like teens. Robbie said, "And then some."

Alicia's cheeks warmed, and she put her head down. She and Robbie never got embarrassed at each other's sexual exploits within the flat. Their rooms were on opposite sides of the hall, so they didn't share a wall, and the bathroom had a lock on it, so it wasn't like they fell over each other. But in this moment of normalcy, Alicia was reminded of her former life. When she was a cool detective, in demand both professionally and personally, and now here she was, ten pounds heavier than last year, frumpy, and hugging a child.

Her child.

Whatever romance awaited her in the future would have

to be worked around this little lady. It was all too much to take in.

"Nice to meet you." And with that, Alicia rushed off to the bathroom.

Stacey enjoyed her bath, with splashes in the little tub which Alicia placed inside the larger, grownup one for the duration. It was a little harder on her back but easier in terms of mess.

After, she placed Stacey in fresh clothes and dug out a sleeping bag for her, fastening her in and cradling her in the dark of the bedroom. An hour later, after a ten-minute feed and an extensive burping session, Stacey dropped off to sleep and Alicia changed into her own PJs.

In the kitchen, she gathered her bag to put her expressed milk in the freezer, but it was gone. Not gone. It was still in the fridge at Sheerton station. She had rushed out after her chat with Ndlove, her brain swirling with white middle-class liberal angst.

"Damn." That pressure built behind her eyes again, the sting in her nose that heralded tears, but this time she pushed it back down before they spilled.

"You okay?" Robbie had wandered in and opened a half-full bottle of wine.

"Fine. Just feeling sorry for some night-shift guy adding my breastmilk to his coffee."

"Left it behind, huh? Well, don't worry, I think you'll have enough."

Robbie opened the freezer section on the fridge and Alicia saw the stockpile with fresh eyes. Almost half a drawer was full of milk packages. Robbie chuckled and closed the door.

"That's a lot," Alicia said.

"When you go back to work full-time, you'll be glad of it."

Alicia pulled out a wine glass and placed it on the worktop where she filled it. "How come you're so patient?"

"You think you're being too … mum-like?"

"I think Stacey's taking over."

Robbie came closer. "Back on Monserrat, before the volcano sent me here, my mom and dad had a kid when I was fourteen. I was part of the family, the oldest sibling. I had a responsibility to make sure my mom and dad could keep running our café and bar. What's happening here, it's nothing. You're busting a gut to show me you can cope, and it ain't necessary. *You're* my family now."

The pair hugged.

"I'm going to bed," Robbie said with a grin. "That Tim, he's got some stamina."

Alicia laughed, embarrassed to admit to herself she was picturing the pair in the act, Tim's skinny bum and Robbie's chunky body enveloping him. "Hey, why'd he have to go? He could've spent the night."

Robbie shrugged. "He has a second job. Works four hours at a pub in town."

"Being a teacher sucks."

"Not this teacher." Robbie left her then, sashaying out in a way that Alicia wished she could pull off.

Instead, she snatched up her collection of letters from Katie and took her wine to the living room, where she flicked on the TV. A soap opera played, and Alicia had to check the time, surprised to find it was not yet eight p.m.

Stacey and Robbie in bed.

Alicia still awake, working.

Drinking wine.

All was quiet.

Alicia reread the notes and found them more depressing

than frightening. A girl acting out now she'd either found out the truth, or suspected it, about her half-sister.

She again picked up the work-issue iPad and considered plugging in Katie's details to track her down. Opening the West Yorkshire Police's intranet portal, an email from Murphy flashed up: a report detailing the movements of all the players that day.

Ernest was keeping his head down, gathering his employees at the cash and carry to deliver a quick talk that ended up with bowed heads and even a little crying. Presumably, he delivered the news of Dean Bicklesthwaite's death to the people who knew him.

Jerzy was holed up at the same Premier Inn where the family stayed the first night. He only popped out to nip into his main office in Leeds, the light blue-and-gold "Golden Start" signage over the door photographed in the report. He returned to his hotel and only emerged to eat at the pub adjacent to the building, before turning in.

Tomaz's friends were placed under surveillance too, concentrating on Greg and Nathan, who got up to nothing illegal. A warrant for electronic surveillance was being pushed through, but Alicia doubted anything would come of it.

Demelza Shine's publicist also doubled as a lawyer and persuaded the police in Blackpool to allow her to perform her show before compelling her to go with them, and since the locals there had little in way of a stake in the investigation they didn't fight too hard. At the time of sending the report, Demelza was a free woman, performing as "Talitha."

Karen's movement caught her eye, though. Alicia had to read it twice before it sunk in. She'd gone to work.

Nothing to flag suspicion, but it was odd that she would be so diligent as to attend her place of work a mere forty-eight hours after finding her father murdered in her living room.

The kids were being watched by her friend, Jenny, at Dean's house.

She was self-employed, though. A business like that runs on efficiency. Dumping a client who brought in the money was foolish, and if she believed her marriage was ending she would likely value her independence.

But...

It didn't sit right. Alicia had imbibed maybe four sips, and now she couldn't manage anymore.

She'd seen grief do some strange things, not least people throwing themselves back into work. But the children bothered Alicia. Would Karen really be so worried about her business that she'd abandon the children following not only their grandfather's death but the burglary too?

A quick call to Sheerton established a car remained at the house after it had been secured, and Jackie remained on site at Karen's request. Another officer shadowed Karen to work but kept his distance.

Alicia knocked on Robbie's bedroom door and entered when called. Robbie was playing a computer game on a PlayStation that Alicia hadn't been aware she owned. Guilt kicked in when she realised Robbie probably played it late at night when Stacey embarked on one of her marathon wailing fits. The guilt doubled when she asked, "Robbie, can I nip out for a couple of hours?"

"Sure, I'll listen out. Where you going? Hot date?"

"No, I ... I'm going to try a new gym."

Jettison Gym wasn't new, of course, but it was new to Alicia. Never one for workouts, she preferred to run with some yoga thrown in, but what with the trauma of her experiences last winter combined with a shallow stab wound, pregnancy, and obsessively tracking down Richard Hague's as-yet undiscovered victims, she'd had little time for exercise. In fact, she struggled to locate her running gear, tucked away at the back of her wardrobe.

Now she entered the glass-fronted unit on the same lot as three coffee shops, a KFC, and a Pizza Hut, just five minutes' drive from the Krasowskis' home. She told the receptionist she wanted a look around before committing to a contract, to be told that like many gyms they only required a monthly commitment, not twelve or twenty-four as had been the case the last time Alicia considered a membership.

"Hardly anyone does that anymore," the lithe, perfect-haired woman told her. "Puts people off joining. You can still have a wander, though, see if you like it."

The woman in Jettison's uniform of light blue polo shirt and navy-blue cargo shorts buzzed Alicia through the turnstile and strode around to greet her, opening the door to her right.

A hundred and fifty square feet of bikes, treadmills, cross trainers, and resistance machines spread out before Alicia, along with a significant-sized corner dedicated to weights. The gym was half-full, even at eight-thirty in the evening. Professionals, more than likely, getting in from work, favouring evening workouts over morning ones. Alicia always preferred the morning for exercise, evenings for relaxation.

The woman held the door. "If you want to use any of the equipment, just let one of our team members know, and we'll sort out an induction. No commitment, and your first session is no charge. It's cheaper if you pay your monthly fee by direct debit…"

She churned on for about a minute, a sales spiel that she must have recited a dozen times, and Alicia feigned interest. Partly to be polite, but mostly to watch Karen Krasowski monitoring a chubby man in his forties pedalling like a maniac on a bike. Dressed in tight workout gear showing off her firm curves, Karen hit a stop watch, and even from this distance, Alicia heard the command to, "Drop it down." The guy reduced his speed and sipped from a bottle.

But it wasn't the chubby fella Alicia had clocked. It was the tall, dark-haired man with light-brown skin, watching from the side. Arabic or south Asian. Clean shaven with sculpted hair that probably wouldn't move in the harshest wind. And he wasn't watching the client. He was watching Karen. Maybe five or six years younger than her, he wore the polo shirt and cargo shorts uniform of the gym, and his muscled arms tensed as he strolled past. A regular studmuffin.

He said hi to the pedalling guy, then engaged Karen in brief conversation. A conversation that meant he placed a hand on her shoulder, stroked her arm, and Karen made a simpering face. As she showed him the stopwatch, the studmuffin stood to the side, and Karen called, "Maximum effort," and the chubby guy's legs sped up until they were almost a blur.

The studmuffin gave a smile and a nod, and Karen clamped her knees together as she waved him off.

"Are you okay?" the receptionist asked.

"One moment." Alicia moved away from the door and out of earshot of the woman, allowing the door to close, and took out her phone to call Murphy. He answered quickly. She said, "You know how we were concerned Jerzy might have killed Dean to cover up an affair?"

"Yes," Murphy said.

"What if it wasn't *Jerzy's* affair that was the problem? What if someone else had a stake in things?"

"What are you talking about?"

"I think I might've found another suspect."

CHAPTER SIXTEEN

ALICIA TOOK her call out into the car park where she could talk more freely, explained what she witnessed—indicators of familiarity, of flirting, of downright intimacy—but Murphy said not to push anything.

"We've got Demelza coming in to clear this up." He spoke louder for emphasis. "If she fingers Jerzy it won't matter what Karen's been up to."

"If she doesn't confirm it's him, we're stuck," Alicia said.

"Get a picture of this ... what did you call him?"

"A studmuffin."

"Okay, well, find a better way to phrase it on the warrant *if* Demelza puts Jerzy in the clear. We'll get his image from the gym records and requisition his phone and finances. Now go home, get some sleep."

Alicia agreed to back off this line of thought but went straight back inside and asked the woman at the desk for an induction right away.

It wasn't that Alicia got off on defying Murphy, or whatever superior made a dubious decision that she couldn't go along with. It was that she simply detected more of a nagging doubt than she'd been able to articulate. There was more going on, and more suspects, and what seemed simple enough just … wasn't. Each time they thought they'd snagged a direct line to the killer, another road branched off.

Murphy didn't know for certain that Demelza would identify either Jerzy as covering up an affair, or Ernest sending a message about a debt. Could be Studmuffin was shagging Karen, then Dean played the protective dad and popped along with some heavies to warn him off, but Studmuffin turned out to be a violent psychopath. And even if he *was* a violent psychopath, there was no real danger from him in the gym. It was public, with cameras everywhere, and dozens of witnesses.

She gambled it'd be the studmuffin who'd carry out the induction, but it didn't matter much if it wasn't since she could just ask about the guy, and the woman he seemed besotted with; workplace romances are seldom secret.

However, her gamble paid off.

The tall, dark, and handsome studmuffin was an Australian called Pete Mahdavi and he smelled slightly of sweat with a dose of Lynx deodorant attempting to suppress it. Alicia wasn't put off though; a guy working in a gym should smell a little bit.

Out in the main body of the place, Karen spotted her almost straight away and gave a frown at first, but Alicia already had her excuse lined up, and made a beeline for her.

"Hey, Karen, don't worry. I'm just here to chat when you get a couple of minutes. But, hey, I need to get back into exercise, so figured I'd make it a two-for-one. Chat to you and work up a bit of a sweat. That okay?"

"Sure." Karen fiddled with her stopwatch. "I'll be about twenty minutes with Hugh."

She tilted her head at Pete, who said, "We'll be done in twenty minutes, no worries."

Alicia didn't feel the need to identify herself to Pete as police, nor did she risk too many questions about him or Karen. Pete first demonstrated, then ensured Alicia could operate the machines: the split speed on the treadmill, the variable resistance on the cross trainers and bikes, how to use the shoulder press, perform bicep curls and many others. He finished in the weights room, then she finally asked about Karen.

"She's cool," Pete said. Coolly. "Good PT."

"PT?"

"Personal trainer."

"I might need one of those."

"The Jettison does an internal program for weight loss or whatever your goals are," Pete said. "We have a PT upgrade if you're interested in that, but I'd recommend a program first. Get you into the swing of it."

"Sure. I'll look into it. What about you?"

"Yeah, I'm one of the PTs, but I'm off here at nine. Donna takes over from me, so I can set you up once she's here."

"Thanks," Alicia said, "but I'll have a chat with Karen first."

"Righto, right." Pete's attention wandered to where Karen consulted an iPad while Hugh disengaged a monitor that'd been strapped around his chest. "Might not be a great time for her. She only came in because Hugh's a regular." His voice became a whisper. "Her dad died recently."

Alicia mimicked the whisper. "I know. I'm one of the detectives on the case."

Pete froze for just a second, then looked hard at Alicia. "And you've come to see her at work."

"Two for one," Alicia said. "I need to fill her in on a couple of things, and I need to sort *this* out." She slapped her backside. Smiled. "Yep, defo need to get working on that."

Pete opened his mouth then closed it quickly.

"What?" Alicia said. "You were saying something?"

"Not something I'm really allowed to say."

"Oh, come on. Was it about my bum?"

Pete chuckled, glanced at Karen and back to Alicia. Another whisper. "I was just going to say there isn't *that* much work needed on it. But don't tell my boss I said that."

Alicia blushed and couldn't reply for a second. Yes, it really had been that long since someone complimented her backside. Although *there isn't that much work needed on it* didn't feel like the most gushing compliment a girl could enjoy, it was far superior to her own assessment. But then, Alicia knew what it looked like pre-birth.

"Thanks," she said. "Oh, looks like Karen is free."

Alicia trotted over, Pete following, and Karen greeted her. "What did you want to discuss?"

Alicia stared at Pete until he excused himself and wandered away. "Thanks!" Alicia called after him. Back to Karen, she said, "This isn't totally police business. It's … look, if you want me to mind my own business, just say so. But when we chatted earlier, you mentioned you got through your post-natal depression, and … you said you lost weight, and that's what got you into this."

"Yes, but what does that have to do with my dad's case?"

"Nothing. I just want to get back in shape. Can you help me at all? I'll pay—"

Karen held up a hand. "I'll give you fifteen minutes for free. Then you can tell me what's really going on."

Karen started Alicia on the cross trainer, five minutes of straightforward back and forth, warming up the joints and muscles, getting her ready for the first real exercise. Next was the treadmill, where she set Alicia to walk two minutes, jog two minutes, then sprint one minute. "Recover, ramp it up, then really burn it. Repeat this five-minute cycle as many times as you can manage. Start with three, which is fifteen minutes, then step it up. When you feel ready, reduce the walking period to one minute and step up the jogging or the sprints."

Alicia went through the walk, asking how she'd been, but stopped as soon as Karen halted and looked away. Sure, she'd popped in to work, but she was far from fine. Alicia changed the subject to how the body burned fat, how she could use this technique outdoors rather than in a gym, and Karen returned to her professional persona.

As the jogging kicked in, Alicia found her rhythm, and Karen advised her on her technique, before the sprint hit. Then, Alicia just went for it. She sweated, she gasped for breath, and almost stumbled once. Karen encouraged her by lying in her countdown, but it worked. Alicia kept going, her lungs burning amid this mediocre workout, and even as she knew the ten seconds remaining that Karen stated were really twenty, she felt sunshine breach inside her.

The worry she hadn't even articulated to herself, the one she couldn't risk speaking aloud, proved unfounded in those moments. Maybe this was all she needed. Exercise!

It wasn't post-natal depression.

She wasn't one of "those" mums.

Not that there was anything wrong with that, but ... no one wanted to suffer like that.

Yes, yes, she'd been down, a bit teary occasionally, but no way was this real PND. *Real* is crippling, all the time. A bit of exercise alone wouldn't give her the endorphins needed to banish it completely. And right now, Alicia's endorphins were flooding her, roiling inside, bursting throughout her whole body.

"And you did it," Karen said, slowing the machine back to walking pace.

Alicia was almost disappointed, but as she struggled to gulp enough air to speak, she figured it was for the best. She'd rev up slowly to a full regimen, but at least she knew there was hope. An end to her blubbing in sight.

"Hey, just saying goodbye," Pete said, passing them. He'd changed into jeans and donned an outdoor coat. "Anything you need, Karen, you know where I am." He made a finger-and-thumb phone sign and waggled it near his ear.

"Thanks, Pete." Karen watched him turn, then asked Alicia, "Was that really all you came for?"

"I did have one bit of news," Alicia said, loud enough for Pete to hear as well. "We found the psychic. They'll be bringing her over here first thing. Should know pretty soon if she was paid to send you home or not."

Karen blinked rapidly, but Alicia watched Pete, hoping for some change in body language, something to indicate he cared. She wasn't certain, but she thought, maybe, there was a hesitation immediately after she spoke. Just a tiny pause in his step.

And then it was gone.

"Thanks for the tips, Karen," Alicia said. "I'll be in touch with any news tomorrow."

CHAPTER SEVENTEEN

DEMELZA SHINE'S epic show as Talitha lasted three hours, half an hour of which was an interval. Since she didn't want to face the police waiting backstage, her encore lasted longer than usual—a little beyond the point where she sensed the audience had finally had enough. Her show wasn't just an extension of her 'Demelza' act. It involved big illusions, close-up magic, and a sprinkling of guest performers. She was an all-round talent who should have been bigger than David Blaine or Dynamo. But, since she was a woman, she had to work twice as hard to gain half as much traction. And the life she struggled to escape was even tougher. It made her more grateful than others.

Although her guest performers were largely made up of rejects from the latter rounds of a popular British talent show on TV, she had no intention of entering herself. She wanted to make it without a public vote. The people who distracted the audience from her technicians setting up her next big illusion were the entrants to that show who clearly had an act but weren't good enough to win, but she was able to use the talent show's logo in her advertising material. Because many in the audience were attracted to the show by a dog or an unusual dance troupe didn't bother Demelza, since she wowed every night. The audience came in not knowing who she was, but they'd remember her.

She was *good.*

Her publicist said she should be aiming for Las Vegas eventually, so that was her ultimate life goal. Her own residency in one of the bigger venues. For now, though, she was building a reputation around the UK, in person and on social media. Her YouTube channel had 1.2 million subscribers from around the world, and material featuring her hashtags and handles were shared hundreds of times a day through Instagram and Twitter. She funded her routines and social media gurus from the sale of her mother's home after she passed away six years earlier, and the smaller, dumber psychic readings in pubs and working men's clubs. Just as she was about to start applying for credit cards, a pair of magicians scheduled to play one of Blackpool's larger venues were caught up in a sexual harassment scandal—one pestering multiple assistants and fans, the other covering it up—so they left a vacancy. Demelza showed the venue owners a compilation of her best illusions, mostly performed individually but compiled into a single show reel. Then she invited them to view her gig in full, *live,* at her expense. When they agreed, she blew the remainder of her savings on the hour-long audition, and once she was certain they were hooked, she showed them her proposal for publicity—that she had licenced limited use of the TV show's brand—and how she would space it out to three hours, making it an all-round variety show, centred around her magic. She demonstrated her much-practiced cold reading skills on three members of the board in charge of making the booking at the theatre, and they were sold.

Unfortunately, she needed a lot more seed money than a couple of credit cards could provide.

Now the police were trying to take it all away from her. If her part in that murder became public, she'd be outed as a fraud and her career would crank into reverse. She couldn't allow that, no matter how much she wished she'd taken no part in it.

After the show, they were waiting backstage. Two in plain clothes here, a pair of uniforms outside.

"I'm changing first," she said.

The woman insisted on waiting inside with her, checked the windows, and then turned her back while Demelza disrobed.

It was all going to shit. She supplemented her lack of earnings from the bigger shows with that stupid medium act. Stupid, but it was her first paying gig. Annoying that she'd already used her real name. She didn't want that coming back to bite her every time she went on TV. *Talitha*. A name she made up out of thin air, one she thought sounded like something out of fantasy fiction. And because she started going only by "Demelza" for the dead-talking acts, she could use her surname on the newer ones.

Talitha Shine.

The most successful magician of the modern era.

Soon. *If* she could keep the pigs from ruining her. And it had all been going so well.

The Blackpool show started two days earlier and had already turned a profit on her initial investment. The running costs had stabilised, and she knew how many tickets she needed to sell for break-even, which was around a third of the theatre's capacity. It was going well.

With the police wanting to ask questions about her show in the Roundhay pub, they only said, "In connection with a serious incident," but refused to elaborate. She'd been too busy to watch the news in detail, and the police weren't saying anything, but once she saw the names, she could guess what went down.

"I'm ready."

Back in her civilian clothes, the cops escorted her out to their vehicle, where they informed her that although she wasn't under arrest, she had the right to remain silent, and a bunch of other things that sounded very much like she was under arrest. Even though she wasn't.

"What is going on?" Demelza asked the female in the back seat with her.

"You'll be told everything you need to know back in Leeds."

"You're taking me all the way to Leeds?"

"Not us. We're taking you to the station. A transport will take you the rest of the way."

"Can I pack some things? My hotel is just around the corner."

The female didn't reply.

The man in front sighed through his nose. "You'll have five minutes. And DC Lockwood goes inside with you."

"Thank you." After a few moments directing them, Demelza said, "Can you at least give me the basics? I honestly don't know what it could be. Why they want to speak to me. Not exactly."

Silence. Then the female must have sensed the barely suppressed panic rising in Demelza. "It's to do with one of your readings. You sent some woman home. They want to know how you did it. Who set it up."

It was worse than Demelza thought. She couldn't give away something like that. Her career would be in ruins. And if the escalation fell through, if the people in Blackpool stopped coming, if she never made it to the City Varieties in Leeds, the Palladium in London, the O2 in Sheffield … she wouldn't even have her bullshit ooga-booga cold reading gig to fall back on.

At the hotel, Demelza found a small bag to pack some underwear, toiletries, and a fresh top, and while DC Lockwood waited by the door, she fiddled under her bed. Here, she found her laptop and opened it up.

"What are you doing?" Lockwood asked.

"Just … I have to drop someone a note. Please. It'll only be a second."

"You'll be able to make a call shortly."

"It's almost midnight." Demelza added strain to her voice. She had to be an actress as well as technically proficient. "I just need to—"

"Do it." Lockwood checked her watch. "Fast."

Demelza booted up the laptop, a solid state one so it worked as quickly as a MacBook, and fired off an email to Jasinda Thanwareth, her publicist and lawyer, asking her if she could possibly block the police from compelling her to reveal her secrets. If it was made public she'd be dismissed from the magic circle, and the bad publicity would end this two-week residency, which was supposed to make her name. If she couldn't prove herself a bankable act, she'd go the same way as so many almost-there entertainers.

She hit send, and Lockwood asked her to hurry. "Mike" wasn't too patient. A knock at the door sounded.

"That'll be him," Lockwood said, and turned to answer it.

Demelza had already opened a browser and typed the words "incident Leeds news" in the hope of discovering what was known so far.

The door opened.

Demelza clicked the first article, which featured the murder of a man in Shadwell.

"I'll be one second," she said, going back to the search results.

"Take your time," came a voice.

Demelza glanced up, expecting to see Mike, the other copper from the car. Instead, she found DC Lockwood leaning against the wall with both hands clamped over her throat, blood oozing from an unseen wound. It coated her hands, flowing in rivers between her fingers and down her front.

"What the hell are you doing here?" Demelza demanded, standing.

"I'd have thought that was obvious." The intruder raced forward too quickly for Demelza to utter a word.

CHAPTER EIGHTEEN

ALICIA ARRIVED last for the morning briefing at eight-thirty. Graham Rhapshaw and Marissa Poole were present, conferenced together up one end, with Murphy, Ndlove, and Cleaver the other. Someone had brought in a Nespresso machine for pod-generated coffee, so after saying good morning to everyone, Alicia helped herself. The hit jolted her with a denser buzz than her half-cup of instant did on her way to Dot's with Stacey.

Her lack of sleep last night had little to do with her adorable bag of noise and poo. For a change, she welcomed the girl's one a.m. feed since she was still amped from one thing or another.

The exercise burst, releasing much-needed adrenaline? Or nervous about disclosing confidential information about the investigation on the off-chance it delivered a tick or a tell that could, maybe, hint at Pete Mahdavi's guilt?

Probably the second one.

"The Blackpool plods are late with Demelza," Murphy said. "I haven't had official comms yet, but ... they lost one of their own last night, so—understandably—they dedicated everything they had to that. I haven't pushed it. We'd be the same."

Alicia swallowed back a spike of fear. Whenever someone was seriously hurt or killed on duty, it was a reminder it could happen to them. At any point. Police officers all over the country would be swapping their profile pics on social media for a black background punctuated by a horizontal blue line.

The thin blue line.

No matter the situation, all police officers, every day, placed their lives in danger. A domestic, a robbery, interviewing a witness. Whenever you're around crime, you don't have to be a gunslinger to walk into a deadly scenario.

"For now," Murphy said, "we'll recap. Alicia found another possible suspect in … what was his name?"

Alicia coughed the catch from her throat. "Pete Mahdavi. I think he's been at it with Karen, but I might be wrong. Could be one of those platonic affairs."

"Platonic affair?" Marissa Poole said. "What on earth is that?"

"It's when two people in a workplace or whatever really fancy each other, might even hang out socially, but because one or the other or both are married or in a relationship, they don't go all the way. Willpower. But they both want to. And they probably will. Eventually. If they don't stop seeing each other. Basically, an affair without the naughty business."

"That wasn't on the logs," Ndlove said.

"Sorry?"

"Your operation last night. It wasn't on the logs."

Alicia sipped her coffee, making adorable angel eyes at the group, and when she lowered the cup she'd pressed her cheeks into service, dimpling with her smile. "No, I popped in to say hi and maybe run a bit. Haven't exactly been active recently. Wasn't official. But I'll be writing it up this morning."

"But it was not sanctioned," Poole said. "In my days as a judge, this would be something a defence lawyer would jump on. A break in procedure, in the chain of command."

"I knew where she was," Murphy said, engaging his officious robo-tone. "You will find a call between myself and Alicia matches the time of the CCTV stamp at the gym, and the conversation entailed my having doubts about DS Friend making contact informally, but she convinced me it was worth it to see this new possible suspect's reaction. I authorised it verbally, and the phone call should be enough to quash any 'reasonable doubt' a jury may have."

Rhapshaw looked sideways at Alicia. He knew how she'd go off on her own sometimes, needing to scratch a mental itch, even when she couldn't see clearly what she was searching for. Her computer often sent her conclusions without the workings-out, so she frequently worked backward, trying to unpack what had been processed without her noticing. She suspected he knew Murphy was half-lying, but it appeared to satisfy Poole, who pressed her mouth tightly closed.

"What was said?" Ndlove asked. "Did you record the conversation?"

"No," Alicia said. "I believed it would be counterproductive to interview a recently bereaved woman under caution while I ran on a treadmill. It was essentially a punt. I wanted to touch base with her, and accidentally came across the suspect. That's when I spoke to DCI Murphy. And Pete Mahdavi gave me enough suspicion to make our interest in him official, just in case Demelza Shine fails to ID one of our current suspects. This will allow us to show a jury..." She made a point of speaking directly to Marissa Poole here. "That we had an open mind all along and were not concentrating on one subject."

Cleaver's mobile rang. He checked the number and slipped off to the corridor to take it.

Back to the room, Alicia said, "So yes, I took a chance. And it paid off."

Cleaver returned quickly, his face ashen. His mouth was a tiny hole, eyes slack and distraught.

Alicia's throat closed. Stomach fell away. Her hands chilled right to her fingers. She swallowed. Could not pull away from Cleaver's slow walk. "But I should also add that DCI Murphy, while he knew of my intent to identify myself as an officer in the presence of Pete Mahdavi and insinuate we were close to a breakthrough, absolutely warned me against revealing we had located Demelza Shine." She turned fully to the room, favouring Murphy. "I chose to disclose that information on my own."

Murphy remained silent a moment, his gaze flicking from Alicia to Cleaver, and back to Alicia. "Oh, crap."

"What is it?" Rhapshaw demanded. "What exactly is going on?"

"Demelza Shine is dead," Alicia said. "Isn't she?"

Cleaver nodded. "Killed in the same incident that the Blackpool detective lost her life. A police officer and our key witness were both murdered."

CHAPTER NINETEEN

THE DEATHS WERE NOT AUTOMATICALLY a direct result of what Alicia did, but that didn't stop the crippling guilt that washed over her. She sat down immediately, hand to her gut, a pain like contractions almost splitting her in two.

The first thing Murphy did was try to mitigate the damage. "Mrs. Poole, Commissioner, I'm sure you'll understand we have a situation to handle here. If you wouldn't mind waiting in my office, I'll bring you an update as soon as I can."

"I am going nowhere," Rhapshaw said. "What exactly have you people *done?*"

But officious-Murphy had abandoned ship and real-Murphy took the helm. "Sir, your guest is a civilian. Here with my permission as a courtesy. We now have a serious matter to attend to and I cannot deal with it when I'm being second-guessed by someone with political ambitions. This is an internal matter. You're free to stick around, sir, but she must leave. And I doubt you'll be leaving her alone in a place like this."

Poole's chin dropped, eyebrows raised; a schoolmarm who wasn't used to such insolence.

But Murphy never backed down when his blood was up like this. "Now, please."

Rhapshaw had known Murphy longer than Alicia, so it didn't take him long to guide Marissa Poole to the door, citing the data protection act, and biasing any potential action that may result from what happened.

Once they were gone, Murphy kicked the team into action. "DC Ndlove, I want scenarios. Could Mahdavi have got from Leeds to Blackpool in time to commit the murder? Cleaver, track him. And Karen. We can't rule her out either. Alicia, did you tell anyone else about her location?"

"I…" Alicia could barely get that one syllable out. "I don't think so. But … Karen could have spoken. Or Pete, if he was in on it. But … I don't think I specified exactly where she was."

"You don't think?"

Ndlove and Cleaver didn't seem to be breathing, awaiting her answer.

She said, "I'm about 75 percent sure I didn't."

Ndlove shook her head and cast her full attention on a laptop, working the keyboard and mouse.

Cleaver waited a moment longer. "I'll go to Jackie Osbourne. Ask her to question Karen cold, like a friendly update, okay? Specifically ask her if she spoke to anyone about Demelza's location. If Karen says she never knew the location, Alicia's in the clear, yeah?"

Alicia was shaking. Not visibly, but that's because she'd clasped both hands in her lap. "Not exactly clear."

"Ndlove?" Murphy said.

Eyes still on the laptop, fingers now still, Ndlove said, "According to the RAC, the fastest route between Leeds and Blackpool is one hour, forty minutes. That's obeying speed limits in average traffic. Eight-thirty at night, pushing the speed up over eighty…"

"She was killed at her hotel just after eleven," Cleaver said. "What time did you see Karen and Pete?"

"Eight-thirty," Alicia said. "Eight-forty-five maybe. But then I had the induction, so add another half an hour."

"Could still be done," Ndlove said.

"They'd need to know Demelza's hotel," Murphy said. "And how to find it. And that there were police present."

Ndlove gave a slight grimace, then reverted to a neutral expression and tone. "First, DS Friend already disclosed the police were bringing her in, possibly a location. Second, if she said the woman was performing in Blackpool, it wouldn't take a lot to ID a psychic's gig. Given there's about a half-hour's play in the timings, it's plenty to make it to the venue, wait, and follow her and her police escort to a hotel. Learning a room number isn't hard. How big was the hotel?"

Cleaver didn't know. "There are a lot of small places there, though."

Ndlove was done. She sat back.

"We'll figure this out," Murphy told Alicia.

"No." Alicia finally breathed normally, a long exhale that almost felt cleansing. "I don't want to be protected from this. I will protect the case, though, and all of you." She lingered on Murphy. "I want to be punished as much as is reasonable. If I got Demelza killed, I deserve everything coming to me."

CHAPTER TWENTY

ALICIA PARKED in the rain outside a house that had been boarded up for almost a year. A semi-detached property a couple of miles from Karen and Jerzy Krasowski's home. Same postcode, slightly less well off. That's not to say poor, either. The houses on this street boasted three bedrooms, but they were *large* bedrooms, with spacious living areas and gardens large enough for five-a-side football, and double garages for their higher-value-than-average vehicles. Top of the range BMWs and Audis rather than sports cars, but still way out of Alicia's bracket.

The house next door to Richard Hague's former residence was up for sale and appeared dark, the owners having vacated the premises after the revelations about their neighbour were made public. Katie was now executor; the doctors having declared her dad would never recover. On the slight, infinitesimal possibility his motor functions were restored, he'd have suffered extreme brain damage, and probably would not be aware of anything; he'd certainly have no ability to comprehend the complexities of property law. A permanent vegetative state was the best prognosis they could offer.

Katie wanted to sell up and move as quickly as possible.

Unfortunately, the only people who wanted to buy were developers with deep enough pockets to pull the bricks down and start over. With another house attached, that wasn't possible. Now that was for sale too, perhaps soon there'd be a glimmer of closure for Katie. Symbols could act as powerful psychological cleansers, as could symbolic actions, like property being destroyed, burning an unfaithful spouse's belongings, or clearing out the closet of a deceased loved one.

Karen would soon be doing that.

And now, too, would Demelza Shine's next of kin. Not to mention the detective who died, a young up-and-comer named DC Lockwood. She was engaged to a cameraman who'd done work for some of the top comedians and even major BBC productions like *Strictly* and *The One Show*.

Richard's house looked lonely. The metallic patter of rain on the car's roof helped her to zone out, to view the house as a child in a playground, cowed and bullied through no fault of its own but because of who owned it. As if, somehow, the sins of the past haunted its present. If Richard had committed murder within its walls, that might have made the house's seclusion understandable, but all he did here was live with a woman he loved so much his urge to kill went away—*Gillian*, if Alicia remembered correctly. He had a child with the woman, whom they named Katherine, quickly evolving into Katie, a vivacious and sports-obsessed teen who knew her own mind and took no crap from anyone. Gillian died of cancer when Katie was in her early teens, though, and Richard raised her alone. Here, in this house.

And that's all the history these bricks witnessed. Katie's disappearance could have infected it with sadness, Alicia supposed, but Richard's spree that followed took place a long way from here: murdering a prostitute and a drug dealer, torturing a witness, and hunting down the serial killer holding his daughter captive. To be fair, Alicia killed the last one. But it was Richard's fault.

If he had just let them do their jobs, Alicia would have found the man. They were on the same route, the same trail to the same culprit. The only question was whether the police would have acted so swiftly if it hadn't become evident someone else was looking for Katie as well as them.

What was clear was that if Richard had backed off, allowed Alicia and the West Yorkshire Police to act alone, Alicia would never have suspected his monstrous past. Or present. She slept with him after days of pent-up tension between them, and knew it was a mistake at the time. Just not what sort of mistake it would turn out to be.

She drove away, getting home early, having been relieved of duty for the day. Murphy logged it as flexible working, that he'd assigned her research that could be done from home rather than present in the office. She knew he'd be pacifying Marissa Poole and Graham Rhapshaw, completing paperwork to send on to Professional Standards, the department younger coppers liked to call IA—an Americanism for "internal affairs" that Murphy had referred to in the past with the sort of colourful language that'd make hardened soldiers blush.

There were two hours until the Dot-Bot was due to relinquish Stacey, and Robbie was going out with Tim straight after work, so for the first time in over four months, Alicia made a pot of tea, placed milk in a little jug, and arranged a plateful of chocolate biscuits on a tray. She carted it all through to the living room, where she put the TV on and went through her stored shows on the Sky+ box, settling on a movie she'd been meaning to watch for about a year. Big stars, small budget, lots of lingering shots of countryside.

Pouring the tea, as the credits rolled, that bloody sneaky

bastard wave of sadness rushed up behind her. It crashed over her head and pinned her down, holding her in place so the tea kept on pouring as she froze in place. As if turning her body to stone would hold back the tears. She shifted the teapot and placed it in the puddle on the tray and allowed the wave to win. It crushed her lungs until she let out a barking, snot-filled wail. She folded in half, lay sideways on the couch, and brought her knees to her chest. Her painful, engorged breasts dribbled inside her bra, milk spreading warmly down her front, so caught up that she hadn't noticed they needed attention. The sensation pricked another part of her psyche and a new wave followed behind the first, swamping her to the point that she could barely breathe. The noises that came from deep within her mimicked whales and monsters from the deep, stirred by the violent tide consuming her. Tears ran hot on her cheeks.

She stared at the overflowed cup.

The TV meant nothing.

Her breastmilk filled her nose with the musty tang of failure.

As a cop.

As a woman.

As a mother.

No, she hadn't failed the last part yet.

The cop in her failed when she shagged a psycho, when she was too fried and busy to grab the morning-after pill, when she got stabbed arresting a suspect, when she almost let a killer trick her with an elaborate double bluff, when she let her computer's conclusion fog her mind and disobey Murphy's order to back away, when she allowed her reputation to keep her going the past year.

The woman in her still looked back on capitulating to her parents' demand for an abortion as a weakness, one she regretted largely because she felt it wasn't *her* decision. She'd slept with more men than the average, not something she ever felt guilty over, but she blamed her inability to settle down on being fussy and rejecting those who tried to change her or who allowed life to get them down. Now her career was about to be flushed down the dirtiest toilet imaginable, making her a jobless single mother.

How could she provide now? With no job, no track record of good decisions? Could she even remotely be a role model for Stacey?

That was what made the tide recede. It's what eased the waves and calmed the water.

Stacey.

No matter her building blocks, no matter what resulted from Alicia's actions last night, there was always Stacey. There was always *going* to be Stacey. And it was Alicia's job to keep the monsters away.

Even if she wasn't a police officer, she'd be able to consult. She could set up at home, be it to advise against criminals through her contacts in Interpol, Europol … heck, she even had a friend in the FBI now.

A private profiler.

That sounded good to Alicia.

She dried her tears. Sat up. The ache was gone.

Switching off the TV, she cleaned up the tea, poured a little back in the pot, and added milk to the cup. She sipped it, enjoying the silence all around. Having the place to herself gave her time to think.

After finishing the tea, she changed her top and bra, relieved the pressure via her electronic pump, and stored the milk for later. All the time, thinking, planning.

Last night was another mistake, yet another poor choice. Whether she was responsible for the two deaths wasn't relevant; her decision-making was what bothered her. And it's what would bother the Professional Standards officers, and rightfully so. If she kept her job, it'd be under serious observation. The notion of coming back after her maternity leave ended as anything but a paper shuffler was ridiculous. She'd be starting again at the bottom and deserved it.

If she kept the job, that is.

So why not go for broke? Why not engineer a clean break? If she was up against the wall for something as irresponsible as disclosing the location of a witness to a potential killer, what harm was there in a simple search using the police system for personal business?

Facing such intense disciplinary charges made other offences pale into near insignificance.

It was why she felt little fear, no doubt, as she logged on to the West Yorkshire Police system via her iPad and looked up all the information it held on Katie Hague.

CHAPTER TWENTY-ONE

IT WAS one of those meetings Murphy hated. He'd even allowed Sergeant Ball to participate, having got permission from Ball's superior to take him in. The man had a network of CIs—confidential informants—that they could really use now a police officer was dead. Ball brought his protégé, Lemmy, with him to the eight a.m. gathering, both having shed their uniforms and dressed in clothes more akin to the other detectives: suits, ties, regular shoes; as if Ball was prepared for this eventuality. Again, Murphy only had the pair for an additional three hours, so he had to make the most of it until they took their mandated eleven hour break away from the workplace. While Ball was as groomed and enthusiastic as Murphy had ever seen the man, Lemmy looked like a kid at his first funeral; his jacket too long, trousers too baggy, tie in a slack knot beneath an open collar.

As deputy SIO, Cleaver stood beside him by a blank whiteboard at the head of a table now occupying their inquiry room; Ndlove, Ball, and Lemmy on one side and Alicia on the other. She looked fine, carefree, as if yesterday hadn't happened.

But it *had* happened. Murphy's hand ached from all the signatures he'd placed on statements and disclosure forms. Until Professional Standards finished their review of her actions, she was still on duty, although Murphy gave her the option to step aside. It was still unclear as to whether what she did made her responsible for triggering the two Blackpool murders, but he was banking on the killer being someone other than Pete Mahdavi or Karen Krasowski.

That one of them might have taken straight off from meeting Alicia and committed those crimes seemed implausible. For now, Alicia wanted to contribute, and Murphy wasn't about to drop her the way Rhapshaw suggested several times the day before.

"Let's start blowing theories apart," he said.

Normally, Alicia would make a joke. He was thankful she didn't. She just said, "The link between Jerzy and Demelza."

"None." Cleaver didn't need notes for this. "Financials don't give a connection. No phone calls that we can find. The only hint he had anything to do with her was his browser history. He visited her site after googling around the Leeds area for somewhere to take his missus on their anniversary night out."

"When did he visit the site?" Murphy asked.

"About an hour and a half before they arrived at the pub. He saw an ad for her show and checked it out."

"So probably nothing there," Ball said.

All agreed.

"More interesting is the burglary," Murphy said.

"Right." Alicia checked a couple of things on her iPad screen. "Tomaz Gortze was employed by Jerzy at his Golden Start agency. They let him go when he blew two jobs in quick succession by not showing up. But the coincidence is too strong. He breaks into Jerzy's father-in-law's house after Dean is murdered, and only steals a couple of items of value and Jerzy's passport. There's … something there. We can't see what, though."

"Jerzy hadn't booked or even looked up foreign travel," Ndlove said. "At least not on the browsers we have access to."

"It's odd, but there's enough to keep Jerzy on the hook." Murphy wrote Jerzy's name on the whiteboard and added the notes "Tomaz" and "passport."

"And the affair," Alicia said.

"Right." Murphy wrote "affair" and drew a line, at the end of which he wrote the other woman's name. "Brenda Williams backs up what Jerzy says. They're involved in a sex-only relationship. Brenda was in Middlesbrough on the day of the murder, and pings suggest she was moving slowly through traffic at the time of Dean's killing. Can we rule out her part in a possible contract job?"

"Not entirely," Ndlove said. "We can't tie her to it, but we shouldn't rule her out. She's close to Jerzy, and Jerzy and Dean both spent time working with Ernest Borek. We haven't actually spoken to Mr. Borek yet."

"I've been digging." Ball opened his notebook to read his handwritten jottings. "He's active in minor scams, and since Jamal Benson sadly passed away, he's been stepping into some of those murkier areas."

"ID theft maybe?" Alicia said.

"He's mostly legit, from what I hear, but yeah, if an opportunity pops up, he'll take it."

Cleaver took over writing duties and placed Ernest on the board. "It doesn't matter if Tomaz had someone for the passport. If he's lying and Jerzy put him up to it, Jerzy has access to people who can make a new passport. Best way is to adapt a real one."

Murphy looked over the board. "Ernest Borek could be helping Jerzy."

Ball nodded. "Still runs unlicensed card games, but nothing big. Can't get a read on extortion, or anything like what Dean used to be into."

"But they all have one big connection," Alicia said. "Bobby Carr."

"Reputed contract killer," Murphy said, as Cleaver wrote the man's name in the bottom corner. "Released from prison a few years ago, now supposedly living a nice life with a woman out in the countryside."

Ndlove started to raise a hand as if in class but spoke instead. "We have no proof of his involvement beyond an old friendship with all three."

"True," Alicia said, "but he has the skill set to carry out all we've seen so far."

"Which you *hope* is the case."

The men all shuffled in place, but Murphy cut through the tension. "It's a theory, that's all."

Cleaver tapped Jerzy's name. "We need to press the Jerzy and Brenda angle."

"Might be a problem. One issue in pursuing that is Brenda is now in contact with Marissa Poole, who likes entrepreneurship. The commissioner sent a memo this morning urging caution in both her case and Jerzy Krasowski's. Brenda has even threatened to sue if we defame her or if any of her potential clients cry off a contract because we've gone too far."

"Too far?" Ball said. "She throws her fanny around, snaring married men, it's not our fault she's implicated in a murder he committed. Or three. Or, sorry ... ones he *might've* committed."

Lemmy yawned. "He defo killed the psychic because she was a phony?"

"All psychics are phony," Alicia said. "Or should I read you again?"

Lemmy held up a hand to decline her kind offer.

"All suspects are out there, all in play," Murphy said. He focused on Alicia. "What is that one thing we've overlooked?"

Alicia waited. All looked at her. When no one else spoke, she said, "I don't know. The lack of forensics is intriguing. Suggests a real professional."

"Like Bobby Carr," Cleaver said.

"Possibly, but I had a look at his record. Nothing suggests more than a street thug with a willingness to do what someone else won't. If it was him, he had help. And someone pointing him at Dean. We find him, like with Demelza, it's a way to work out who hired him. If he'll talk. He probably won't."

"We'll interrogate the trail," Ndlove said. "There'll be enough of a link to one of them."

"And we've also overlooked one guy," Alicia said. "Well, not overlooked, but we've held back for some reason."

"Who?" Murphy asked.

"The bookie." Ndlove glanced at Alicia for confirmation.

"Right." Alicia nodded. "Ernest Borek. We keep seeing his name, but it's always in small ways. A conversation, a loose friendship, some illegal business that's only a smidge illegal so we don't really care that much. He's slipping through the cracks. We need more on him."

"We're up, Lemmy." Ball gave Lemmy a nudge, the younger man jerking as if waking from a half-sleep.

Murphy said, "Take DI Cleaver. Lemmy, you're relieved. I think you'll be more use after a good night's—day's—sleep. Go home. Come back refreshed. There'll be plenty to do tonight."

Lemmy stood, head bowed, a slight moan escaping him. "Thanks, boss."

Ball looked annoyed for a moment, then appeared to

realise his mistake in pushing the kid. Murphy didn't need to say anything as the younger man exited.

"Alicia, you work through intensive profiles of everyone left. Jerzy for starters, Ernest Borek when we learn more, Dean himself, even Karen and Brenda. Ndlove, I want as much background on Pete Mahdavi as you can get without a court order. Anything you can get, no matter how thin, you let me know and I'll start on the application to grab his bank and phone records. Questions?"

There were no questions, and Murphy dismissed them. He had to check on two other teams, so he, too, exited.

That left Alicia alone with Ndlove. Alicia rarely felt uncomfortable around people, even those who had expressed a lack of engagement with her. Ndlove was a blockage in Alicia's throat.

Ndlove broke the silence. "Ma'am, I just wanted to say I'm sorry about the other day. I didn't mean to be … insulting."

This dislodged Alicia's obstacle. "It's okay. I appreciate your honesty."

Ndlove nodded. Sat silently.

"I do think you've misunderstood me, though," Alicia said, her confidence growing. "Let's go for a drink. Me and you. Now."

"Now? We have to…"

"No. There's a coffee shop around the corner. Five minutes. Bring the laptop if you like. The place has great Wi-Fi."

"May I ask what for?"

"Change of scenery. I think there's more to come from you, so want to know why you *really* don't like me when everyone else thinks I'm brilliant."

CHAPTER TWENTY-TWO

THE COFFEE SHOP was called the Has-Bean, an independent place dominated by long wooden tables that encourage people to share the space, a trend Alicia hoped would spread to more establishments. While Alicia ordered the coffees and pastries, Ndlove picked a smaller table with more comfortable chairs in a corner formed by a bookcase. Alicia delivered Ndlove's flat white and her own mocha with red cherries and said the barista would bring the pastries over when she'd warmed them through.

"So," Alicia said, knowing full well her first sip had given her a cream moustache. "What's the story? We girls should be sticking together, not tolerating one another's company."

Ndlove left her coffee alone and crossed one leg over the other. "Fine. Ma'am."

"Nuh-uh, no ma'am. Alicia."

"Alicia. I don't know what it is you hope to achieve here."

"Openness." Alicia wiped her lip. "I feel like you're a damn good copper who would benefit from smiling more. I cured Murphy of being a constant grump. I don't see why you can't enjoy life a bit more too."

Ndlove picked up her cup and sampled it, pulled a face, and placed it back down. "Too hot." She sat back, nervously eying Alicia.

"I'm not trying to trick you," Alicia said. "I'm just good at this. And what you said the other day may have been a part of how you feel about me, but I'd like to get a deeper read."

"You want to know why I don't get on with you as well as others? The others who think you're brilliant?"

"Something like that."

"Girls have to stick together." Ndlove spoke the words with disdain, as if they were stupid. "You're coasting, ma'am—Alicia. You are using your talents and ability to minimal heights, while others like me have to try so much harder to achieve much less."

"You think I'm not committed enough?"

"No, that's not what I mean. I mean, people like Marissa Poole get to be MPs. While someone like you … you could make such a *difference* at higher levels. But you do nothing of the sort."

Alicia held her coffee cup just for something to do with her fingers. "I don't think I'm coasting. I'm doing my best. I have a baby now, and I'm just getting used to it, working out what I'll be able to do—"

"I'm not talking about this week, Alicia." Now she used Alicia's first name, and it wasn't easy to tell if it was natural or if she was using what she'd learned in the service. Placating an interviewee. She said, "I worked with you before then. I saw what you were like. Joking, making deductions no one else was seeing, flirting around—"

"Flirting? I don't flirt."

"Not sexually, but it's the same thing." She switched to a high-pitched "bimbo" noise. "*Look at me, I know all this stuff, but I'm going to push my ideas like a dizzy blonde instead of a professional police officer.*" Back to normal, she fell silent, sipped her coffee, then said, "Sorry, I shouldn't do the voice."

"No…" Alicia wasn't sure how to respond. She'd had similar comments in the past, but even the grumpiest grump usually came around. And it wasn't the impression Ndlove did that hurt Alicia the most. It was the coasting comment. "I sustained injuries in the line of duty last year in Yorkshire. I was stabbed whilst on business in America."

"It's not your commitment I'm questioning. It's your ambition. Even with a baby, even with a knife scar, even with the inquiry into the serial killer case being made to look political … there are bigger issues at stake. It's not about us being women, either." She paused to take a drink, then resumed at a less frenetic pace. "At this level, as a detective sergeant, you can be the go-to girl. As an analyst at the SCA, you can avoid being tenured back to uniform because you specialise, which will happen, when? Five years?"

Alicia worked it out. "Three."

"You are everything good and everything bad about women on the force. You could be a detective inspector, a DCI. Heck, with your intelligence and ability you could be the *commissioner* next time the post comes around. You could be the difference, not just for women, but for all of us."

Alicia had barely considered those things before. *DI Friend.* In charge of murders rather than just giving insight or settling with being the most valuable player. She got to break these cases without having the spotlight shone from above, or below. Her position avoided much press handling, something she was somewhat phobic about, and although it was never easy as such, she was definitely firmly ensconced in her comfort zone.

Plenty for Alicia to think about.

"Thank you," she said to Ndlove as the pastries were delivered by the young girl with a nose ring and sleeves of tattoos. When she was gone, Alicia asked Ndlove, "What's your son called?"

Ndlove smiled, allowed the tension to ease from her shoulders, and resumed her coffee. "Eric. I have pictures if you like."

Alicia said she'd love to see them and settled in for a chat about anything that didn't remind her of work.

CHAPTER TWENTY-THREE

THE TRUTH WAS, Cleaver hadn't liked Sergeant Ball that much when they first hooked up in the inquiry room, seeking out the kidnapper who took four girls, murdering three. The fourth was saved thanks to him and Ball, and of course Alicia and Murphy. It was the case that made Cleaver's name. He found Ball unkempt and slovenly, imprecise in his techniques, preferring the methods of an era that was still looked back upon by many with real fondness, but never really existed. The days when an officer could use the word "tart" to describe a sex worker, or "darkie" as a catch-all for everyone with skin less than creamy white, and to strong-arm witnesses and suspects into giving up information.

Cleaver never bought into any of that.

But he liked a pint and a laugh, and Ball enjoyed the same, and although they knew each other in passing, they'd never worked together directly until that case. Cleaver, like Ball, had been languishing at detective sergeant, and since his divorce had put on a fair bit of weight. He had some catching up to do before he equalled Ball's girth, and it was perhaps Ball's inadequacies that he saw reflected in his own creeping age.

When Cleaver started seeing a younger woman who he met on that fateful case, Darla, he kicked himself in the arse to get fit, which reinvigorated his mind and his attitude to the job. Then when Ball got tenured back to uniform, that kicked Cleaver even harder to push for a promotion, which came off thanks to Murphy's own boost to DCI.

The case on which Cleaver met Alicia really saved him.

It was odd to think of it that way, of three dead and one traumatised girl helping fix one's career. Of course, it had had the opposite effect on Ball.

He'd been hurt during that time, and he took to drinking more heavily and being more "laddish", like being knocked unconscious triggered a midlife crisis. Although neither Cleaver nor Murphy were his direct superior, they voiced their concerns, and Ball was forced to attend therapy sessions. Confidential ones, so no one knew what went on there, and Ball never spoke of them. Yet, shortly after, as he was made to wear the uniform again and hit the streets, although he protested, it seemed to be what he needed.

Now, like Cleaver, he was a stone and a bit—almost twenty pounds—lighter, and as they waited in the corner of a busy greasy spoon cafe called The Skinny Pig while Ernest Borek polished off his breakfast, Ball asked the question Cleaver was expecting.

"What do you think it'll take to get me back out of uniform?"

"The usual route," Cleaver said. "When a vacancy comes up, apply. Might be a little soon, though. Don't you need a year or more?"

"Usually." Ball poked the remnants of his own breakfast around; a 99 percent fat-free sausage, poached egg, low-salt low-sugar beans, and rindless bacon. "But something like this. If it goes on a bit, they might need me."

"It won't go on a bit." Cleaver had already finished off his low-fat low-salt sausage bap and was working on his coffee. "Couple of days and we'll either make an arrest or it'll start to die. Me and Ndlove'll take it over as one of our roster of cases, and Alicia puts her feet back up for another six weeks."

"Think she'll go down?"

"Nah, she always lands right."

Cleaver risked a glance over at Ernest Borek, a ruddy man in a light-blue suit, no tie, and brown shoes. His head was smooth, and he had one of those wanky thin beards that circled his mouth like a pencil sketch. His companions were large men, like nightclub bouncers. He reminded Cleaver of the old time gangland types, who made a show of strength by employing bodyguards to shadow their every move.

Cleaver said, "Lot of muscle for a respectable businessman."

"Yup." Ball went for his mug of tea. "Think he's made us?"

"Hope so. That's kind of the idea."

Ball and Cleaver couldn't look more like a pair of CID detectives if they wore their warrant cards on their foreheads; their simple suits and plain ties, their very manner.

"Why do you think he needs them?" Ball asked. "No one I spoke to mentioned security."

"We've mentioned Bobby Carr, right? Well, he's gone dark. His last known address is out toward Ilkley. A former farmhouse. He supposedly had a missus up there, someone he was with in the golden days of stickups and assassinations."

"Ahh, the good old days."

"Yeah, well, if he's disappeared, even though he's supposedly reformed, and someone around here is going after former members of Ernest's and Bobby's crew, what might that mean?"

"Might mean Ernest thinks he needs additional protection."

The trio finished their food. Cleaver and Ball watched them conspicuously, not trying to hide their interest. Letting him know they were there. Like in the good old days.

As he was exiting, one bodyguard ahead of him, Ernest Borek paused, turned, and locked onto the two coppers. He came over, his shoulders down, the two heavies waiting by the door. "Hello, detectives."

"I'm not a detective," Ball said.

"I am," Cleaver said.

Borek indicated a spare chair. "Should I join you for interview now, or wait for arrest?"

"No interview," Ball said. "Just keeping an eye on you."

"For your safety." Cleaver opened his hands like a book.

"My safety?" When Borek lowered his voice, his Polish accent thickened. His English got worse too. "Why I need police keeping eye on me?"

Cleaver led, as pre-arranged. "Because one of your friends was killed by Bobby Carr recently."

Borek swallowed, pulled up a chair, and sat. A bead of sweat formed on his scalp as he lowered his head into his shoulders like a turtle. "I cannot talk of this here."

There were a lot of people around, and the place was cramped. At least seven or eight would have heard Cleaver declare Bobby Carr's name, adding pressure to Ernest Borek.

The Pole said, "Can we talk elsewhere?"

"Nah, I haven't finished." Ball indicated his plate where a sausage and a puddle of beans remained. He stuffed half the remaining sausage and a scoop of beans into his mouth and spoke as he chewed. "Why did Bobby Carr kill Dean Bicklesthwaite?"

Cleaver sipped his coffee.

Borek puckered his lips for just a second, then again, and finally placed both hands on the table, fingers interlinked. He spoke in tones low enough to evade the nearby tables. "He did not. I do not think so, anyway."

"How come…" Ball hadn't swallowed yet, but was about to, so he waved his soiled fork in the direction of the large men at the door.

"Why them?" Borek finished for him.

"Mmm." Swallow. "Them."

"Reassurance. Rumours about Bobby have reached me, and some of my partners." Now he'd resumed his regular tone, albeit quietly, his English suddenly improved. "Although I despise all crime, I used to have associations … perhaps not all legal ones … but I do not participate. I just watch. Listen. And do my business right."

"Of course," Cleaver said. "We're not recording this conversation, and you are not under caution. Nothing you say here is evidence. Speak freely."

"Free as you like." Ball speared his final bit of sausage.

"Okay." Borek swallowed. "Bobby Carr is a good man now. No way he killed Dean. Total new character. I hear he did bad things ten years ago, but he is reformed."

"Then why the muscle?" Cleaver asked.

"Just because I do not believe Bobby Carr is the one who did it, does not mean someone else from the past thinks, wrongly, that I was a part of something."

"Something?"

"I do not know. This is truth. I promise." He'd reverted back to the broken dialect, and Cleaver was beginning to suspect this was some sort of tick, a tell that betrayed when Borek was being dishonest. "I am fully legitimate now. Cash and carry food. Transport network. Better money than counterfeiting." He stumbled verbally, his sweat beading in greater quantities now. "Not that I profit from counterfeit goods. Is wrong to rip off people, even the rich. Okay."

Ball ingested his final mouthful and clunked his knife and fork on the plate. "Yes, mate, don't worry about it. You haven't incriminated yourself. Much."

Cleaver laughed gently. "Of course, if we need to interview you formally, you understand we might have to bring up certain past transactions."

Borek frowned. "You said you would not—"

"We said you're not currently under caution. Doesn't mean we can't dig. Now if you were flogging Armani imported from Vietnam or making swill and sticking it in Chanel No. 5 bottles here in the UK, it might sound like small time stuff, but we know it goes higher in the modern world. Counterfeiting is big business for jihadis and other terrorist groups."

"No, no." Borek wagged his finger like a teacher instructing a child to quit a dangerous activity. "I am not part of jihad network. Do not go there."

"We're not. I'm just emphasising the point that because a lot of these terror networks are funded through counterfeit goods, drugs, pornography, pirated films, et cetera, there's more focus on it these days. It's not just a slap on the wrists, and away you go. You need to give up suppliers, routes, that sort of thing."

Borek shook his head. "I do not know these things. I pay, the goods arrive, I sell. I mean…" Again, he stumbled. "I *used* to."

"Of course." Cleaver made a mental note to pass on Borek's details to the relevant division. This guy was digging himself deep. Stress will do that to a person. "But you still fear for your life. Despite your … *legitimate* status now."

"Yes."

Ball slurped his tea. "Is Jerzy Krasowski involved? In your business?"

Borek shook his head. "He supplies people. For my wholesalers. He sometimes sends boys my way who are less interested in those jobs, and I give them … other work."

"Work that pays cash?" Ball winked and rubbed his thumb and forefingers together.

"Sometimes is easier to pay cash to people who do not trust their banks. It is their responsibility to declare income, pay tax, yes?"

Cleaver placed his empty cup down. "Actually, if it's regular paid work, it's the employer's responsibility to collect relevant tax and national insurance. According to HMRC, anyway. But I'm not a tax lawyer, so maybe you should check."

"Self-employed!" The bald man gave an open-handed grin. "They are all self-employed workers who do occasional jobs for me—"

"Okay, okay, we're getting off track," Ball said. "Spill some names, Ernest. If not Bobby Carr, then who beat the shit out of Dean Bicklesthwaite, then took a blade to him?"

A long, drawn out lull followed, voices from all around merging into one block of white noise.

Finally, Ernest Borek said, "Truthfully, I do not know. But if Dean is dead, and now Demelza Shine, I cannot be sure. Not me. Not Jerzy. Not Bobby Carr."

"Did Dean help run your side businesses?" Cleaver asked. "Could it be someone muscling in?"

Borek's mouth turned down, genuine grief, genuine worry. "I really do not know."

Ball had frowned several seconds earlier. "Demelza Shine."

"Yes?"

"You said Demelza Shine."

"I did."

Cleaver saw where he was going, and let him run with it, a charge of excitement building.

Ball said, "We never mentioned Demelza Shine, and her name hasn't been released to the press. How did you know about Demelza?"

"Gossip," Borek said. "She was a friend of ours a long time ago. Her family was informed, so her death made it back to me, of course. Why...?" Borek twigged suddenly. "You did not know?"

"Know what?" Cleaver said.

"I assume this is why you have interest in me suddenly. Demelza was a friend. More than a friend."

Cleaver flashed back to his conversation with James in the Gable House pub. Specifically his mention of the female who hung out with them sometimes.

Local lass, took no crap, y'know.

"More than a friend?" Ball said. "What? She blew you behind the bins after closing?"

Borek chuckled, sat back in his seat. "No, detectives, nothing like that."

"I'm not a detective," Ball said again, louder this time.

"Demelza was not some whore or casual acquaintance. What, you think a Polish immigrant can get started with big counterfeit sales on his own?"

Weird girl, weird nickname, like she's trying to fit in with the Polish fellas.

Cleaver leaned in closer, voice low, containing his urgency. "She was part of the operation?"

"No." Borek now looked happy, deeply satisfied. "She was the boss. Demelza ran the whole thing. Like me, like Dean, Bobby Carr worked *for her*."

CHAPTER TWENTY-FOUR

ALICIA BELIEVED the connections were all slotting into place and insisted they needed more intel before raiding Bobby Carr's house, but the order came down from on high—not directly from the police commissioner, but all assumed he who applied pressure to DCI Murphy's boss.

By the time evening hit, an armed response team assembled, and once Alicia arranged for Robbie to take over mum duties from the Dot-Bot, she hitched a ride so she could be there too. Her indiscretion the previous day was forgotten for now, at least amongst the rank and file, and even Ndlove, but she would be swimming upstream against the people charged with maintaining police discipline and lawfulness. Alicia didn't let it cloud her for now.

A roadside restaurant and petrol station served as their staging post, closed and boarded up for several years, but large enough for the eight-strong armed unit to equip themselves, lay out a map, and familiarise themselves with Bobby Carr's property. Two distinct groups: armed police at the centre of the huddle, and non-armed police on the outside.

Alicia's competency with weapons was limited, and she'd

allowed her permit to lapse, as had Cleaver and Ball. Having hit his bedroom following the Borek revelation about Demelza —deemed irrelevant by the brass—Ball surfaced to see through his intel. Lemmy and he were not supposed to be on duty for another four hours, but Ball had roped his young charge along too.

Ndlove was suited up in body armour over her regular clothes, with a helmet and visor on top, and a Glock 17 on her hip. Alicia caught Cleaver's frown and how Ndlove caught him staring; Cleaver's protégé was going to be first through the door with the testosterone junkies.

DCI Murphy would be alongside.

Although he wasn't part of the initial team, he still sported a sidearm and body armour. Alicia pegged it for a semi-midlife-crisis, his advanced driving course and diligent firearms training crying out that the older man yearned to be a geri-action hero like Liam Neeson.

Cleaver said, "Guess I should reapply."

"They give you a gun," Ball said, "you end up at the sharp end of these ops. I'll hang back and be happy about it."

Lemmy, in his baggy suit, looked excited. "I'm gonna get trained, soon as I can. Looks seriously cool."

Alicia stayed quiet. She still worried about the consequences of what she did the previous day, whether she got Demelza and DC Lockwood killed. The only thing that kept her going was how each morsel of new evidence pushed that scenario farther away.

The farmhouse was no longer on a farm. At least, not a farm as most knew it. The land was sold to an energy company that erected six windmills against the wishes of locals and those who visited on a regular basis. An eyesore, according to the many doomed petitions that cropped up. The company also installed a field of solar panels and held licences for fracking. They had not yet exercised that latter permission, but Alicia suspected it wouldn't be long.

Bobby bought up the farmhouse and outbuildings before the land was sold. From what Alicia could see as they pulled up to the perimeter, the windmills and solar fields were far enough from his windows to still call the views "idyllic". If he was facing the right way, of course.

They approached from the idyllic end, the windmills up ahead on a hillside on which sheep once grazed. Alicia, Cleaver, Ball, and Lemmy all held back at the first checkpoint, all apart from Ball apparently frustrated with their backseat roles. Murphy looked back only once.

Now wearing a big helmet as well as his vest and gloves, she couldn't read anything in there. Fear, hope, excitement, regret; nothing registered, nothing Alicia might have expected. Just a blank canvas staring at her.

Donald Murphy was shitting himself. Breaches like this became a near paramilitary operation, these men trained not only to break down doors and take out suspects who might be in possession of a firearm, but to confront terrorists of the ilk who might instigate a mass killing via machine-gun or machete. They were tough, and Murphy was happy for them to run this part of it.

He'd never fired a gun on official duty and had only participated on a handful of these ops. Each time, he was last through, totting up points for experience. When he volunteered to tool up for this, he assumed Alicia would also be there, and wanted to be sure she stuck close to him, otherwise he'd have let the big boys handle it. And he felt like crap that he didn't offer Ndlove the same sense of protection he did Alicia. He reasoned it was because of Alicia's attitude, her fragile state, whereas Ndlove struck him as a stronger person, her desire to sign out a firearm here echoing his own need to grab hours of live operational hours.

Minutes, in reality, but they measured it from the point at which the Glock 17 was signed out to the time it was signed in. An officer was, correctly, responsible for that gun throughout the period it was in his or her possession. Logging hours wasn't just about action; they had to prove themselves trustworthy.

Alicia hadn't been on the range or renewed her licence to acquire a weapon, so here he was, with only Ndlove for company. The pair trailed the ARU, tuned in to their radio frequency, currently silent and running on hand signals.

"Okay, boss?" she asked.

"Good, thanks, you?"

"Sure."

Bobby Carr's house was located up a drive that wound in a quarter-circle from the road, affording him privacy and granting the police a longer run up than would otherwise be an option. The use of force was approved first by the chief constable, then Murphy's chief super contacted Margaret over in Bradford, Ilkley being a small part-time station without armed response facilities. Being on Vijay Badesa's patch, though, as inspector nominally in charge of Ilkley station, he also accompanied them, falling in the rear beside Murphy and Ndlove. He hadn't spoken since the op commenced, and barely to Murphy anyway. He was along for the ride. A courtesy. Nothing more. And he probably knew it.

The standard cops all took cover as two men geared up the battering ram, while what looked like the sole woman on the team counted them in. "Three … two … one."

Crash.

The door split around the handle and burst open. In ran

the unit, one after the other, each one covered by the previous breach in a show of precision usually reserved for watchmakers. They must train all day every day.

Murphy sure as hell wasn't a patch on them.

He listened in as they cleared each room, then scouted out back. It took four minutes until the all clear came through.

Vijay Badesa removed his helmet and holstered his Glock. "Well, thank god for that." Sweating, he waited for Murphy and Ndlove to agree.

"Better than the alternative," Murphy said. "But our suspect isn't here. Which means a wasted journey and manpower."

Badesa closed his mouth as Murphy passed him and peeled off his own helmet, Ndlove at his heels. Inside, the unit spread out to cover windows in case the suspect was hiding outside and allowed Murphy to call through to those waiting without guns.

"We're in. No apparent suspects present. Proceed with caution, though."

Alicia proceeded with caution all the way to the house, and inside. Ball and Lemmy waited out front at Murphy's request, Murphy citing the 'too many cooks' analogy. They'd be allocated duties as soon as Alicia gave her take, and Cleaver agreed to their next course of action. Probably collecting every bit of paper and photographing each corner, anything to help find Bobby Carr and question him.

The hall was a mess. Not unusual when a group of armed cops smashed the door in and ploughed through bothered only by the instinct to not die. With Cleaver and Ndlove in another room, Alicia snapped on a pair of gloves and picked up a photo that had fallen flat on its front. It featured the

Bobby Carr they'd seen in mugshots alongside a slight woman, his arm around her in front of a waterfall. Alicia recognised the waterfall as being up Skipton way, but not the woman.

"Any idea?" she asked.

"Nope," Murphy said.

"Where's that nice man gone?"

"Who?"

"Vijay. Where is he? He *seemed* nice." She called out in a singsong voice, "Vijay! Where *are* you?"

Vijay Badesa appeared from the kitchen. "Yes, you need something?"

"Just your lovely eyes. And your brain." Alicia showed him the photo. "This woman, do you know her?"

"I know her," Vijay said. "She lives here with Mr. Carr. Linda-something."

"You know everyone in town?" Murphy asked.

"No, not everyone. It's small, but not that small. But this lass, yeah, I know her. I know of the main resident here, Bobby Carr. Knew he had form, so I took an interest in who he was hanging around with."

From another room, Ndlove's voice carried. "Got blood!"

Alicia gazed around now, taking in more of the hallway. It wasn't the sort of pattern you got with a breach. Ornaments had fallen in different directions, and when she progressed to the dining room with its positively huge kitchen and a table large enough for the von Trapps, there were even more indicators of a struggle. Pots and other items spilled on the unfinished floor, smoothed down as if preparing for tiling or linoleum.

"Your people didn't do all that, did they?" she asked the team leader.

"No," the hairy sergeant answered. "We haven't touched

anything except a couple of things might've fallen over when the doors came open."

Came open.

Or were kicked in, as they had to.

Ndlove crouched by a reddish patch on the floor with more on the wall. A dark maroon, almost black on the brickwork.

"*Suspected* blood," Cleaver said.

"Right, suspected." Alicia got up close without standing in it. "Blood."

"Suspected," Murphy said. "We'll get SOCO in."

"More here." Ndlove had wandered away, finding a couple more stains on the cement floor. "Someone has tried to clean it up, but bricks and cement are porous. Isn't so easy."

"What do you know about Linda?" Alicia asked, absently following Ndlove alongside Vijay Badesa.

"Not much," Vijay said. "Quiet. Had a child from a previous marriage, so I heard. Turned up a few years back with the teenage boy in tow. Lad's all grownup now. Troublesome little shit, but nothing major. Nothing that *stuck* anyway. Bobby Carr got him in line, though, near as I can tell. Or the lad moved away. Something happened, anyway, because one day we stopped picking him up. Bobby Carr did some program a while ago, and that sorted him out. Maybe he did the same with the lad."

The faint blood trail led into a utility that housed a washing machine, tumble dryer, and chest freezer. Ndlove drew her gun.

"Rebecca, is that necessary?" Alicia asked. "You're not in an American TV show. Nothing's going to jump out of the freezer."

Murphy joined them now, a tight squeeze. "Okay, back off. Sergeant, I need you to witness something."

The man with the beard and the body armour reappeared and noted the blood. He drew his gun too.

Ndlove gave Alicia an *I told you so* look, and Alicia backed out, only her head poking around the frame.

Gun holstered, Murphy crouched forward, reached to stretch his arm out, fingers on the chest freezer's handle. In a swift motion, he flipped it up.

A cloud of icy air plumed upward.

Ndlove and the hairy sergeant aimed at the container.

Nothing jumped out.

Both armed officers and Murphy peered inside. Murphy beckoned Alicia, who beckoned Vijay and Cleaver. Six people stared into the freezer.

On top of the waffles and rock-hard meat, a woman lay in a flimsy-looking nightie. Her stomach had been sliced open, her chest stabbed three times, and half her face was a bloody mess. A frozen bloody mess. And her throat had been cut wide open.

"Linda Grout," Vijay said, his brow hanging low over his eyes. "I remember now. Strange how that happens sometimes. But I'm certain. Her name was Linda Grout."

CHAPTER TWENTY-FIVE

"LOOKS like she's been beaten for a prolonged period on one side of the face," Alicia said. "Sustained, too. Like bam, bam, bam." She mimed her arm going like a piston.

"Conscious?" Murphy asked.

"Can't tell. I don't think we'll ever know. The freezing of the body will make it impossible without a confession from whoever did it."

It was only the three of them: Murphy, Alicia, and Cleaver. Alicia requested some time to look at the body in peace, so Ball and Lemmy were let in and Ndlove passed on orders to them from Cleaver to start combing the house in search of guns, knives, anything that could link the crimes. Everyone was now booted up, gloved, wearing hair nets, the armed personnel outside, guarding the perimeter. Bulletins were out for Bobby Carr, but they found no vehicle registered to him or anyone by the name Linda Grout.

Alicia needed this time. "Things are swirling," she said. "I hate when things swirl. Except when I stand up too fast or drink just a tiny bit too much. That's good swirling. This is bad swirling."

"Any sign of it straightening out?" Murphy asked. "Because I have some thoughts of my own, believe it or not."

"I never examined Dean's body in person, just read the reports: badly beaten, which may have indicated torture, before being stabbed several times, then cut open. Eventually, his throat was cut."

"Just like this girl," Cleaver said.

"She's a woman," Murphy said sternly. "Forty at least."

"We initially believed the wounds on Dean were frenzied," Alicia said. "He was attacked, beaten up for information, then a knife came out. One on one was unlikely, wasn't it? He was a big man."

"Unless the attacker was big too." Murphy gave his moustache a thoughtful rub. "And Bobby Carr fits."

"Let's just go back a bit. To Dean. Let's *assume* for a minute that Bobby definitely did it. Bobby somehow enters the house."

"It's back from the road," Murphy said. "Could be why no one saw him."

"And Dean knew him," Cleaver said. "Could've just knocked."

"After following him to his daughter's address?" Alicia said.

"Watching the house? Saw Dean go in?"

"Meaning what? That Bobby was interested in *Karen's house*?"

"Or Jerzy." Murphy was pacing now, an occasional glance at Linda Grout. "They all knew each other."

Alicia stared at Linda. "When Demelza Shine was their boss."

Cleaver stuffed his hands in his pockets. "According to some half-remembered evenings by a guy who must've taken the odd kickback from whatever they were flogging in his pub. He might've been part of their group, at least on the outside.

Turning a blind eye, receiving a hefty tip for his trouble. But he said Jerzy didn't start hanging around the place until later. Could be why he didn't recognise Demelza that night."

"Back to that evening," Alicia said. "Whatever his reason for doing it there, Bobby gets in, beats Dean. Stabs him. Dean tries to defend himself. Bobby gets him down and opens him up. Guts spill. Then, when it's over, he cuts Dean's throat."

"And, what?" Murphy said. "Comes home and offs his missus?"

Alicia leaned into the freezer again. "I can't tell. The autopsy will work out how long she's been frozen, if it was in the last couple of weeks."

"Why only the last couple of weeks?" Cleaver asked.

"You really should know that, *Inspector.*" Alicia gave him a mildly amused look, but not so much it disrespected the body. "You *do* know, don't you?"

Cleaver held still, thinking. "The crystallization of the blood. After a long time in deep freeze, it's difficult to age it. The window gets wider and wider."

"Right. There's blood on the bottom of the freezer, so she was still bleeding when she went in, so it must have been soon after she died. Her colour is relatively even with only minimal discolouration of the skin where she's lying, so the blood flowing to the lowest point of her body was arrested. By the cold. But, if she went in yesterday or the day before, we should be able to tell, and if it was a week ago, we should learn that. Two weeks, it'll be tough to nail down a day. Three or four, we're looking at a wider margin of error. Then over a month, it'll be hard to age within more than a few weeks."

"We'll get Vijay to run CCTV sweeps," Murphy said. "Get her last movements in the town."

"We've got blood outside," Cleaver added.

Alicia pushed forensic thoughts from her brain. Like all

detectives who investigated murder on a regular basis, she had experience in that area, but it wasn't her specialty. "Let's go at this another way."

"Which way?" Murphy asked.

"The way that makes me show off and you get to gasp when I'm right."

"Can't wait."

Alicia steadied herself, zeroed in on the centre of the swirl. "Even in the most methodical of serial killer cases, there are never identical murders. They might favour an approach, like strangulation, or they may favour a method of body disposal, but they don't mimic other crimes with this degree of accuracy."

"How accurate?"

"I'd bet if you pull up the file on Dean, there'll be three wounds to his chest. Just like Linda Grout here."

Cleaver stripped off a glove and pulled out his phone, one of the larger variety that was almost the size of a tablet and started dabbing at the screen.

"It's blow for blow the same, except Dean was hit on both sides of the head. Probably due to him fighting back and not playing the game Bobby wanted him to play."

"What game's that?" Murphy asked.

"Revenge," Cleaver answered for her, having checked on his phone. "Three wounds."

Alicia went back to the body and waited for the men to join her. "What if Dean Bicklesthwaite did this to Linda? What if he came here to settle something with Bobby Carr, but Bobby wasn't home?"

"Or Dean wanted something from Bobby," Cleaver said, continuing Alicia's train of thought.

Murphy straightened his neck, stretching taller, as he frequently did when Alicia suspected he was contemplating the darkest corners of the human condition. "Tortured Bobby's girlfriend in front of him to get it."

"It's a heck of a leap," Alicia said.

"Not inconceivable, given Dean's enforcer days. We assumed it was small time, but small time is all we know about."

Alicia joined Murphy in his contemplation. "I'm picturing Dean begging for mercy as Bobby opens him up and makes him watch as his intestines spill onto the floor."

"Gross," Cleaver said.

"But it fits." Murphy attended to his moustache again. "The reformed hitman reverts to type, can't let this lie. He goes after the person who did it, set things up with Demelza. Maybe blackmailed her rather than bribed her. Or just got her to do a favour for an old pal. Which leaves one serious question."

"More than one." Alicia held up three fingers and counted them off. "Who else was involved? What were they after when they came here? And who's next."

All processed this.

"Not quite gasping," Cleaver said.

"But you are impressed, aren't you?" Alicia asked.

"A bit."

"Then prepare to be amazed with my next enormous leap of logic."

Murphy now rolled his eyes. "How much is a guess and how much is based on evidence?"

"Total guesswork. But logical. Please ask Sergeant Ball to come down and bring any documents he might have dug up."

Cleaver complied, summoning Ball via the radio.

"Where is this going?" Murphy asked.

Alicia felt weird beaming wide and bright with a corpse so close, so she limited herself to punching Murphy's arm.

"If I'm right, your heads are going to explode with amazement."

"Do we wait for Ball or will you tell us?"

"Well, Vijay said the victim's name is Linda Grout. *Grout.* That sound familiar to anyone?"

"No."

"No," Cleaver said, looking puzzled.

"Right." Alicia again checked she didn't sound too jolly. "The lovely Vijay doesn't know her too well, and despite the exotic name he's as Yorkshire as any of us. Rural Yorkshire. Meaning he might not do too well pronouncing foreign names."

"Inspector *Badesa* might have trouble with foreign names?"

Ball arrived, holding a bunch of bills in a clear evidence bag. "You need these?"

Alicia closed her eyes. "No, don't let me see. Let me guess. It's Eastern European?"

"Ehh, yeah. Looks like it."

"Not Grout."

"No," Ball said.

Alicia opened her eyes and saw Cleaver and Murphy were almost in the same place as her. "This lady in the freezer, murdered by persons unknown, is not Linda Grout. She's Linda *Gortze.*"

"Yep," Ball said. "Linda Gortze and Robert Carr."

Murphy's face creased in thought. "It's circled around again. Linda was Tomaz Gortze's mother."

CHAPTER TWENTY-SIX

THAT EVENING, they delved into Tomaz's past. Alicia only had until nine p.m. before she had to get back to the baby, and she needed to move quickly. She got Murphy to put his advanced driving skills to the test and hurtle to the remand centre holding Tomaz in record time. Meanwhile, Cleaver and Ndlove would tackle the paper trail of the lad's past, cross-referencing any and all names that had cropped up since Dean's murder.

It was becoming a closer-knit affair. Less about a sprawling criminal enterprise, and more personal. Did Bobby Carr hold back a stash of proceeds from their former life? Did Dean want paying? Did Ernest?

Did they go there to get what was owed? How did Bobby afford such a nice house? Was it through his hoarded profits? And was Demelza even aware of what she was getting into?

"Why didn't Jerzy recognise Demelza?" Murphy asked as he blew through a red light in the marked police car, sirens blaring.

"Maybe he did," Alicia said. "Maybe he was in on it too."

They took a roundabout pretty much on two wheels,

although when she complained Murphy swore to her it wasn't. As they batted questions back and forth, one thing was clear: there was a lot of lying going on.

Tomaz was currently located at a remand centre almost equidistant between Leeds and Wakefield, awaiting trial for the burglary of Dean Bicklesthwaite's home, where he'd been kept under observation for a day and a half but showed no signs of the concussion he'd been faking. He'd been allocated a lawyer and the pair waited in a visiting suite, a sedate space with two cheap couches, a cheaper chair, and a corner for tots to play. When Alicia and Murphy walked in, following a rigorous search and check on their IDs, Tomaz was wearing grey sweats with a smaller bandage now circling his head, his hands cuffed before him, indicating it must have required a physical effort by the staff to coral him into the room. His lawyer, in a brown pinstripe, introduced himself as Colin and urged them to go careful with his client as he was recovering from a serious injury. No mention of an altercation on his way here.

Murphy set his phone, reeled off the official spiel so a jury would know Tomaz consented to the recording, and opened with, "I'm sorry to inform you, but we found your mother this evening."

Tomaz frowned, sat forward. "Found her?"

"There's no easy way to say this … but your mother is dead."

Tomaz's bottom lip wobbled for a moment. Then he buried his face in his hands, let out a whimper, and proceeded to cry. They let him. Gave him a minute to absorb the news.

Alicia sat beside him. "It's awful news, I know. And it's even worse, I'm afraid. She was murdered."

"Murdered? How?"

"Strangled."

Tomaz suddenly ceased crying and sat stiffly. "Strangled?"

"Yes." Murphy nodded, a sombre undertaker on duty. "It isn't easy to ask you this, but we need to know if you can think of anyone who might have wanted her dead. Or your stepfather."

Tomaz shook his head.

"We think Dean Bicklesthwaite killed her," Alicia said. "The man whose house you were caught burgling."

"No," Tomaz said. "Can't be."

"Who put you up to breaking into that house?" Murphy asked.

"I can't." Tomaz shook his head rapidly.

Alicia gave him her best wide-eyed nice-girl look she could summon. "Was it your step dad?"

"Was it Jerzy?" Murphy asked.

Tomaz stared. "This is a fit up. You think I killed my mum and that guy in the house. You wanna pin it on me."

"No," Alicia said. "We need to know the background. What happened? Why was your mother stabbed to death?"

"I don't know, I swear it. I don't know anything. I broke into that house because I heard the owner died. I picked shit out at random, but that bitch beat me unconscious. I'm gonna sue, you know."

"We'll leave you now. With your lies. Your secrets. But you need to know, we don't believe you." Alicia patted his leg and stood. Joined Murphy. "When I said she was strangled, you looked shocked. When I just mentioned she was stabbed, you weren't. Just went with the flow of conversation. You know what that means to me?"

"I don't like where this is going," the lawyer said. "Badgering my client. Tricking him with wordplay when his mother has just died. I think I'd like a copy of that recording."

"He already knew," Alicia said. "Didn't you, Tomaz? You

already knew she was dead. And you're in a stable state, meaning you've had time to process it. When we get the autopsy results, we'll find she's been dead a long time. A month or more. You're the link, Tomaz, the key to this whole thing. And I'm going to find out how."

Having got what she came for, Alicia spun on her heels and made to leave.

But Tomaz's response was a tut. A sigh. "Just like last time."

Alicia twigged just as Murphy joined her in leaving. She spun back to Tomaz. "What last time?"

His lip curled into a snarl. "The last time you pigs tried to pin a murder on me. Didn't work out too well, did it?"

Alicia looked to Murphy. There was no record of that on his file, but she didn't want to give away that they were again looking at a curveball. She said, "I wasn't on that case, Tomaz. What do you think happened?"

He grinned. Toothy. Defiant. "Some tramp got burned back home. Rough sleeping smackhead. They put a petrol can on Bobby's land and pushed some idiots to say it were me who did it. It wasn't. And the judge tossed their statements. Let me out."

"How old were you?" Murphy asked.

"Sixteen. Fifteen when I burned— I mean, when you thought I burned him."

Alicia's stomach turned. She'd seen this attitude before, the near-slip of his words confirming that he'd got away with the crime. "You burned a man to death?"

"Accident." Tomaz folded his arms and smirked. Minutes after supposedly learning of his mother's death. It'd help condemn him if he was a part of this. They were still recording. "Ruled the guy must've had enough and tried to get warm using petrol. Fumes ignited some he'd spilled on himself."

"Not a chance they'd arrest someone, then let it be ruled an accident."

"Well they did."

Alicia closed her eyes a moment, then left without another word.

She generally didn't let the horror of human nature get her down too often. There were enough wonderful people out there to see off the truly evil ones many thousands of times over.

"You're thinking it was all Tomaz?" Murphy said, reading her.

"I don't know." Alicia sent a text to Cleaver to get Tomaz's juvenile records included in their sweep.

All the names. Everyone involved. Witnesses. Cops. Lawyers. The works.

As they reached Murphy's car, she said, "A lot of killers go undetected for years. Could be as simple as a sick kid fighting back against people he hated. If his mom found out, and he killed her; she disappears. Bobby turns to his old network to track him down. Dean gets killed, Bobby goes dark … it's all too…"

"Swirly?" Murphy offered.

"I need to sleep."

"I'll drive you home. Your car'll be fine at Sheerton."

Murphy drove toward her place via A-roads, at a rather more sedate pace than the journey here.

"I wish I could stay late with you guys," Alicia said.

"You have more important things to deal with."

"It's all going to change, isn't it?"

"Different doesn't mean worse."

She couldn't look at him. "I should be with you guys."

"Cleaver will call with anything they find."

"I know." She held her breath until the hot pressure at the bridge of her nose passed. No tears spilled.

Murphy's phone rang. It was Cleaver. Alicia pushed the speaker button and it tuned to the patrol car's Bluetooth kit.

Cleaver's voice echoed around. "Ready for another coincidence?"

"Another?" Alicia said with a hint of amusement. "I'm getting a bit bored of them."

"Tomaz was accused of murder. Even went to trial. Three years ago. Bobby was there, Linda too, and a lawyer called Freddie Milton. Know him?"

"Big fees," Murphy said. "Bad acquittal rate."

"Only bad for us," Cleaver said. "If you're guilty as sin and can afford him, he's shit-hot. And guess what?"

"Tomaz walked."

Alicia saw the swirls ease for a moment. "So that could be what caused Bobby's old friends to ask where he got that money. And when they found his nice big house in the country—"

"That's not why I'm calling," Cleaver said. "That's background."

"What's the big news?" Murphy asked.

"The judge who kicked Tomaz loose. It was our police and crime commissioner's new best friend. Marissa Poole, MP."

CHAPTER TWENTY-SEVEN

ALICIA WAS, again, grateful for Stacey's insatiable appetite. She fed the girl until ten p.m., then at three a.m., she was summoned to provide sustenance once again. Unfortunately, the pounding of links and coincidences had kept her alert and thinking for way too long, and the three a.m. session was less productive. No new insights. No new theories.

Her mum agreed to babysit in the flat the next day, so Alicia caught the bus to the train station, then the train to Leeds, where she tapped up Rebecca Ndlove to pick her up from the town centre. They discussed the discoveries from the day before, but all it did was repeat known information.

The pair made it to Sheerton. While Ndlove went straight to the inquiry room, Alicia headed for Murphy's office where she had arranged to meet the man sat sipping a coffee from the Has-Bean. Graham Rhapshaw. He wasn't alone as she'd instructed, though; he'd brought two uniformed coppers with him, a couple of guys she'd never met before.

"Alicia." He spoke affectionately and stood to greet her, dismissing the pair of uniforms.

"Graham." Her eyes flitted to the door, which she closed behind the departing constables.

"Oh dear. This is your serious face, isn't it? I'm not sure I like your serious face."

Alicia forced a smile. "How about this?"

"Worse. Sit down, you must be exhausted." Once Alicia flopped down, he sat opposite her. "How's motherhood?"

"Hard. I'll need to be a lot more organised when I come back full-time. *If* I come back full-time. I still haven't heard from Professional Standards."

"No. Alicia—"

"I know, I know, you can't comment on an ongoing inquiry. It's fine. I need to ask you something. And please, please can you answer without getting all puffed up and grumpy? I'll explain all in due course, I promise."

He considered it. "Okay. But I like the sound of that about as much as I like your serious face."

Alicia had rehearsed how she'd phrase what she had to say several times since he agreed to meet her here alone. Now, her brain had gone blank, the hard drive wiped. So, she drove her mouth blind. "Marissa Poole."

"What about her?" His hackles were rising already. Bad sign.

"She used to be a judge. And there are some question marks over her decision-making at the moment."

"Yes, the press are really going for her."

Alicia shrugged. "That's the business, I guess."

"She'll take it. She'll have to."

"If she wants to be home secretary."

Graham tapped his nose. "Rumours and gossip, Alicia. What about her?"

"I don't want to add any fuel to what she's going through. That's why I came to you directly."

He raised his chin, looking down at her. "What is it?"

"Can I have your word you will let this go where it goes?"

"If Mrs. Poole is guilty of wrongdoing, and not just the nonsense in the gutter press, I'll let the chips fall in the appropriate places."

Alicia had to decide.

Trust him or not? They'd known each other years, and despite their careers taking very different trajectories they'd remained friends. They'd retained their respect for one another.

She said, "Her name came up in connection with Tomaz Gortze. She dismissed evidence of a dreadful crime, but—"

"There's evidence of corruption?"

"We went through it just now, on the way in." She outlined the actual crime, a rough sleeper in Ilkley, burned alive in the middle of a park by the river; a horrific act of violence committed by a person who either had no heart, or a jet-black one. "The case revolved around both physical evidence and witness testimony. A lot of the witnesses were the lowlife types, but their accounts matched CCTV sightings of Tomaz, and the type of petrol can he used. Poole ditched them. Wouldn't allow the statements because a couple of the guys had records. Burglary, muggings, small time stuff, but some offenses were committed against upper-class types. Other than their record, there was no reason to deny the statements."

"Why not? If they're proven to be unreliable?"

"The jury would've heard of their pasts. They should have been given the opportunity to make up their own minds. But it never made it to a jury. The case collapsed."

Graham mulled it over. "Did they ever get anyone else for it?"

"No. The coroner initially said murder, but when the police could offer no other suspects, he had to rule it 'unexplained.' Some said one theory was he did it himself. Misadventure. The coroner never ruled it an accident as Tomaz said, but in his idiot brain, he got away with it."

Graham's hand enveloped his forehead and wiped it down his face. When he was fully revealed again, he looked tired. "Corruption. Bane of my bloody life."

Alicia thought that an odd response, but she pressed anyway. "There are so many secrets dropping right now. It's like birds falling out of trees when a cloud of poisonous smoke passes over."

"Very poetic."

"Thanks, I rehearsed that one. But the thing is, we need a true picture. I'm going to need to question her."

"Who? Marissa?"

"Mrs. Poole, yes. We're going to requisition the financials of every person with any connection to this. Anyone with a hint of skin in the game. And with Mrs. Poole's current accusations of corruption hanging over her, if she's implicated in this big, swirly case, we'll see what she has to hide."

Graham turned to stone. She almost heard his skin creaking and groaning as it coalesced into an unbreakable husk. Then he moved, human again. "Corruption. Like I said, the bane of my life." He huffed, sat back, deflating. Odd, since he'd been a rock moments ago. "Everyone seems to be corrupt nowadays, Alicia. Mates in high places."

"Not everyone, sir."

"Everyone has their own little bit of corruption. Even you."

"Me? I don't think so."

"I buried what you did."

Alicia's turn to solidify. She didn't dare shift in her seat in case she cracked and fell apart before his eyes. Gradually, she risked movement in her jaw. "I told Murphy not to hold back."

"I know. And I told professional standards that too. But it looks like you didn't send the killer after Demelza. The time-line is doable, Leeds to Blackpool, but after PSB got Jackie Osbourne to talk to Karen, it looks like you never revealed a location. Not even a region."

While that lifted a fraction of the weight holding her in place, Alicia needed more. "I still did something that—"

"Something that shouldn't sully a good detective if there were no real consequences. They agreed to move onto other things, providing neither of the people you told is implicated in the deaths." Rhapshaw clasped his hands together. "But just because they chose to move on—at my *strong suggestion*, don't forget—doesn't mean you didn't benefit from an element of corruption. No matter how small."

Alicia's neck reverted to bone and muscle and skin. She shifted her head, looking away from Graham, both grateful and furious, happy and sad, guilty and blameless. "I didn't ask for it."

"No, but there is the other matter. One I'm not sure I should cover up for you."

Alicia faced him. "What other matter?"

"I haven't been in this job long. I was Chief Superintendent Rhapshaw just a year ago, back when a certain Richard Hague was slipping around my patch. Remember him?"

"Of course I do." Alicia cut herself off before she said too much; Graham didn't have the first clue about her relationship with him, and as far as she knew he didn't know she ever visited his comatose body.

He said, "It was a mess. Mostly a victory, thanks to the girl being found alive, but lots of other factors. A serial killer who got away with his spree in America mounting a vigilante mission to rescue his daughter from a different serial killer. It has confusion and failure written all over it."

Alicia didn't argue.

"It's for that reason, Alicia, that I placed a flag on anything and everything relating to the man known as the Century Killer."

"Oh," Alicia said.

"Yes. *Oh.* I wanted to be informed personally of any over-stepping of bounds. I admit I was mostly worried by the press digging for salacious accusations or mistakes that might hamper my campaign, but that flag stuck around. A colleague kept it in place after I resigned, and today I got a message on my phone via something called WhatsApp. Imagine what I thought when I was told one of the investigating officers on that case was looking up personal information regarding the whereabouts of the victim in that case. Katie Hague. Richard's daughter."

"It's … nothing. I swear. It's nothing you need to worry about. Katie is … troubled. She needs help, and the mental health facilities in Britain, they're failing."

"Except, Alicia, it *is* something I need to worry about. You accessed the police database for personal reasons. Do you know how many man hours went into checking up on you? Making sure you had an alibi?"

"Alibi?" Now Alicia's throat tightened. "I did it. I put in a request for the information. I got her personal details straight away, and added a phone trace, background, but I haven't received it yet. Haven't read it. Certainly, I haven't acted on it yet—"

"Alicia." Graham held out a flat palm, a *stop* gesture. "Why did you need to perform an illegal search of the police database for Richard Hague's daughter?"

"I've been receiving poison pen letters. I'd been in contact with her before she moved to Wolverhampton and I worried she'd made me the focus of some of her grief and anger. I just wanted to reach out. Talk to her." She braced herself. "Your turn."

"What?"

"I've been either here, at home, or in the presence of other police officers, so my alibis are in place. I'm not worried about that. But why would I need one if you already have my confession?"

Graham wet his lips, a nervous tick inherent in many humans. No one knew its function, but Alicia once wrote a paper guessing it may be to do with symbolically lubricating the passage through which bad news was about to pass, to let the speaker eject the words more easily.

He said, "Five days ago, the police in Wolverhampton found a body in woodland, adjacent to Katie's college. Two days ago, just hours after you looked her up, that body was identified as Katherine Hague."

CHAPTER TWENTY-EIGHT

KATIE HAGUE WAS REPORTED MISSING a fortnight previously by her roommates in Wolverhampton, but it wasn't completely out of character for her. She lived in halls, a kind of apartment block designed and built specifically for students; communal kitchen, living room, hall, and four small bedrooms, one apiece, equipped with a single bed, a desk, and TV stand. Each flat had enough furniture and appliances for four people only. Essentially, the basics, with minimal distractions from studies. Some students take to this life, and when they all settle in, most take up residence in a house with the same group of people. Katie, it seemed, kept to herself. At times she'd be gregarious and fun, at others withdrawing into her room for days at a time. Her roommates called her "odd" and one even said she was "rude" and none of them questioned whether she might have been experiencing mental health issues.

When you're young, you don't. If three girls want to go out drinking, and the fourth wants to sit in her room, crying, or watching TV in a numb stupor, the three take it as a personal insult. Actually, it's a sure-fire sign of depression. But no;

people think you can "just snap out of it" or "try *not* being depressed" or some such. Like you can "just snap out of" having flu. Or cancer.

And Katie's depression, it appeared, was a cancer.

The body was ID'd by her roommate Claudia, although a second belt-and-braces DNA test had been ordered. Not unusual when no immediate family member can verify a body. Grandparents from her mother's side would provide a sample which would be compared for a familial match, much like the one taken to confirm Karen's ID of Dean and allow her to claim the body.

Alicia did a spot of arithmetic in her head. Two weeks since she'd been seen. Body found five days ago.

"Katie's dead?"

"Yes, and once I've left and official channels take over, you'll be suspended," Graham said.

"How long?"

"They don't need to make it an official suspension, Alicia. They *could* write it off as stress, insist you get some rest. If I *strongly suggest* it. Your 'keeping-in-touch' week is over, obviously, so we can clear all this up as bad judgement on your part and see you back at work in a month or two."

"Actually, I meant … how long was Katie dead for? Before they found her?"

"I don't know. A week, I think? They're still conducting tests. But you know how it is with that level of decay. A week in a wooded area, no humans. Animals and insects with her undisturbed…" He looked like he had more imagery to speak of but withheld it.

"That's … worrying. How did she do it? Hanging?"

Graham swallowed. "Not quite. She stabbed herself."

"*Stabbed* herself?"

"It's not as uncommon as you might think. In this case,

she bought an honest-to-God *sword* online, set it up so the handle was buried in the ground, and fell on it. Drugs and alcohol in her system—"

"There needs to be a full investigation. We need—"

"There *has* been a full investigation. And it will remain open until the coroner rules it murder, or suicide, or something else. *You* need to stay away. We can make this official if you prefer. If you don't drop it. Otherwise, go back to your baby, and forget this."

"I can't forget this. I got her a good therapist, she was getting better. I need to know what happened."

"When you come back to work, it'll all be cleared up. Just walk away now. I can only help you so much."

The swirliness was amping right up. No, not amping up. *Adding*. It was *adding* to the swirliness already inside her. A new swirl, not a bigger one. The Dean case, now Katie.

Because if Katie was dead a week, then in a morgue for five days, that was twelve days. Within those twelve days, Alicia received not one but *two* letters. From Katie.

Timing.

Arithmetic.

It was conceivable she sent the first before killing herself but not the second.

"I'm sorry." Alicia stood shakily. "I'll … go back to my own therapist too. I think … I think maybe this week was a little much for me. Too soon after the baby."

Graham nodded along, satisfied.

She continued telling him what he wanted to hear. "I'll see you in a couple of months. You know where I am if you need a statement."

"I do." He stood and extended a hand.

And even though she knew he was pressing her for no other reason than to protect his closest ally, someone who—in the Home Office—would be able to convey serious powers to him and his ilk, whose endorsement would benefit him to no end should he choose the parliamentary route following his time as police and crime commissioner … despite all this, she shook his hand. "Thank you, Graham. I appreciate it."

On her way out, planning to not even say goodbye to Murphy, she focused on the immediate issue. She couldn't possibly wait months to close this off. She couldn't even wait for that DNA test. It needed clearing up *now*.

No matter the consequences.

CHAPTER TWENTY-NINE

MURPHY WAS ALMOST RELIEVED when Graham Rhapshaw asked him to pop up to his own office and delivered the news that Alicia had agreed to fall out of the case and resume her maternity leave. She was plainly stressed, struggling with the lurch from copper to new mum to full-time working mother. She'd cope, once she worked out a routine. Most women did. Not easy, especially alone, but he was confident Alicia would do what she always did: she'd find a way.

He was less relieved when Rhapshaw moved on to other subjects. Frankly, Murphy was on the verge of calling up the deputy chief constable to complain. Rhapshaw seemed to think he was still on the job. The goodwill he still fostered would only go so far. Murphy let it go for now.

Back in the inquiry room, Ndlove and Cleaver worked alongside Ball and Lemmy, having readjusted their body clocks from night duty. Murphy placed his phone face down on the table and told the four detectives that Alicia was no longer working with them, gave the vague reason of "exhaustion" and revealed where they stood on the case.

"The issue with Marissa Poole has been cleared up. Her

interest in the case was, partially, to do with the young man who the Crown failed to prosecute after she rejected evidence. She has apologised for not disclosing that information. But Commissioner Rhapshaw has suggested she is in the clear. He will not support a warrant application."

Ball, Lemmy, Cleaver and Ndlove all awaited his verdict.

When he didn't continue, Cleaver asked, "Does he have the power to block that?"

"Not officially, no. But he'll be speaking to the chief super, and the chief super *does* have that power. Marissa Poole will speak to me, and only me. *Off* the record."

Ndlove shook her head. "Bitch."

"It was always unlikely she'd have anything to do with Dean Bicklesthwaite."

"But still. She's being investigated for sentencing minorities more harshly than white kids. This is a white kid who got away with murder. She deserves the scrutiny."

No one spoke for a moment.

It was Cleaver who broke the silence. "I agree. But that's not our job."

Lemmy was frowning. "Thought it was worse sentences for poor people, not minorities."

"Minorities are more likely to be poor," Ndlove said.

"Yeah, but it's not racism, is it?"

"Not directly. Maybe not her intent. But that's the effect it has. Minorities are more likely to be poor, so picking on poor people means a disproportionate sentence for minorities."

"Look, I'm not big on politics." Lemmy leaned on his elbows. "But if you take away race and just look at their background, the people she sentenced are scrotes. Scumbags. More likely to reoffend than someone with a decent job to go to. Or parents who can keep 'em in line."

Ndlove spoke slowly and calmly. "A white kid with a dad

who's not only reformed after prison but clearly has money ... he gets away with *burning* someone to *death*. While a black kid with a mum who has a history of drinking and minor violent scuffles ... he's dealing a bit of weed to his mates and goes down for *two years*. That sound fair to you?"

"No, but—"

"Okay, that's time." Cleaver clapped his hands. "This isn't our place. We gather evidence. We put it to the CPS. They make the cases. Judges have to obey the law and sentencing guidelines from the government. If she's clean on all that, maybe an off the record chat is all we need."

"It's all we'll get," Murphy said.

He noticed that Ndlove was tensed, her body pointed away from Lemmy. Lemmy, meanwhile, was still relaxed. He hadn't even noticed how his words had affected his colleague. Another thing for Murphy to collar Ball about later.

"For now, we have two avenues to explore. The Jerzy line isn't put to bed yet. He still had an affair, he might not have known Demelza directly, but could have set up the hit."

Ball raised a hand. "But Linda Gortze—"

"Could've been killed by Bobby too. But that's our other line of enquiry. Someone came to rob Bobby, tortured his girl-friend for information, and whether they got what they wanted or not, Bobby is coming for those responsible. He enlisted the help of his old pal Demelza, but then killed her to keep her quiet. That's the one I like. But, as ever—"

"Keep an open mind," Cleaver said, finishing for him.

"We're sandbagged on Poole?" Ball asked.

"If anything new comes up that puts her in the frame for either the Dean Bicklesthwaite murder, or if we can prove she took a bribe to kick the witness statements on the Tomaz case, then we're back on her like flies on a turd." Murphy held up his phone, his palm over the screen. "I have to make some calls. You all know what you're doing. Dismissed."

With Ball and Lemmy interviewing other people of interest in Ernest Borek's former circle of petty thieves and counterfeit retailers, Ndlove was to collate everything into a form that could be presented to the CPS, leaving Cleaver to work the numbers. He'd requisition Darla, Murphy's niece, and Cleaver's current girlfriend, to adapt an algorithm that would pull out relevant data. After that, if nothing helpful emerged Cleaver would spend several hours and a lot of coffee and takeaways going through every bank statement, prison record, and mobile phone bill to tie Bobby to Dean or Jerzy.

Alone, Murphy turned his phone over and said, "You get all that?"

"I did, thank you," Alicia said via the speaker function. It sounded like she was driving.

"Think we'll build a case against Jerzy?"

"He could still have drawn attention to the murder through Demelza to get home ASAP. Sparing his children the sight of their dismembered granddad might have been a condition of him taking part. Getting Karen out, getting Dean to a place they felt comfortable killing him. Dean's place is a little conspicuous. Houses closer together."

"Revenge. It's the simplest explanation."

"You're not buying it, Murphy?"

"Is it impossible? No, it's just … that thread."

"Yeah, that's annoying. The Poole thread, linking to Tomaz."

"It's dangling."

Murphy sighed through his nose. "But you have what you need. You don't need to keep checking in here. Take your medicine on this. They'll make the case if you don't. If you stay away, they'll drop it."

"You're keeping someone on Pete, too, right? In case it turns out he and Karen were having the affair?"

"We've flagged his phone and we're looking at his other background, but why would he kill Dean? Even if Dean knew about it, surely he'd side with his daughter? I think that thread is tied off."

"Yeah, it's better to go with Occam." She sounded disappointed through the white noise of the car on her journey home.

"Come back next month, Alicia. I'll bring a Chinese round, maybe treat you to an old malt. *Once it's over.*"

"Hey, one thing." She paused, but Murphy got the sense she wasn't waiting for him to speak. "Think you'll have a place for me at Sheerton?"

"Not going back to the SCA?"

"I'm just thinking … I'd make a good DI. Don't you agree?"

Murphy found the political aspects of the job difficult, so Alicia would be doubly hindered by them. DI, possibly, but DCI? Unless she changed her approach, that was unlikely.

"Murphy?" she said. "You don't think I'd be a good inspector?"

"I think you'd be an outstanding one. I'm just not sure *you* would like it." But he couldn't deny she'd be useful to have around. And she clearly needed some hint of hope for change. "I'll find a detective sergeant post for you, and you'll get as much mentoring and support as you need to make DI. Rest is up to you. Okay?"

"Sounds good. Thanks, Murphy."

"If there's a space."

"Of course."

"And I'll make sure the application is completely neutral so there's no favouritism."

"Of course." Her tone changed, and Murphy thought maybe she was smiling.

"About Marissa Poole," she said. "She's still dangling, and we don't like danglers do we, Murphy?"

"No one likes danglers, Alicia."

"You going to leave it?"

"Of course. I'm not insubordinate, unlike someone I could mention."

"I don't know what you could possibly mean."

She hung up, and Murphy just hoped she wasn't going to do anything *too* stupid.

CHAPTER THIRTY

NOT WANTING to burden her mom or Robbie, and with no idea what time she'd be home, Alicia dropped in on the Dot-Bot who seemed a little too relieved when she announced she was taking the rest of the day—and the rest of the next couple of months—off work to focus on things at home. She'd burdened her friends and family enough. She promised to drop by her dad's place with Stacey, and Dot suggested setting up a family dinner for all of them, allowing Alicia's two brothers to spend a little more time with their niece.

Alicia hadn't seen much of her brothers in the last few years, their busy lives limiting interaction to family occasions like birthdays or Christmas, and major sporting events like the World Cup, the latter a tradition they continued from childhood. They skipped Wimbledon this year, and Alicia worried they might be drifting too far. Their homes were spread across Yorkshire, not far enough to lose touch completely, but too long a journey to casually nip in for a cuppa.

Today, she announced, was a girls' day. She was taking Stacey on a little road trip to visit an old friend. Dot liked the idea, again a little too enthusiastic, as if she'd been waiting for such an announcement for a while. Perhaps she'd been concerned at Alicia's lack of socialising.

For now, Alicia put that out of her mind and concentrated on bigger issues. Her "old friend", of course, was Katie Hague and the "road trip" was popping down to Wolverhampton—a two-hour journey not accounting for traffic. She wasn't exactly sure what she hoped to achieve by showing up in person, but sheer bloody-mindedness meant she had to. That, and an echo from the past that irked her.

She kept Stacey awake and amused with nursery rhymes all along the M62 over the Pennines before a sharp left turn took her down the M6 to her destination. Just before turning off, she stopped off at a motorway service station, brought Stacey out for a stroll, then sat to eat at a KFC. When the baby started pawing at Alicia's chest, Alicia obliged by feeding the tot in a quiet corner of Starbucks whilst sipping a decaf latte, before resuming the journey.

As expected, the full tummy and the motion of the car sent Stacey off to sleep. Not a method she could employ all the time, but one essential to this afternoon's aims.

After a crawl into the city, Alicia found the morgue was part of a grey police station from the seventies, all boxes of concrete and steel, like the Millgarth station where she first met Murphy. She secured Stacey into a wraparound fabric carrier and entered the reception area, flashed the ID that no one thought to relieve her of, and asked to speak to the detective in charge of Katherine Hague's death.

DI Rick Spencer was a man of average height. In his shirt-sleeves, though, the muscles in his arms, shoulders, and chest were pronounced. He'd been expecting someone from Leeds to come with the grandparents but not with a baby in tow. Alicia just shrugged, not wishing to lie outright that she was on official business, while not correcting his assumption. Since Katie was being returned up north, her place of residence, the coroner would rule from that district; it was open and shut, so no wonder Ricky Spencer seemed eager to sign off on the paperwork.

Should she call him Ricky?

Probably not.

He let her through the locked door from reception into the station proper. A musty corridor waited, and Spencer led the way. "What's with the baby?"

"It's my day off," she said.

"Ah, the luxury of overtime."

Again, Alicia didn't correct him. In fact, she caught herself looking at his arse as he led her through to what she assumed would be his office. He almost caught her too, as he scanned his pass to let her through a door.

"You sure you want to bring a kid in here?" he asked.

"Oh, she's been in police stations before."

"Yeah, but…" He pointed as they turned a corner.

Alicia followed his finger to where a sign for the morgue pointed the way. She halted. "I didn't think we'd be going there. I was hoping for … pictures. More than I could pull off the system."

In truth, she had no access to the system, which was partly why she had to make this trip in person. Although she kept hold of her physical ID, her sign on credentials were revoked. And those echoes from the past meant she *had* to see for herself.

"There's no more," Spencer said. "Just what's on the case file."

"Can I maybe see them again?"

Spencer didn't reply straight away. He seemed to be considering something, and Alicia immediately noted suspicion in the way he held himself.

She quickly said, "I got stiffed on the childcare, but…"

The suspicion remained.

Alicia shrugged to keep it casual. "Would the photos be okay?"

"I've sent the hardcopies on to Leeds already. The digital ones are in the system. I can give you a desk for an hour or two—"

And he'd expect her to use her own sign-in details. "Is that in a busy squad room?"

"Yes, sorry." He now looked at Stacey. "I can try to get you a private office, but—"

Alicia waved him off. "Okay, look, as long as she stays asleep, she'll be fine. Even if she wakes up, she probably won't know what she's looking at, right?"

"Right." He resumed walking and Alicia followed.

"You sure it's suicide?" Alicia asked.

"It's all in the file." Mr. Suspicious resumed his squinty looks.

"You know who she is?"

"Katherine Hague. Daughter of the Century Killer. Sad case. Guess the stress was too much. You didn't read the file?"

"Not fully. I'm … you know who I am?"

Spencer nodded as they reached the double doors leading to the cold room in which the bodies were stored. "You were on the original case. Killed the guy who took Katherine the first time, didn't you?"

"Yes, that's me." She noted he held his pass above the receiver that would open the morgue doors but hadn't unlocked them yet. "I only heard about Katie this morning. I called in a couple of favours to be the one to come, and that's why…" She gestured to Stacey, aware she was lying outright now, not simply by omission. "I just know a body was found, and you can't age it precisely because it was so decomposed. A person who shared her flat ID'd her, and you're waiting on DNA to confirm."

"And you're here ahead of the grandparents because…?"

"Echoes," Alicia said. "I just need to be sure."

Spencer made up his mind and swiped his card to let her through.

They entered the sterile space. It was chilly, but not refrigerated. Stacey was fine in her wrap and if Alicia wasn't shivering it couldn't be *that* bad. Any bodies would be stored in the six lockers facing them, the autopsies themselves performed in a room at the end of this one. Gurneys were lined up nearby.

Without needing to check the inventory, Spencer went to the end of the six lockers, plucked a pair of gloves from a basket nearby, and filled out a form. "She's our only resident right now. What's this about echoes?"

"When we were investigating her kidnapping, a body turned up. We came down, thinking it was her. *Assumed* it was her. It wasn't."

"And you're worried it won't be her today."

"I'm *expecting* it to be her. I *hope* I'm wrong."

Spencer finished his paperwork, got Alicia to sign to say she'd entered—technically the body was part of the chain of evidence—and then he opened the locker. He slid the tray out on which lay a sealed bag made of a thick, heavy compound like rubbery plastic.

Alicia checked Stacey was still fast asleep, then nodded.

Spencer pulled open the zip. "You know this won't be pleasant, don't you?"

"I do." Alicia stepped forward as the bag opened.

The girl inside was unrecognisable. Not only as Katie, but as a human being. It was like someone had pulped an alien. Her skin was almost blue. The body frame matched Katie's, her hair, her age. She'd been cleansed of blood and grime, and a Y-shaped incision over her chest proved she'd been examined. There was only a light smell, thanks to the refrigeration and the removal of the rottenest bits of flesh. The lethal wound was dry, like a large fish's mouth, beneath the sternum.

One, single wound.

"Irony?" Spencer said without humour.

"Because that's how her dad killed?"

"That's what we're thinking."

"Single wound. Richard stabbed through the ribcage, or directly through the sternum."

"That's one reason we're thinking suicide. Go up from beneath, into the heart, and it's a lot easier. No bone, just organs."

"Did she reach the heart?"

"The edge of it. Bottom quarter. Clean, though. Not a direct hit, but … it wasn't a long death."

"And the scene?"

"Buried the sword up to the hilt, used a homemade vice out of two lumps of wood to shore it up, steady it. Rocks to stand on."

"And there's no doubt?"

"There's always doubt. Coroner's verdict at the moment appears to be inconclusive. Pitching it back to Leeds is just to get it off our books and back with the family. We're a small operation. But that doesn't mean we just sit on it. We're tracing Katie's movements, all contact made with others, both in person and electronic."

Alicia was relieved nobody appeared to be skimming on it. "It's your patch, your murder."

"We don't think it's murder, but we won't make the assumption."

"Too late."

"Too late?"

"You've already made the assumption. You're ticking boxes with the trail." Alicia leaned closer, careful not to let Stacey come into contact with any surface in here. The smell was stronger, so she pulled away; if she was sensing the aroma of dead flesh in the air, Stacey was breathing it in too. "I don't think it's her."

"DNA isn't in yet, but we got a preliminary ID."

"I know, but … Katie was drinking, not looking after herself. This isn't the body of someone living that way."

"She plays a lot of sports."

"Not recently. This person, her breasts are too small, her legs are too thin…"

"She was doing a lot of drugs. There was acid, ketamine, and a truckload of booze. If she hadn't pushed herself on the sword, she'd have been a hospital case from the toxins. Plus … the skin retracts in death. She wastes away—"

"*I know!*"

Alicia shut her mouth tight. She hadn't meant to shout, and now she was concerned Stacey might wake up. The baby didn't so much as stir.

"I'm sorry," Alicia said.

"It's okay. You wanted her to be alive."

Alicia could not help but stare at the gory mess in the bag. "It just … I mean…" She hoisted Stacey a little higher to ease the pressure on her lower back. "If Katie dies here … everything we did last year … all we went through … it was for nothing."

"But if it isn't Katie…" He zipped the bag up and pushed the table back inside the locker.

She didn't need to elaborate on Spencer's unfinished words. "If it isn't Katie, then looking at the MO, the profile of the victim, and Katie nowhere to be found … it makes Katie the prime suspect in a murder."

CHAPTER THIRTY-ONE

IT SHOULD HAVE BEEN SIMPLE. Murphy sat in his office overlooking the squad room that contained four detectives working six cases, one of them a less senior DCI borrowed from missing persons. He ripped the latest sheet from his A4 notepad and started again, jotting notes that kept leaping into his brain even when advising the other detectives on the next course of action. Two were out making an arrest thanks to his approval on their work. He'd delegated all his other cases now, thanks to his fellow DCI agreeing to step in for a couple of days and was now concentrating on this alone.

Before, it had seemed—yes—simple. A guy has an affair, his father in law discovers it and demands he confesses, so the guy kills the father in law. Dumbass plan, but it fit. It worked.

Until it didn't.

The discovery of the body of Linda Gortze threw it all on its head, her cause of death now found to be the throat cut resulting in massive blood loss. Initial analysis of the house revealed a lot more blood in the bathroom, where the killing presumably took place, raising the question of why they bothered to move her to the freezer. Murphy figured it was probably Bobby who moved the body, preserving it until he carried out his revenge.

Rhapshaw still wanted him to concentrate on Jerzy, that he could have been a part of both killings, but the problems of interconnectivity remained.

First, he jotted the heading "Facts" and below it listed everything they considered indisputable:

Dean Bicklesthwaite was murdered in Karen's house.

Dean, Bobby Carr, Ernest Borek, and Demelza Shine were all friends running a counterfeit clothing scam before Bobby was sent down for killing a man.

Jerzy Krasowski became friends with Dean AFTER the counterfeit business died. Appears legit.

Unlikely Jerzy knew Demelza.

Jerzy is/was having an affair with Brenda Williams.

Psychics are not real.

Demelza was part of the murder setup.

Tomaz Gortze was on the books at Golden Start.

Tomaz Gortze burgled Jerzy's house, stealing his passport.

Tomaz Gortze's mother was murdered BEFORE Dean, but in the same manner.

Tomaz was accused of murder several years ago but released by Marissa Poole.

Tomaz Gortze's mother is Linda Gortze, Bobby Carr's girlfriend.

He then wrote a heading "Prime Assumptions" below which he noted things they strongly believed but could not currently prove:

The murder is tied into this circle of friends.

Demelza Shine was murdered to stop her revealing the identity of the killer.

Linda Gortze's death triggered Bobby Carr's return to violence.

Bobby Carr killed Dean Bicklesthwaite
Tomaz knew about his mother's death, so he helped Bobby.
Bobby also had help from Demelza.

That last point caused him to pause and reconsider. Why would Bobby Carr want Karen to go home early? Would he care about a case of PTSD in Karen and Jerzy's kids? Was he just doing it for a laugh? Irony in a sociopath?

Also, if Bobby and Tomaz were working together, why did they need to take Jerzy's passport?

Murphy left that alone for now, and moved on, writing "Theories" for a list of things that were not clear yet and required some leaps in assumption.

Dean plus someone else (Jerzy? Ernest?) realised Bobby had more money left from their gangster days. Came to collect.
Dean and others tortured Linda to get the money.
Fail? Succeed?
Bobby either got free, or they let him go when he paid them.
Money? Where is it?

"A mess," Murphy said aloud.

It was supposed to be *simple*. Most murders were. So why was this one not?

They wouldn't know until they located Bobby Carr.

Murphy's phone rang. It was nearly seven p.m. and it was Alicia on the line.

She said, "Hi there, Uncle Donald! I need you to sing to Stacey."

CHAPTER THIRTY-TWO

WITH STACEY WAKING IMMEDIATELY upon exiting the station in Wolverhampton, she screamed for twenty minutes in the back of the car as Alicia drove around aimlessly, considering whether the body in the morgue was a murder victim or an elaborate suicide engineered to emulate Richard Hague's modus operandi. The mishmash of wailing infant and incomplete facts meant Alicia stopped the car to both shut up the child and treat herself to a cup of posh coffee. Feeling guilty about viewing Stacey as little more than an inconvenience, she then played with her in a playpark that she spotted close to the coffee shop. Strong enough to sit up, Alicia tried Stacey in a swing for the first time, squeezing her in, supported by the furry all-in-one snowsuit and nudged her gently from behind.

The motion quietened her.

Bitterly cold even in her best duffel coat, Alicia proceeded with the activity whilst trying to work out whether she'd *deduced* it wasn't Katie back there, or just really *hoped* it wasn't.

Echoes.

Spencer and Rhapshaw were correct about suicide by stabbing being less rare than most people would expect. Disturbed minds often don't consider the pain, or else they anticipate it. Welcome it. Using its accuracy is better than hanging which can go wrong for any number of reasons: leaping from height or in front of a train gives too many opportunities to chicken out; pills can be ejected through involuntary spasms whilst unconscious, or else do-gooders might find you and call an ambulance, whereupon a person can be revived but often with irreversible kidney damage—a scenario that simply adds to a suicidal person's reasons for wanting to die; and guns are not as easy to obtain in the UK as movies and TV make out. No, when researched properly, in the absence of being able to obtain a gun, a knife is more precise for someone who is serious about ending their life.

If that *was* Katie, Alicia suspected anticipation was a factor, punishing her father via her own flesh. She would have imagined an outpouring of wonder at what she did, of people marvelling at her intelligence and bravery for aping her dad's killing method, of turning it on herself. The blade sliding into her might even have brought a serene smile to her lips, a final sensation of peace settling through her troubled body.

A fertile imagination in a disturbed mind was a dangerous thing indeed.

Alicia could have obtained her own DNA sample from the corpse and compared it to Richard's, or even Stacey's for that matter, but she chose to wait. No point muddying the evidence. Spencer had her phone number.

But them sending the body back to Leeds so quickly did stink of them reaching a conclusion they shouldn't have leapt to, no matter what Mr. Sexy Arms said. Yes, they were looking into her movements, into who she met with, her communications, but it felt half-hearted.

"That's such a cute smile," someone said nearby.

Alicia snapped out of her thoughts and paid attention to

an Asian woman in a heavy coat and a headscarf that tucked in tightly under her chin. She was with a toddler of around two years old, running for the slide. The woman smiled again, nodded at Stacey.

Alicia came around the front of the swing, presented with the biggest smile she'd ever seen on her daughter. Positively *gurgling* with delight at the shallow pitch of the swing.

"She loves it!" Alicia said.

"They do," the woman said. Then in a knowing tone, she added, "Good luck getting her out." She followed her son to the small slide.

Alicia watched Stacey some more, pushed her a little higher, and when she came back down, the squeal filled Alicia with sunshine and happiness. She laughed too. Stacey went back again on the momentum, and this time waved her arms around as the returned to Alicia.

Away. Smile.

Back again. Whoops of sheer delight.

It was one of those moments all mums anticipate. Discovering an activity that generates unmitigated fun, pure love, joy radiating from every pore. Stacey had inherited Alicia's dimples and they shone brightly from her, digging deeper with each squeal.

Alicia couldn't resist it. She plucked Stacey from the swing seat and gave her the biggest hug she dared. Couldn't stop smiling.

Then she did stop.

Because Stacey almost lurched out of her arms. Alicia held her away, tightly enough to be sure she couldn't squirm out, and the face Stacey pulled was full of hate and spite. She screamed again, pushing Alicia, trying to wriggle from her arms.

"You're kidding me." Alicia glanced over at the other mum, who returned a sympathetic look. "Right then."

She placed Stacey back in the swing, turning off the waterworks like she'd flipped a switch. The girl kicked her legs and thumped the swing's rail, frowning at the infernal device until Alicia pulled the seat toward her. Stacey smiled, waving her hands. Then Alicia let go.

Squeals again.

Alicia stood up straight and nodded back to the woman, whose sympathy, if anything, had deepened. On the plus side, Alicia could pick up her coffee and mull over the Katie situation some more.

She still hadn't told anyone but Murphy about Richard being Stacey's dad, and could not risk it as a blemish on her record—personal or professional—so she hadn't told Katie either. It could have set her therapy back. But if she somehow found out, as the letters seemed to indicate, that might push her in the opposite direction.

As Richard withheld his true self from her, now Alicia was holding back Katie's only chance of a sibling. Twenty years her junior, but still a sibling.

And what *about* the letters?

The postmarks proved they originated in a mix of Yorkshire and the Midlands, and the latest one was mailed only days earlier. After she disappeared. Dating the body was never as simple as in the movies, so there was a grey patch in which she could have gone off the grid, holed up for a while, sent the letter, then skewered herself.

Alternatively, she could have experienced a complete psychotic break. The letters may have acted as a temporary pressure valve, but she'd have been bottling up so much more. When that valve finally burst, suicide or incredibly reckless behaviour wouldn't be out of the ordinary. Unusual decision making. *Bad* decisions. All driven by a psychosis, mixing her prescriptions with things like ketamine and hard liquor.

In fact, it was beginning to dawn on Alicia that, maybe, Katie committing murder was a more likely scenario than suicide. She'd never see the inside of a jail, though. A mental health facility, maybe, but not jail. Not in the state she had to be in.

And yet.

There was still no DNA confirmation. And that meant Alicia's own decision-making in coming here was questionable. Especially bearing in mind the giggling, dimple-bragging four-month-old currently swinging back and forth before her.

Alicia needed to keep Stacey awake for at least two more hours or she would never fall asleep in the car, which would mean multiple stops on the way back, and a frazzled brain to boot. She couldn't spend all that time just whizzing the child back and forth on the swing. Could she?

Stacey answered for her in the form of her reddening poo-face. A look of concentration and then sheer effort. Then relief. And tears.

At least it got her out of the swing.

Alicia carried her back to the coffee shop and bought a fruity tea to drink on the premises, changed Stacey, and spent another twenty minutes playing with her on her lap, alternating between her favourite plastic giraffe and Alicia's car keyring and house keys to keep her settled. A feed beckoned, and since the place proudly declared they were breastfeeding friendly she sat right there while she did it. Another quick burp, then a deeper one heralded an end to that session, so she wandered back to the car, pulled out the pushchair, and spent the next hour trundling around the park, banishing pointless thoughts, and concentrating on how to keep in touch with the developments concerning Katie.

She could ask Murphy, but that'd get him in trouble.

No. That wasn't the answer. He'd already tried to back her a lot this week, so she should give him space. And she had Stacey to deal with, after all. She needed to think more about the baby and less about the murder. Less about Katie. Alicia wasn't the world's greatest detective, even though certain aspects—profiling mainly—did make her one of the most in-demand, and she understood DI Spencer was probably not slacking off, that she viewed his actions through a blurry lens of uncertainty.

She would let it all drop.

Buy a swing for Stacey.

Wait, where will I put it?

Alicia lived in a first floor flat and there wasn't even a communal garden. She could install one at her mum's, although she wasn't sure the Dot-Bot would want such a thing amid her geometrically perfect vegetable patches. Her dad would welcome it at his place, but she only got over there on certain days; he was the sort of granddad who played with babies, not the sort who looked after them and fed them and basically kept them alive. His generation of men had barely looked at a nappy let alone changed one.

Detective *Inspector* Alicia Friend could probably afford a mortgage. She had savings. Not enough for a deposit on a mortgage in a nice area, but the Bank of Mum & Dad would surely facilitate a loan to cover the rest.

Alicia leaned over the pushchair and when Stacey saw her, she gave another dimple-heavy smile. "I'm thinking about a mortgage. You made me old."

Instead of murder and death, Alicia concentrated on a life plan. Of what she might afford, where she might buy a house, how many bedrooms, how she would tell Robbie…

Could Robbie live with her? Or was Alicia getting too old

for a roommate? Mid-thirties. People tended to have moved on by then. All her friends from school and uni were either living alone or with partners or spouses, one had even got married, birthed three kids, and was now divorced and living with her parents.

Time to grow up?

Maybe.

She got in her car after the requisite four hours of awake time, making it seven p.m., so she might miss the worst of the M62 traffic. Stacey was clean and fed, so with any luck she'd be able to just rouse her at home, change her into pyjamas and clean nappy, give her a quick feed, then put her straight down. Until one or two a.m.

Good plan.

And yes, she did nod off minutes into the journey. Alicia figured it was a good end to a bad day. She'd failed at the murder of Dean Bicklesthwaite, leaving it for Murphy to close; Katie was either dead or so deranged she'd taken the life of someone who looked a lot like her; but Stacey had found a physical sensation she adored, and Alicia made a firm decision to move out of the flat she had shared with her best friend for nearly a decade and buy an actual *house*.

Then, an hour into her journey, where the M6 met the M62, traffic ground to a halt. Stacey murmured.

"Oh, no…"

The little one hated being stationary in her car seat. Seemed to take it as a personal insult and reacted with combined panic and anger. Alicia wondered if the angle of the seat gave her wind, but when moving the vibrations eased it. Whatever the mechanics, Stacey woke up and filled the car with noise. The giraffe eased her temper for a short while, but as the car crept forward a few inches at a time, she threw it and screamed some more. Alicia tried singing, which worked for about five minutes, then her nursery rhyme CD, and then she checked the traffic news on her phone while Stacey yelled and wailed.

They were stuck here for at least another thirty minutes.

She couldn't take it. Dimples or no dimples, she had no choice. She tuned her phone to the car's Bluetooth, dialled Murphy's number, and when he answered, she came straight out with it. "Hi there, Uncle Donald! I need you to sing to Stacey."

"Sing to her?" he replied. "Now?"

"Yeah. Can you hear her?"

"I can hear her."

He'd be deaf not to.

"I'm in the squad room," he said.

Alicia noted the time. "It's late."

"I'm busy. I can't sing to her."

"*Please?* I'm stuck in traffic and she's making my brain sag. I think it might dribble out of my ears if you don't."

"Did you see her?"

Alicia poked a finger in her ear closest to Stacey. "See who?"

"Katie. We had a call checking up on you. They now know you used your ID when not on duty."

Alicia closed her eyes. Maybe DI Friend would never come to be. Too many mistakes. Too many snubs to procedure and authority.

A new level of rage cried out of Stacey, so Alicia shifted swiftly in her seat. "Would you *please*, just for *one minute*, shut your *bloody mouth*!"

Both Alicia and Stacey froze in place. Alicia's wide eyes stung, unable to blink. The anger surging through her ebbed to her extremities, a hand rising to her mouth. She tried speaking, but nothing came. As the surprise waned, Stacey picked up where she left off, crying in a higher pitch, seemingly intended to shred the last of Alicia's resolve.

Alicia settled back to her seat, noticed the car in front had shifted several feet, and edged onward herself. Numb from the outburst. Wondering what she could do to make up for it. But that racket. That incessant, unending scream grated right through her. She couldn't go all the way to Leeds like this, she—

She heard singing. Soft, deep, melodic.

The lyrics to *You Are My Sunshine* rolled from the speakers all around. Although Stacey took at least another five seconds to hear it, once she did, her wailing eased a fraction. Within ten seconds, the noise she made abated to a simple hick-hick sucking of air.

Traffic still only moved feet at a time, so Alicia edged to the next lane, then onto the hard shoulder, where she parked and removed her seatbelt, reached over and unbuckled Stacey. The baby's face had turned blotchy, as it always did after prolonged tantrums, and Alicia simply held her as Murphy's smooth voice rolled over them both. When he finished, he didn't need asking to go through it again, and Alicia wondered how many police detectives were listening to him as well.

That gave her a warm feeling.

She checked on Stacey, who was no longer ramping up for more tears, and buckled her back in her seat. She rejoined the queuing cars, and after a third rendition they were moving at between five and ten miles per hour.

"Once more, Murphy?" Alicia said.

She pictured him sighing, but the words came through again, slower, with a melodic grace that gave Alicia the idea to make Murphy's next birthday a karaoke night. As they sped up to almost forty, the blend of song and movement eased Stacey back to sleep, and the turn-off for the M62 was in sight.

"Thanks, Uncle Donald," Alicia said. "And … I'm sorry. About … I never shout at her usually. I just…"

"It's okay," Murphy said. "Tough day."

"It wasn't her. Katie. It wasn't her."

"We'll know soon enough."

"DI Spencer won't be calling me with the DNA results, will he?"

"No. But I'll get them. And I'll call you."

"Thanks." Alicia felt selfish for that, but she needed to know. And Murphy wouldn't get in trouble if he kept his over-view official and only contacted Alicia via his personal phone. "It can't be her."

"Like I said, we'll find out for sure soon."

"I'll hang up now."

"Okay."

Alicia didn't hang up. There was more going on in the back of her brain than she realised.

"Alicia?"

"Yes?"

"Do you want to talk some more?"

"Not yet. But stay on the line. I'm processing."

"Processing what?"

"I don't know." She ran back through what she just said to Murphy. About Katie. About Stacey. "Murphy, what's the progress today? At your end, I mean?"

"Slow. I had Ball and Cleaver ask Jerzy about Demelza Shine, and he still says he didn't know her. Seemed surprised we were asking. He maintains he did not set up Karen with the reading and was not involved with Ernest's shadier stuff, not until after he went into proper business. We can't find anything to refute that."

"Right. Slow."

"There are so many connections, so many possibilities, it's

almost impossible to make sense of it. Unless someone confesses, we'll have to dig up another witness."

"Run through it. Really quick." She was on the M62 motorway now, almost empty, the opposite of the M6. "Don't think. Just hit me. Bullet points. Every detail. In order."

"Okay." He didn't sound sure. "Karen and Jerzy are at a psychic show. While they're there, Dean Bicklesthwaite is beaten, his stomach sliced open, and throat cut. While they're at the show, Demelza Shine—an old mate of Dean's—tells Karen something horrible has happened and she needs to get home straight away. At home, they find the body. DNA confirms it's Dean Bicklesthwaite. Jerzy, it turns out, is having an affair with Brenda Williams, but we have no evidence that Dean knew about it."

"And we can't confirm with any certainty he didn't," Alicia said.

"While they're moving their things temporarily into Dean's house, Karen finds out about the affair and kicks Jerzy out. Later that night, Tomaz Gortze breaks in, steals valuables plus Jerzy's passport. And only Jerzy's, not the others that are also nearby. Tomaz was on the books once at Jerzy's Golden Start recruitment agency, along with a couple of minor league weed dealers. Karen herself may or may not have been seeing a work colleague, and later the same night as we learn this, Demelza Shine is killed alongside a police officer. We learned Dean was a heavy for some small-time crooks, and when they went down he hooked up as a bouncer for some of Ernest Borek's backroom card games."

Murphy took a breath.

"Keep going," Alicia said.

"Ernest became friends with Dean and introduced him to a local importer of counterfeit goods, Demelza Shine. Plus a chap called Bobby Carr. Ernest, it seems, was involved in flogging those counterfeit goods, but later goes legit. Demelza was the brains behind the business. Bobby Carr was involved in much higher-level gangster stuff, though, an enforcer and gun for hire who went to jail for a killing unrelated to anyone involved here. While everyone goes legit—a wholesaler, logistics transport, psychic and magician—Bobby serves his time and gets out, reforms, and starts a relationship with Linda Gortze. She is also Tomaz's mother. Linda, though, is murdered. Killed probably weeks before Dean. Tomaz was, at one point, accused of murdering a homeless man, but released without charge and no one else was sought in connection with it. Bobby Carr hasn't been seen since at least the time Linda was killed, so finding him has to be the priority."

"He's the one," Alicia said.

"I think so. He answers the 'who' question. We don't know the 'why'. Or, frankly, the 'how' just yet. We're running down known associates tomorrow."

Alicia's brain bubbled away, concentrating on the road. "Murphy, I need to sleep on this, to think it through properly. What if there's a good reason for all these connections? What if it's so loose and baggy for a reason?"

"I'm not following."

"Go home, Murphy. I'll talk to you first thing. Right now, I'm having a ridiculous idea. But it might just swing things for you."

CHAPTER THIRTY-THREE

WITH ALICIA DECLARING she was no longer working, the Dot-Bot arranged to go to the seaside for a couple of days with her friend, so the following morning Alicia had no childcare to fall back on. It worked out well, though. If HR found her on the premises whilst on maternity leave, she'd be marched out with no choice in the matter but showing up with Stacey at a police station to show off the new-born gave her a short window.

"You shouldn't be here," was Ndlove's first words as Alicia breezed in, Stacey in a car seat.

"I'm not working." Alicia placed Stacey on one of the inquiry room's tables, drawing attention from Ball, Cleaver, and Lemmy. "Would I bring a baby to *work*? No, of course not. So, I'm not working. Now turn away while I get my boob out."

She hooked Stacey up and did what was necessary whilst sat at the table, and texted Murphy to say she'd arrived. He showed up, and they went through the same conversation as Ndlove, which he reluctantly accepted.

"Social visit," he said. "Can't object to that. Keep your

head down, though. Rhapshaw is in the building, no doubt scouting for his puppet master."

"I'll be so subtle you'll barely notice me." Alicia adjusted the muslin cloth covering Stacey and her nipple, which she'd learned made some people uncomfortable. "So—Dean Bicklesthwaite."

"You cracked it for us?" Ball asked.

"Not quite. But I did do a lot of thinking last night. A lot of 'what if' questions that I was hoping might blow a hole in all that swirliness."

Ndlove frowned. "Swirliness?"

"Did it?" Cleaver said.

"Not even close." Alicia was thankful for Cleaver staying on track. "But it gave me a couple of ideas. And they're, like, far out, man, so bear with me."

"Can't wait," Murphy said.

"Dean, Ernest, and Demelza. All start non-criminal businesses around the same time as Bobby Carr goes down. After, when all is going well, and it's just Dean and Ernest, Jerzy makes contact with Ernest again, his old friend from their days working manual labour for minimum wage. I get that right?"

"Correct," Ndlove said, a hint of scepticism in her tone.

"Which got me asking, 'What if?' *What if* the legitimate businesses were never intended as the main income? *What if* they took off and they made more money that way, and so they ditched the bad stuff for profit reasons?"

"I'd say, so what?"

"Then the economy tanks. The pound slumps. Importing is suddenly more expensive. But you know how to make your side-business profitable again, going back to the old ways."

"Any evidence?" Cleaver asked.

"Just asking questions." Alicia checked Stacey. She'd be okay for a while. "Next: *what if* someone was going to testify against someone else? *What if* they wanted to stay legit, so were willing to sell a mate down the river?"

Thoughtful expressions all round.

"Unusually, everyone has a motive for staying clean, and if they go dirty everyone has a motive for killing to stay out of jail. Of these, who is most likely to revert to their old ways?"

Murphy reverted to his moustache-stroking habit. "Ernest would be most affected by a dip in the economy."

Alicia drew a tick in the air with her finger. "Correctamundo!"

"But Bobby has a violent streak," Cleaver said. "Reformed or not, we know they often crack."

Alicia traced another tick next to her first.

"But what is the thing that keeps sending us in circles?"

"Too many connections," Murphy said.

"Right. Old friends. Family ties. Burglars who have family and personal ties."

"It pivots around Tomaz," Cleaver said.

Alicia thought again. These were just brainstorming ideas. She only had questions. Ones that might push them the right way, ones they hadn't yet asked. This was often how she found answers, though, so she ploughed on with her biggest *what if* yet. "What if this is more to do with family than we realised? We've been looking and looking for Bobby Carr, but he's not shown up since … ever. He was seen around Ilkley with Linda weeks ago, but nothing since then. And we're relying on locating him to break this open."

"And?" Ndlove sounded impatient.

"And, what if he's dead already? What if, through Jerzy's checks for his agency—remember Tomaz was a client—Ernest figures it out? Then someone learns Bobby has been holding back money from the old days? What if Dean discovered one of his close friends owed him money? What if … *what if* they knew of a psychopath who was unable to hold a stable job, and who was clearly mental enough to burn a person alive for shits and giggles?"

"That's a hell of a leap," Murphy said.

"If Dean was pushing for the illegal business to start up again, and he had nothing to lose, he'd need someone like Bobby on side. But if Bobby said no, he wasn't interested in investing, maybe he'd find another way to apply pressure."

"When he asked Jerzy about candidates, they found Tomaz? A family connection."

"Why?" Ndlove asked.

Alicia was slowing down, her gears turning more stiffly. "What if ... and this is a biggie. *What if* Tomaz isn't just Linda's son? There has to be a sperm donor, doesn't there?"

"Dean?" Cleaver said.

Lemmy's first contribution was, "Wouldn't that have shown up when we took Tomaz's DNA? After his arrest?"

Murphy shook his head. "We only needed to match Dean to Karen. The test was for a familial match only."

"Just familial?" Ndlove said. "Not a full analysis?"

"We didn't run that deep. Wasn't necessary. And it's..." Murphy pulled a sour face, one that suggested he hated himself. "Expensive. Full DNA workup is expensive."

"Okay, it's big question time," Alicia said. "Was a new business underway? Was Dean Bicklesthwaite the new Mr. Big? Did he lose control of what he thought was a neat replacement for Bobby Carr?"

"That would make Tomaz—"

"A really awful psychopath," Alicia said. "It'd mean he killed that homeless guy, his own mother, Dean Bicklesthwaite and, probably, Bobby Carr too. What's the betting some of that former farmland turns up a big, bloated body with its throat cut?"

Ndlove tutted. "We've gone from too many connections to one theory pulled out of the air."

"Two theories," Cleaver said. "Bobby Carr taking revenge for his girlfriend's murder, or a killing spree by a crazy kid who hates the world."

She focused on Murphy. "Only one way to untangle all of this."

Murphy nodded, miserable. "I have to spend a lot of money."

CHAPTER THIRTY-FOUR

HAVING LEARNED GRAHAM WAS PRESENT, Alicia insisted on tracking him down and speaking privately. They used not Murphy's little room, but the chief superintendent's office on the fourth floor. It was wider and had nicer furniture. She'd winded Stacey, so she felt it was safe to plonk her in Graham's arms without asking him first.

He opened his mouth to object, but Alicia got in first. "Look, she likes you."

Stacey's chubby hand enveloped one of Graham's super-shiny buttons. Buttons it was questionable he should be wearing. Alicia wondered if maybe Graham regretted the civilian role, and yearned to return in a more hands-on capacity. It would explain his insistence on being here so often, in a uniform she wasn't sure was appropriate for him to wear anymore. A sentiment Stacey appeared intent on enforcing as she twisted another button.

Graham let her, repositioning her in the crook of his arm. "Alicia, while it's nice to see you, I have to question exactly what you're doing here."

"I just wanted to apologise. Sincerely. I was out of line,

and I must admit … I was under a lot of stress, and … I will not besmirch a good politician's name." What she didn't say was she wouldn't hesitate on besmirching a *bad* politician's name, and since Marissa Poole appeared to occupy the darker shade of grey on the good/bad scale, Alicia would keep her word. "Murphy authorised an expensive DNA make up between Karen, the body from her home, Tomaz Gortze, and Jerzy Krasowski, plus Bobby Carr's sample taken when they incarcerated him. We're hoping to get a voluntary sample from Ernest Borek."

"Yes, I read DCI Murphy's note just now. How many familial matches do you think there are?"

"Impossible to say right now. Could Dean be Tomaz's dad too? The original test only matched Dean to Karen. Does it even matter?" She shrugged. "You know how long these full examinations take. It's a thorough study, not a quick scan into a computer."

"Meaning you have to kill some time chatting so you'll be around when the results come in?"

"It'll be tomorrow," Alicia said. "At the earliest."

"So, this really is a social call?"

"Not exactly."

Stacey started on the coin-sized medals on Graham's chest which prompted him to shift her to the other side, where she appeared satisfied with more of his shiny buttons.

He said, "Then what?"

"Katie Hague."

"Oh. Yes." Graham moved to the window overlooking the car park. On a clear day, hills were visible in the distance just outside the city, but today was not clear. "I've been kept abreast of how that went."

"And?"

"And you shouldn't have gone there."

"I know."

"The only thing that kept them from pushing for disciplinary proceedings was that you're officially on maternity leave and such sanctions would have to wait until you returned. They found the prospect of waiting that long … inefficient. Plus, we know you haven't quite been yourself lately."

"It was her, wasn't it?" Alicia said. "They matched the DNA."

Alicia was getting bored of talking about DNA now. It was a great tool, but so slow. So annoying.

Graham turned from the window. "The DNA taken from Katie Hague's grandmother did *not* match the body in their morgue."

Alicia didn't know whether to be elated or scared. "They're certain?"

"They're doing a second test against Richard Hague himself, but there's little doubt. They'll be pushing to match her dental records and more DNA tests on missing persons in the area. As for Katie, well, she is now an official missing person herself. But, Alicia …"

"Yes?"

"Take your baby. Go home. Put your feet up. Do not interfere in this in any way. It is your very last chance."

Alicia nodded, actually meaning it. She could not get involved with Katie, not that deeply. She would hand over the letters to Wolverhampton and leave them to do their jobs. If Katie did what Alicia feared, they would conclude the same. If the poor body in the woods was actually a suicide, maybe there was hope.

She accepted Stacey back from Graham. "You know, they never officially ended my keeping-in-touch week."

"No," Graham said. "That would mean a lot of paperwork,

and a trail that may reflect badly on any promotion you apply for."

She noted a pull at one corner of his mouth. "Murphy said something?"

"Anything discussed between me and a senior detective in this station would have to be confidential. You'd probably understand that better … if you were a detective inspector."

Alicia manoeuvred Stacey out of reach of Graham's uniform. "Thank you, sir."

"But one more slip up, one more misuse of police resources, I won't be able to keep it off your record. Understood?"

CHAPTER THIRTY-FIVE

ALICIA HEADED TO THE GYM. It was close by her dad's and she trusted him to watch Stacey for ninety minutes, which he was delighted to do. She changed her first and fed her so all that remained was for the occasional wet burp that may or may not occur, but otherwise they could lie on a mat together and bat dangling objects around.

And yes, of course it was the gym where Karen worked.

Alicia warmed up on the cross trainer, then hit the tread-mill, repeating the workout Karen showed her of walk-jog-sprint three times. Halfway through, the exercise endorphins kicked in and, although she detected a wobble in her arse and thighs that wasn't there pre-Stacey, she felt *good*. So good. Then she moved to a machine that involved pulling down a bar from over her head and performed two sets of ten reps. It was while she was resting before her third that Karen approached.

She wore a loose-fitting tracksuit, hair in a ponytail. "Looking for me?"

"Just working out." Alicia pointed at the machine.

"Really?"

"Really," Alicia said. "I'm a police officer. If I wanted to speak to you, I'd come speak to you. I had no idea you were working today. I just liked this place."

"Okay." She said it with an inflection that indicated she wasn't sold on Alicia's lie, but settled next to her on a machine that worked the inner thighs. "I'm not working today. Just … toning."

"Cool." Alicia reached up and commenced her final set.

"Single again," Karen commented, unprompted.

Alicia counted to six. "You don't think you'll work it out with Jerzy?"

Seven … eight…

Karen worked her legs slowly with a high weight. "He was already on his final warning."

Nine … ten … and rest. "He did it before?"

"Prostitute four years ago. A mutual friend, two years before that. I'd just had Lincoln when he went on a trip and I partly blamed myself for the hooker. I was really down, and … you don't want to hear about this. I'm sure you've got a smashing fella back home."

"Not really." Alicia moved to the machine adjacent to Karen's to work the outer thighs. "No fella."

"Ran out on you?"

"Died."

"Oh, I'm sorry. Must be tough."

"I'm taking it slow." Alicia commenced her first set, unsure why she lied again. Unsure why the lie felt like a revelation. "Or maybe I'm not. Maybe that's why it's been so hard."

Karen started on her next set too. "It's not the answer."

"What isn't?"

"Work. Exercise. I mean, it helps. It keeps the blues away, but they're just around the corner, waiting. There's no single answer to getting rid of them completely."

"Is it that obvious?" Since last night, when she shouted at Stacey, Alicia accepted she had, indeed, become one of "those" women. Someone with health issues relating to her screwed up hormones, to the massive change in her life, to not having a father to her little girl; a situation in flux. If Richard *was* dead, it'd be easier. If the dad really *was* the Aussie spunk she told everyone she shagged on New Year's Eve but never learned his name, she could eventually track him down. "Yeah, it's not easy."

"Everyone's different. Keep going with this, though. It helps."

They ended their sets, resting for the next.

"We've been looking at some other people from your dad's past," Alicia said.

"Jackie told me. That fat guy … sorry, that … bigger cop…"

"Nominative determinism."

"Sorry?"

"Ball. He's called Sergeant Ball. Like someone called Baker selling cakes for a living. Ball became a Ball. Geddit?"

Karen smiled and started her final set. "Anyway, yeah, he asked me all sorts of questions. Bobby-something, who I didn't know. Ernest, who's a sweetheart but, y'know, a bit dodgy."

Alicia pressed the pads apart, tension in her legs. "Dodgy how?"

Karen wafted it away. "Just little things. A cheap winter coat if you need one, decent shoes for your kids, school uniforms for half the price the school sells them. That sort of thing."

Alicia nodded, hoping for a ray of light to break through. Nothing. "Are you sure your dad never mentioned Bobby Carr? Robert? Anything like that?"

Karen halted mid-rep, turned her head to Alicia. "Why?

Why all the same questions? About Jerzy, about this Bobby Carr guy? If I start asking around my old neighbourhood, am I going to find something out? Because even my liaison officer won't tell me shit."

Alicia shook her head. "No, and … I'm just making conversation. I'm not here officially, remember?"

Her words prompted Karen's workout to restart, but Karen's reaction meant a glint of light through the clouds. She was holding something back. And so was Alicia.

Something she'd held back from her what-if session. And now, with Karen's hackles up, Alicia wasn't sure she could do what she needed to.

Sergeant Ball and Lemmy stayed on the husband, who was meeting with Ernest Borek in the Oarsman pub, doing some sort of business. With Jerzy Krasowski. It was a large enough space for Ball to remain relatively inconspicuous, although he was forced to break his self-imposed beer fast to blend in. He mussed his hair and undid his tie, and told Lemmy to do the same, having joined Ball on what was supposed to be his day off. It was Ball's day off too, a forty-eight-hour transition from nights to days, but since Murphy had already acquired him, it wasn't needed. Because Ernest knew Ball's face, he kept his back to the little powwow, relying on Lemmy, who fit in here better than either Ball or Cleaver ever would.

"So *why* can't we listen in?" Lemmy asked. Again.

"Not authorised." Ball sipped his pint of bitter. God, he'd missed this. Beer before noon. *Mmm*. He was not just flabby; he was *unfit*. Now, having cut out beer and cut *back* on the takeaways, he was slightly less-so. And needed to be if he was to get that damn uniform off permanently. Right now, though, the pre-noon beer was a prop, one he wouldn't finish if it meant progress. He needed to do a damn good job on both mentoring the lad and demonstrating his investigative prowess wasn't dulled by his tenure. "We got metadata and location tracking on phones and bank cards. But listening in means specialists. Murphy thinks we're on the verge of cracking this without. What's happening?"

Lemmy moved his eyes instead of his whole body, as he'd needed to be reminded several times already. "Since Jerzy gave 'em the envelope a minute or so ago? Nothing else since then."

An envelope. Thick enough to contain money. Passed from Jerzy on one side of the corner table to Ernest on the other, one bodyguard beside him, the other standing sentry.

The lads Alicia described the other day were also present, three tables away, plainly watching the scene. What wasn't clear was if they were involved or simply observing something going down on what they considered their territory. The large men accompanying Ernest might make them think twice about trying anything, but if these youngsters worked for someone with more clout, there might be a scene any moment. Ball even used his phone's earphone and mic to call back to base. Currently, there was a small unit standing by around the corner, ready to spring into action should the need arise.

"They're talking," Lemmy said.

"Sitting upright, chatting? Smiling?"

"Nah, no smiles. Upright, but, like, hunched."

"Like us?"

"Hand gestures."

Ball's frustration spread through his arms and legs. He'd been following Jerzy, not Ernest, so didn't want Ernest spotting him just yet. No one figured Jerzy would be watching for Ball out of uniform, so it was safe for him to take the lead. No one expected them in a near-empty pub at eleven-thirty in the morning, either, so not being able to observe for fear of recognition meant relying on an inexperienced probie to relay any visual feed.

Screw it.

Ball knocked his phone to the floor. Waited a beat. Bent over to pick it up, twisting enough to see the meeting for himself. He smiled. Sat up.

"The hand gestures don't mean they're mad with each other," he said. "They're positioned so the fingers and hands swipe in front of their mouths every half-second or so."

"Why?"

"Guess."

Lemmy took another look. "So they can talk more quietly?"

"Lip-reading. They're worried lip-reading punters might eavesdrop, or we might be filming them from here, or outside."

"Meaning they've made us?"

"Maybe. Or they might just be paranoid. Safety first."

"Man, that's nuts."

"People started doing it a few years ago. An article circulated about the FBI in the US using deaf people to interpret videos taken without sound. There was a TV show too, I think. And don't get me wrong, it's *feasible*, if the camera's close enough. But even zoom lenses don't usually have enough definition to allow full translation. Maybe now, with 4K resolution. Or soon, anyway."

Lemmy watched a bit longer. "But I get what it means."

"What does it mean?"

"If they're that paranoid, they have something to hide."

Ball gulped his pint down to the halfway mark. "Well done, my young apprentice. We'll make a Jedi out of you yet."

Ndlove and Cleaver had to trace Tomaz's activities, working back from his arrest, and create a chronological timeline based on the intelligence wrought by his electronic signature. Darla provided the means, acted her usual impatient self—a persona Cleaver had come to know was purely an act she liked to project; the IT genius with no time for tech-Muggles. She made things look easy, and the shorter fuse she demonstrated, the more people assumed her tasks were indeed simple to her. Cleaver wasn't sure she knew she was putting on an act, though, and didn't dare broach the subject in case she started second-guessing herself at work. And no one was better at mining credit card data, phone logs, or CCTV than Darla.

Despite her curt, "Here you go, knock yourself out," before standing abruptly so Cleaver could take the helm, he knew she meant it affectionately.

The "helm" in question was a readout of cell phone towers that allowed them to view the approximate location of Tomaz's mobile phone, the latest iPhone which an unemployed scumbag shouldn't be able to afford. Normally, a youth embarking on a criminal path would use a jail-broken stolen model, but Tomaz's was bought for cash in Leeds and ran it via a SIM-only contract.

"Nice of him to help us out like that," Ndlove said.

He did not, however, own a single credit card, relying on cash and his debit card to get by. Not a problem. He received a cash injection each month from Bobby Carr's account, totalling £750, which he had usually spent by around three days before the next deposit.

An allowance.

Not a huge amount, and plenty to live off when his bedsit was paid for by the state along with a small amount of unemployment benefit. Because of Tomaz's slack attitude to attending job interviews and training courses, though, his employment benefit was frequently cut off and sanctions imposed, which should mean a more frugal month, but Cleaver suspected those would be the times he indulged in a little burglary or other similarly criminal enterprise to get by. His phone did ping in the exact spots for three break-ins over the past two months.

And now, having found little obviously suspicious in his finances, they ascertained Tomaz moved around the city a lot. His phone interacted with both Jerzy's and Ernest's, but hardly at all with either of the contract phones traced back to Linda Gortze or Bobby Carr. Except once.

"He goes home once in three months," Ndlove said.

Murphy traced the route, approximate though it was. "Bus route from Leeds."

Ndlove checked the bus company's website and agreed. "He takes the bus out to his mum's house six weeks ago."

"When was the estimated time of death for Linda Gortze?"

"Without bugs or blowfly eggs, it's hard to be sure. But the body was frozen between four and eight weeks ago."

Cleaver checked the other phone trails. They never expected anyone to have headed to Blackpool, or to be in the vicinity of Dean's murder, or Bobby Carr's house, and that's exactly how it panned out.

"Think he was there?" Ndlove asked.

"I think a person dumb enough to take his phone on a burglary and carry it with him to a place his mother was lying dead … or would soon be dead if he planned to do it himself … would also be dumb enough to take it on a murder. If Dean's murder was just Tomaz breaking in and going nuts, replicating what he did to his mum … where's Bobby Carr in all this?"

"If Tomaz is this crazed maniac…" Ndlove clamped her mouth shut. "I mean, if he's doing all this … the rough sleeper, Dean, his own mother…" She couldn't finish the sentence.

Cleaver understood. "There'll be others. Hidden. Ones we haven't detected. Or unsolved killings. Maybe not cut the same way, but … yeah. I think if Tomaz did this, we're looking at a bigger case. Lucky he's already in custody."

They both returned to the screen, processing in their own way.

"What do we know from this?" Ndlove asked.

"One thing that doesn't add up. The money. The allowance from Bobby. It means Tomaz has some sort of a relationship with Bobby Carr. A decent one—"

Darla, who should have been lining up CCTV footage to link with the phone trails, not listening in, gave a huff that made both Murphy and Ndlove turn. She said, "The opposite."

"Opposite?" Ndlove said.

"If he only went home once in several months and had no interaction with his mum or step-dad, maybe the money was this guy's way of keeping the psycho little shit away."

Cleaver considered Darla's cynical take. "Makes sense."

"When he goes home…" Ndlove didn't need to finish the sentence.

———

DCI Murphy remained stuck behind his desk, coordinating. During the months of his secondment, and then the permanent role, he'd been a more hands-on DCI than some. Certainly, more than the chap he replaced. Some DCIs were happy behind a desk, generals pushing pieces about on a board. Others got out and about, elbows deep in as many investigations as they could. As he'd been advised by various colleagues, Murphy tried to strike a balance, and succeeded for the most part.

Muggings on an estate were being blamed on a group of African migrants who came to the UK as orphaned minors but who were now all grown up and had no jobs, no prospects, and "no respect for the country that took them in." A verbatim statement from an elderly woman interviewed during a door-to-door. The direction that investigation had taken suggested it was a single, young, Congolese kid who'd got involved with a small group of British born lads and was trying to impress them by harassing locals. They all stepped up their game, one-upping each other, eventually pooling their resources into a sort-of business. Five arrests were imminent—four Brits and just the one African.

A spate of stabbings—one lethal, others just life-threatening—had plagued the estate half a mile from the muggings. At first, police feared a gang war, but it turned out to be a macho initiation into the local gang. Get stabbed, earn a scar, a colostomy bag for bonus points, and hit the streets again. "The more scars, the more badass, the more pussy you get, innit," said one witness, defending the craze, and showing off his own wound. It had to look like it might kill you, too, or it didn't count; no arms or legs. The one who died was still considered "a legend" by his gangmates.

Other issues were piling up, too. Emails from detectives inviting his input, requesting approvals for certain operations, but the murder of Dean Bicklesthwaite was so tangled, so wrapped up, Murphy felt like he wasn't in control. He was leaning too closely into it. Passing his elbows and touching his shoulders, his chin getting nearer every hour.

He read the reports from Cleaver. Listened to voicemail from Ball. Added it to his log. Replied to authorise continued surveillance. He wrote an email asking again for a rush on the

DNA, but deleted it, knowing they were already eating up the overtime budget.

Perhaps his time management skills needed a refresh. Maybe he'd apply for a course once it was over.

Of most concern was what he hadn't heard. He hadn't heard from Alicia.

It wasn't really a risk. Despite Graham's warning that Alicia should adhere strictly to protocol, she had every reason to be waiting in the gym's reception. Having taken the morning off to sort childcare, her chat with Karen was unofficial, but again that wasn't a tough place to scramble out of. No way she could have been sure Karen would be there. She simply showed up, and so did Karen, and their unplanned conversation elicited an idea that she hadn't yet dared voice.

The idea she had last night but didn't dare raise earlier with either the detectives or with Karen herself.

When Karen emerged, freshly showered, Alicia stood and ran off her excuses, reiterating this wasn't part of some elaborate deception, and when Karen appeared to be at ease, she hit her with what she needed.

"Another DNA swab."

"Why?" Karen asked, her wall going up again.

Jackie Osbourne waited outside for Karen. The family liaison officer motioned with her thumb, and Karen waved back to say everything was okay.

"To be thorough," Alicia said. "We have your sample but used all the material. We just need to check on a couple of other things. To eliminate all DNA from the crime scene where Demelza Shine was killed. We know yours won't be there, but—"

"Okay, okay, let's do it. Should I come to the station?"

Alicia beckoned Jackie Osbourne in. The FLO cautiously obeyed. Then Alicia dipped in her gym backpack and withdrew a DNA kit and evidence bag.

Jackie eyed it all the way. "You really just happened to have a swab kit on you?"

"Of course," Alicia said. "Don't you?" Without further questions, she went on. "Mrs. Krasowski has agreed to let me take a new DNA sample. I need you to witness it."

Jackie glanced at Karen, again with concern, but again Karen waved it off.

Alicia asked Karen to open her mouth. She took out the swab, and scraped the inside of Karen's mouth, sealing it in the test tube, and the test tube went into an evidence bag. All witnessed by Jackie, the FLO said, signing her name on the form Alicia produced for her.

Alicia thanked Karen for her time, and as she exited, she glanced inside the gym. Pete Mahdavi was watching.

CHAPTER THIRTY-SIX

WITH NOT MUCH ELSE TO DO AFTER dropping off the evidence bag, Alicia stopped by her dad's place to attend to Stacey, waited for the baby's next poo, and watched on, stunned, as her father volunteered to change the nappy. He retched only once and completed the task with real pride. It wasn't a bad job at all.

"See?" he said. "Not just your mother who knows how to take care of her."

While she should have been annoyed that he'd only done it because he felt the need to compete with his ex-wife, Alicia used the opportunity to school him in heating up Stacey's bottle using water—never the microwave—and how he shouldn't refreeze the bagged breastmilk provided, and nor should he attempt to thaw it separately. "Keep it in the fridge and it'll melt in the bottle as you heat it."

"Okay, okay, don't worry." Her dad was a shorter than average man, although not as short as Alicia, with wiry arms from a life of manual work. He also deemed himself more competent at all tasks than he was in reality, from woodwork to car maintenance. Should she trust him with Stacey?

"Call me if there's anything," Alicia said. "Anything at all. Okay?"

"I promise."

Alicia didn't like guns, but she liked being around guns even less when she wasn't allowed to carry one, a realisation brought home by the op over in Ilkley. She found someone she knew in the firearms section and talked him into squeezing her in for a test which would renew her licence. All he needed to do was phone through to Janine Paulson in the SCA—her direct line manager despite answering to Murphy during her secondment here—and got the approval quickly. Paulson asked to speak to Alicia, and rather than chewing her out about her recent misdemeanours in the procedure department, she just asked about Stacey, and some personal questions that were not usually forthcoming.

The reports couldn't have crossed her desk yet.

Alicia passed her refresher with flying colours, afterward placed a call to DI Ricky Spencer in Wolverhampton where she apologised for her deception the previous day. He eventually forgave her and confirmed Katherine Hague was a missing person and would liaise with West Yorkshire and everyone in between to try and find her. They still hadn't ID'd the body but were confident they would soon, and given Alicia's disclosure of the poison pen letters, would take a closer look at the "suicide."

"It *is* the sword Katie bought on eBay," Spencer said.

"She has a habit of disappearing," Alicia said. "She's been doing it on and off for a while."

"And coming back unharmed, we know. But this length of time is unusual even for her. We'll find her. One way or another."

A call waiting beeped. She thanked Spencer and took the next call.

It was Murphy. "Our DNA matches came back early. They're arresting Jerzy and Karen Krasowski. But it looks like Karen is going down for the killing."

CHAPTER THIRTY-SEVEN

Incident Room, Sheerton Station, 5:30 p.m.

MURPHY STOOD before the assembled detectives, plus Ball and Lemmy, and Alicia awaited the verdict.

The DCI said, "This is complicated, so pay attention."

Notepads came out all round, including Alicia.

Interview Room 1, Sheerton Station, Earlier

Alicia sat alongside Murphy, opposite Karen Krasowski. Karen stared hard at Alicia. She waived her right to counsel.

Alicia opened. "Mrs. Krasowski, we matched the DNA sample you gave on the night of your father's murder to confirm his identity."

"Of course you did," she replied. "He's my dad."

Murphy opened a folder and turned to show her results no one expected her to understand. He said, "But we also matched Tomaz Gortze's to your dad."

Karen's mouth gaped, staring at the technical readout as if she could deny the facts.

"Here's the problem, though," Alicia said. "When we look more intensely at the comparison between you and Dean, it does confirm a family tie. But it isn't father-daughter."

She seemed even more shocked, but Alicia had seen liars do amazing things before.

Incident Room, Sheerton Station, 5:30 p.m.

Murphy said, "According to our samples, Karen is Tomaz's half-sister. But Tomaz isn't cooperating."

Family Room 3, West Yorkshire Remand Centre, Earlier

Cleaver and Ndlove took the chance to asses someone they already pegged as a murderer of more than a homeless man. And when the staff brought him through, the smirk of a man who'd gotten away with something was ever present.

Once the duty brief arrived, one Sarah McKee, Cleaver asked him whether he knew he was burgling his own father's home.

"Don't be daft," Tomaz said. "Wouldn't rob that place."

"I meant the place you were arrested," Cleaver said.

"My dad don't own that house. It's the dead guy."

"Right."

They waited a moment for the penny to drop.

"No, no, wait," Tomaz said. "That bloke who got killed?"

Ndlove flashed a DNA report on an iPad. "Did you think Bobby Carr was your father?"

"Nah, I mean, I call him my dad, but ... he's not. He's a

dick. Me mum never told me who the guy was. She was a hooker, y'know? No way of telling."

"Doesn't it bother you?" Cleaver asked. "That the man whose house you burgled turned out to be your biological father?"

Tomaz thought about it, jaw jutting, eyes tightly focused on the table.

Cleaver asked the question again.

"*I heard you.*" Tomaz slapped the desk. "And no comment."

Incident Room, Sheerton Station, 5:30 p.m.

"Tomaz Gortze refuses to be drawn on it," Murphy went on. "He insists he didn't know. That it was a coincidence. He will not give up the name of the person who put him up to it, and maintains he just knew where to go. That it was his own idea."

Interview Room 2, Sheerton Station, Earlier

Ball hit Jerzy with the same information being bandied around: according to the DNA tested so far, Karen was not Dean's daughter, but she was *related* to him. Tomaz, however, was definitely Dean's son.

"But we did find Karen's biological father," Ball said.

Jerzy played with his fingers. Nervous as hell. "Who?"

"Karen is Bobby Carr's daughter. Dean and Bobby are cousins."

"No…"

"You were set up because you'd been banging that ex-army chick for so long behind Karen's back."

"It wasn't that long. Just a few weeks—"

"Tomaz is Dean's flesh and blood, not Karen. Did she find out? Did she hold Dean responsible for what happened up in Ilkley?"

Jerzy squinted, shook his head. Confused now. "What *happened* up in Ilkley?"

Incident Room, Sheerton Station, 5:30 p.m.

"No one had told Jerzy about the murder of Linda Gortze, and he seemed genuinely shocked. He is completely at sea."

"Unless he's an incredible actor," Alicia said.

"Same could be said about them all," Ndlove said.

Murphy leaned in. "What are we seeing here?"

Interview Room 1, Sheerton Station, Earlier

Karen remained stone throughout the rest of the questioning.

"Did you find out before Linda was killed, or after?" Murphy asked.

"I didn't know," Karen said.

"Did Bobby kill Dean?" Alicia asked. "Or was it Tomaz?"

"I don't…" Karen choked on a sob and real tears flowed. "You can't possibly think…"

"We were so blinded by the friendships, the connections to the business, we never thought to check on the most potent motives for murder. Jealousy. Money. When we did finally ask about the cash, the businesses that led to the group going legit, it made a bit more sense. Now, when family comes into money, or there's money at stake, it causes a lot more than just a row over the Christmas turkey."

Karen bowed her head. "I didn't do anything. If you're accusing me of this … I want a lawyer. Now."

Incident Room, Sheerton Station, 5:30 p.m.

"So, without anything more from Karen," Murphy said, "with Tomaz clammed up tight, no probable cause to arrest Ernest—who declined our request for an interview—and Jerzy insisting this is all news to him … we're stuck again."

"I bet Alicia can clear it up," Ndlove said.

"With all our current information," Alicia said, "my only working theory is this: Dean is a Mr. Big type. Tomaz is Dean's illegitimate son and Karen is *not* Dean's daughter. She found out she is actually Bobby Carr's daughter, and somehow blamed Dean for his being jailed, and withholding it from her. She figured her fake dad's insurance money was decent compensation. Somehow, she concocted the plan with Bobby to get rid of Tomaz and his mum Linda, who was now pressing Dean for maintenance money. Karen couldn't have *any* of her entitlement going to Tomaz, so got Bobby Carr to infiltrate himself into Linda's life, eventually killing her.

"Once it was in place, she concocted a night out with hubby, a psychic she knew Jerzy wouldn't be able to resist. One *she* knew from her old neighbourhood through her fake dad, an old boss of the group who needed money to keep her big show going. It was also Karen's alibi.

"And remember our original theory? That the idea was to get them home before the kids saw the body? That holds double if it's Karen. She needed an excuse, and slipped Demelza some cash, with more to come if she disappeared and kept her mouth shut.

"Finally, the evidence pointed at Jerzy because she *knew*

about the affair. And she's the one who tipped off the layabout Tomaz about the house and valuables, hoping to implicate him with his business connection to Jerzy. The passport and the botched murder trial make Tomaz look insane."

"To simplify," Ndlove said. "Karen planned it. Bobby executed it. Jerzy and Tomaz take the fall. Karen gets the money."

"Two birds," Cleaver said. "One stone. Everyone is implicated but her."

"Bobby Carr goes underground until she gets the cash?" Ndlove suggested.

"She's free and clear," Ball said. "Clever bitch. No cheating hubby, a ton of cash to live off, and a new dad."

"It's the only thing that makes sense," Cleaver said.

Murphy stood to indicate the meeting was over. "Now we just have to prove it."

DCI Murphy's Office, Sheerton Station, Later

With only Alicia, Murphy, and Graham Rhapshaw present, the blinds were down, and Alicia insisted on only using a desk lamp, making the room dark.

"Why?" Murphy asked.

"Ambience," Alicia said with a grin.

"We need ambience?" Graham said.

"For what I'm about to tell you, yes. I need to clear up a couple of things first, but if the extra sample I took from Karen today tells us what I'm worried about—"

"You took an additional sample?" Murphy said. "Why?"

"If I'm wrong, then based on the evidence we have at the moment, our conclusions are sound. But, with not one of them cracking, with all of them shocked at what we're putting to them, I think it's worth it to check one last swirly dangler. But I might need someone to spin it if things don't work out."

"That's where I come in?" Graham said.

"No one but me needs to take the flack."

"And me," Murphy said.

Alicia didn't argue. It'd be useless.

"I'll do what I can," Graham said. "What do you expect this test to show?"

"Nothing, or everything. The nothing option means we stick with what we have and everyone is peachy. The everything option … means all we concluded today is bullshit, and we'll need to be sure no one else on the case gets dumped on."

DCI Murphy's Office, Sheerton Station, Later Still

When Murphy and Alicia were alone, Murphy asked, "Are you sure this will work?"

"No," Alicia said. "I'm actually less sure than Graham is. But we have to try."

Then her phone bonged with a text from her dad:

She won't stop crying. What do I do?

"See you tomorrow, Murphy. Bring your big-boy pants. This might get rough."

CHAPTER THIRTY-EIGHT

BRENDA WILLIAMS LIKED HER WEEKENDS. She still worked but with less intensity. Emails she couldn't be arsed replying to in the week, rereading proposals to go out on Monday, reviewing cash flow. She did all this sat in her pyjamas near a window, sipping coffee in the low morning sun, iPad in hand.

Frankly, she was happy to be free of Jerzy, who'd texted her a couple of days ago to say it was all over. His guilty fumblings, his speeches explaining why he'd just screwed her, his excuses as to why he had to leave her without cuddles … it all got a bit too much. Boring. She liked it the first time they slept together; he was drunk and so confident, but latterly he'd been reticent, like his mind was elsewhere. And she knew why he screwed her already and had never been particularly fond of cuddles. Sure, on the rare occasions a man injected excitement into her heart as well as her loins, a bit of holding was nice. Jerzy wasn't a man like that.

He knew his way around a vagina and didn't treat her breasts like a stress toy, so she put up with his annoying habits. He was better than a vibrator, but only just.

No matter. She'd find someone else soon enough.

Of course, throughout all his bumbling excuses, how he insisted on explaining his actions, he never once asked why *she* was screwing *him*.

The doorbell rang.

This better not be lover boy, she thought, rising from her comfy chair, and padding to the front door.

She checked over her shoulder and twitched the curtain to peer through her window, close as it was to the pavement. Another irritation she'd be happy to leave behind now the Jerzy affair was done with.

A little blonde thing waved back at her. Pigtails. Nice trouser suit with shoulder pads. Flat shoes. Same one that caught her and Jerzy together although it took a moment to recognise her. Today she was dressed like a detective, but could've been a twenty-year-old cheerleader.

As Brenda took in the sight, the blonde thing mimed opening the door, her grin so wide and gaping it *must* have been a wind up. Except it wasn't. As her police ID pressed up against the window proved. That she then pressed her face up against it too negated the seriousness slightly, but Brenda stood, smoothed her pyjama top flat, and mooched to the door.

Opened it.

"Hi, I'm Detective Sergeant Alicia Friend. Remember me?" She still had the ID out and the big ol' grin.

"Of course." Brenda stood aside. "Come in."

DS Friend entered and looked around, her head moving quickly. "Ooh, cosy." A peek in the living room. "Nice." She pointed down the narrow hallway to the kitchen. "Can I have a quick look?"

"Why?"

"I'm in the market for a house now, and I think this is

probably about the size I could afford." As she wandered toward the kitchen, she called back, "Oh, and I needed a quick word. Official police business, not house hunting."

She entered the kitchen and took it all in, before heading for the window over the sink.

Brenda caught up. "Would you like a tour?"

"Nice garden. Just big enough to enjoy, small enough for a single gal to manage."

"I like it."

"Bigger than you'd expect from the front."

"Could we get on with your 'word'?"

DS Friend pulled a thoughtful expression. Looked at the door on one side of the kitchen and one on the other. "Why two doors?"

Brenda figured it'd be quicker to indulge her than protest, so she stepped over to the first door and opened it to the toilet, sink, and bathtub. "Bathroom." She pointed to the other. "Garden."

"A bathroom downstairs?"

"Yes. It's an old house."

"You have another upstairs?"

"No. Two bedrooms and a box room."

"One toilet? Next to the kitchen? Eww."

"Like I said, it's an old house. Can we get to the … 'official police business' please? I have a few things to do."

DS Friend perched herself on the same stool as the last time she was here.

"It's just a courtesy," DS Friend said. "Under new Home Office guidelines, we're obliged to fill you in. Karen Krasowski learned about her husband's affair with you, and set about orchestrating a way to rid herself of several problems: cheating husband…"

He hadn't planned for a copper to die. Not before, and not today. But if this little pixie-type detective forced his hand, he'd have no choice. At first, he wasn't nervous, assuming there were some loose ends to tie up regarding Jerzy and Brenda, but as he listened through the floor, she reeled off some nonsense about Home Office guidelines requiring her to disclose the whole case to a peripheral witness. There was no such thing, making it clear she was here under false pretences.

He wished he had a gun but buying one locally might attract the attention of a snitch who didn't know him, one who'd earn a pretty penny dropping a tip to the cops. No, without connections in the area, it was nigh-on impossible for him to go exploring. That's why all he could use was the knife in his hand. A razor sharp blade, serrated on one side, nine inches long.

It didn't matter how he did it though. It just needed to get done.

DS Friend finished her convoluted story and waited as if due a round of applause.

"Okay … thanks?" Brenda tried, impatient now.

"You're welcome." The little detective hopped off her stool. "Now, how about that tour?"

"Tour?"

"Of the house. I'd love to see upstairs."

Now Brenda found the need to assert herself. "That's not really appropriate. It's a mess, and I want you to leave. I have work to—"

"Yes, work to do, but I really need to see upstairs."

"Why?"

A creak sounded in the hall.

"That's why," DS Friend said.

Brenda sidestepped, away from the hallway door.

"What are you—"

"He's here to tie up his final loose ends." Then DS Friend adjusted her jacket, loosening a button and moving her position so she angled toward the door. She called, "Hello, Deano! Come on in."

The door eased open, and there, pressed against the wall, was Dean Bicklesthwaite, wielding a ridiculously outsized hunting knife.

CHAPTER THIRTY-NINE

"DEANO, MY MAN!" Alicia said. "Good of you to finally make an appearance." She opened her jacket, slipped a Glock 17 from the holster, and placed it on the tall table. "Have you been here all along or did you just break in this morning?"

Dean stepped into the room, swallowing at the sight of Alicia's gun. He wore a polo shirt and jeans, his hair unkempt and his face unshaven. He smelled musty even from across the room.

"You've been staying here," Alicia said, glancing at Brenda. "Bed hair does nothing for you."

Although Caucasian, he gave off a dark hue, like he was cloaked in shadow. Handsome, but being unable to go outdoors for several days had taken something of a toll. He was broad, tall, and although he sported a bit of a gut, he moved as a solid mass, like a rugby player.

"Sorry," he said. "I have to."

"Have to what?" Alicia said. "Kill us?" She patted the Glock on the table.

"*Are you crazy?*" Brenda screeched. "Do something!"

"Oh, okay." Alicia placed her hand on the gun. "You

know, that was the plan. I was supposed to come in, get proof Dean was here, and then call in the cavalry." She held up her sleeve to show the clip she needed to press to activate her radio. "We wondered if it was a hostage situation—"

"It is!" Brenda said. "He threatened to kill me."

"Lying bitch." Dean stepped forward.

Brenda appealed to Alicia again. "What are you waiting for?"

Alicia smiled. Nice as pie. "I'm expecting one last attempt to kill you, Brenda."

Dean smiled too. And whipped his knife toward Brenda Williams.

Instead of dodging away or cowering while the blade sliced through her flesh, Brenda stepped into the arc of his swing, hooked her arm around the crook of his elbow, and slammed her fist into Dean's throat. Knee to the groin. Upper cut elbow to his jaw.

Blood popped from his mouth.

"Do something!" Brenda demanded.

"Nah," Alicia said. "I think you're fine."

Dean went at her again, this time lunging with a stabbing motion. She parried him expertly and chopped an open hand to his neck, hammer blow to the side of his head, and planted a solid heel through his jaw.

He dropped. Groggy, but he still held the knife. He blinked, rolled, and then he was up again.

Brenda said, "Fine, to hell with this."

She swiped a long knife out of the block on the counter-top, and this time she attacked. A dummy kick, which retracted, then slashed at Dean, cutting his chest open. A proper kick to his knee sent him wobbling, and a second pinpoint strike sliced through his wrist.

Dean dropped the knife.

Brenda geared up for a final strike, jabbing at his cut chest, pushing him against the wall, and pulling the knife back. No doubt in Alicia's mind what would happen next.

"*Freeze!*" Alicia shouted. "*Armed police!*"

She pointed the gun at Brenda, who did as instructed, and froze. Dean slumped to the floor, cradling his wounded wrist.

Brenda held onto the knife as she faced Alicia, a devilish grin to her now. "Self-defence. No matter how you paint it."

"I know." Alicia was only six feet from Brenda. "I just needed to see if you could handle a big man like Dean. Or Bobby."

"Clever." Brenda hefted the knife. "But stupid too. This was a dereliction of duty. You failed in your duty of care to me. Allowed this man to attack me—"

"You offer solutions," Alicia said. "Corporate, communications, or *other*. When Ernest and Dean went back to their old contacts to restart their enterprise, they looked at their sales and, because they're better businessmen now, discovered Bobby and Demelza stashed more than their share of their old profits. They wanted them back. And your specialist service sounded right. What they didn't realise, though, was just how far you would go. They didn't know you were a cold, hard, war profiteer."

Brenda's downturned eyes found the knife in her hand.

Alicia firmed the pressure on the first part of the Glock's trigger mechanism. "You went to extract the info. Must have been serious cash."

"One-point-five million." Dean sputtered blood.

"*She* killed Linda. You didn't expect her to go that far, did you, Dean?"

Dean sat upright. "Ernest. He brought her in. Six weeks ago. It was wrong. We knew it was wrong. I tried to stop her—"

"Shut up, you idiot." Brenda forced the words between gritted teeth.

"And you trying to stop her let Bobby get away? You still helped kill his girlfriend, and what, threatened his stepson? But he vanished, didn't he? And you knew he was coming for you."

No response from Dean.

"You trusted Brenda here to clean things up. Linda, Bobby, the family. Then there was Tomaz. Troubled little man who Jerzy tried to help. And Jerzy too. That link, that connection, was everything you needed."

Brenda shook her head. "You can't prove any of that."

"I won't need to. Will I, Dean? It went so much further than intended. Setting up Jerzy to take the fall wasn't hard. You never forgave him for the prostitute, or that your daughter kept taking him back, so after Linda dies, and Bobby goes AWOL, Brenda engineers an affair, one even Jerzy doesn't realise is a part of the setup. You can't escape the torture of Linda, though, can you? And luring Bobby Carr to your house seemed like a great idea, where Brenda killed him for you."

"I was in Middlesbrough. In a traffic jam."

"You have plenty of employees. We checked. You left on time, and yes, the traffic helped, but I reckon if we look hard enough we'll find someone who says they had to take your phone to your house that night. Just so you have that electronic alibi."

"You won't prove a damn thing," Brenda said.

"We will. I promise." Alicia then spoke into her sleeve. "It's a go. I say again, it's a go."

CHAPTER FORTY

THERE ARE some moments that go on for an eternity. Some are fleeting. Then there are those that rush by in a blur, and yet at the same time seem to stretch, elongated beyond normal human consciousness. That morning was one of those for Alicia.

The big risk had been in going in alone, but she had the mic and she could hit the panic button any time. Murphy insisted on her being armed, which she was relieved about. She was going to ask for a gun, despite not liking them particularly.

Even though no firearms were in play, Brenda Williams was highly trained, having spent a decade in the British Army, with several years in the Royal Signals. Comms specialists. But she also tried out for the SAS, one of the first women ever to do so, failing only on the psyche exam. They believed she was too prone to violent solutions.

What rushed by was her entering the house. How she used her real-world thoughts of entering the property market to look around discreetly, hoping she would be wrong. Hoping Dean was not hiding here after all.

But he was.

Brenda arranged it all, as per her company's USP, how she could come up with a solution for whatever problem you might have. And Dean's problem was huge.

It was called Bobby Carr.

"It was the bodyguards who did it," Alicia said. "Ernest hired your guys. Officially you are a corporate body, and that part of your business is sound. Comms solutions. But you also provide close protection officers. *Bodyguards* in layman's terms."

Brenda held the knife still.

"And don't forget how it was you who mentioned Demelza Shine's act to Jerzy. Casual, but you knew how he believed that stuff. Something Jerzy said the first time you and I met. 'She even said she wanted my anniversary dinner to go well.' I asked him. He confirmed it. You pushed him to go to this act. *Recommended* it, even. A gamble, but if he didn't take the bait you'd just have needed to wait for another chance."

"Nonsense."

"It's not cast-iron proof, but Dean will sing like a bird, and Ernest won't be far behind. They're not murderers. Are they? They wanted to do it right. The violence was all you."

The door crashed in. Calls of "Armed police" filled the house.

Brenda's eyes flashed again. From Dean to Alicia, to the knife.

The men in armour pounded down the hall, more coming in the back.

And Brenda leapt toward Dean, knife hurtling toward his throat.

Another moment in time that should have been lived in slow motion. But life doesn't work like that. It flashes by. It drags you through at such speeds you can barely hold on by your fingertips.

In one moment, you are shagging a handsome albeit evil man, the next you are giving birth, followed by a whirlwind of on-the-job training about how to keep the child alive, and then you're back at work, and promoted, and buying a house, and sending the child to school, then she's leaving, and you're all alone again.

Basically, Alicia pulled the trigger three times.

Brenda bucked twice.

She was pretty much dead by the time the third bullet hit.

CHAPTER FORTY-ONE

48 hours later

WHENEVER A POLICE OFFICER is involved in a shooting, especially the pulling-the-trigger part, that officer is relieved of duty for a while, and the incident is voluntarily referred to the Independent Police Complaints Commission, who investigate neutrally with the intent of finding an unbiased truth. They seek neither to condemn the person shot, nor exonerate the police.

Alicia agreed to an interview under caution despite officially resuming her leave. It had been a long week.

"When I reviewed the interviews taken originally, I noticed one simple timing that seemed insignificant. One that Jerzy repeated in the interview the day before the shooting.

"It wasn't that long. Just a few weeks.

"We hadn't factored in that Jerzy's affair started within the period that Linda's body was first frozen. When I realised that, I knew we needed to push as hard as we could. Who would Ernest go through all that for? Covering up? Refusing tests, refusing interviews unless under arrest? Why the bodyguards?

A FRIEND IN SPIRIT

"My biggest what-if of all: *what if Dean was still alive?*

"That question was so daft that we went with that nonsense about his daughter, which will cost the police a false arrest suit—sorry about that—but it'll be worth it.

"Brenda wanted the money and was happy to strong-arm Bobby and Linda for a steep percentage of what Bobby embezzled from the others. She used that old business, and all their connections, from Demelza through to Tomaz, to do it. And even though Bobby got away that night, they still robbed him of the money he'd stashed.

"By the way, did I mention Tomaz came home at Bobby's request? Because Bobby wanted his help getting some old mates off his back? That's right. He wanted Tomaz around as backup in case this meeting that his friends called for turned nasty. But, Tomaz being slack, got there late. Late enough for Brenda to convince him *she* was there for the same reason: backup. With Linda slaughtered and Bobby in the wind, she said his dad needed his help. They had to conceal Linda's body until the scum responsible had paid. Tomaz agreed to stay out of the way until it was all sorted, and they'd call on him when needed.

"Why not just kill Tomaz?

"No one really knows for sure. Dean *says* when Tomaz turned up as they were cleaning the mess, he asked Brenda not to kill Tomaz. Dean didn't have a plan but didn't want any more death. Said Tomaz could be useful alive, and he'd explain later. He came up with the burglary once Karen moved into his own house.

"What no one realised was that Bobby was, for real, Tomaz's biological dad. That's what tripped everything up. Bobby was one of a few candidates from back then, but they never did the test. Tomaz looked a little like Bobby, and Bobby was nice to Linda. According to Dean.

"But with this getting out of hand, Dean wanted to disappear. And with Bobby free, and presumably getting ready to hit back, that was his chance. Dean lured Bobby to the house to give him the names of everyone involved and return his money.

"Knowing Bobby would try to kill him, Brenda waited. Killed Bobby instead. He was a big guy, but not trained the way Brenda was. She did it the same way as Linda, so it hinted at Tomaz being a serial killer.

"Oh, and there was one part we guessed right. *Half* right, anyway. They set up the psychic, sent Jerzy to the pub knowing he'd never met Demelza back in the day, and it really was that simple: Dean didn't want the kids finding a corpse.

"Brenda had followed Bobby so she could tell Dean what he was wearing, and they knew Karen would ID him because she had her dad on her mind when she burst in, panicking.

"That's the other half of the psychic's part in this: make Karen believe it was her dad by instilling it in her mind before she even opened the door.

"All that was left was to ensure Karen's DNA got swapped out for someone related to Bobby, and no one would know. They'd think it was Dean who died, and the businessmen get to keep Bobby and Linda's money, and Karen is free of Jerzy and rolling in dough from Dean's insurance pay out."

"Back up a little," the man interviewing her said. He wore a hat. Indoors. He smelled of cigarettes. "Assuming this is proven, that the DNA swap took place, that means Karen is innocent in all this. She didn't know about the body switch. How, exactly, did the DNA swab get mixed up?"

Alicia wanted to be there for this bit, but she was now playing things by the book, so was happy to sit here and talk instead. "I believe DCI Murphy is taking care of that."

Murphy got Sergeant Ball's roster from the duty sergeant and took responsibility for the next arrest himself. He didn't want to wait, not with the IPCC taking statements, tying things up from the public's point of view.

He never begrudged the independent body doing its job, but he did object when they came flying in, demanding to take up officers' time without a thought for ongoing work. They might get answers in the case on which they were working, but how many others had to be delayed because of lack of manpower?

Murphy taking Cleaver out with him wasn't exactly the best idea, but he knew Alicia could keep them talking for a ridiculous amount of time. And he wanted to be the one who did this. He wanted Cleaver there.

Professional Standards would get a full report in time, but he had to see it with his own eyes, hear it with his own ears.

Ball was due to pop into a newsagent who'd been broken into the previous night and take statements and acquire the CCTV footage. He was emerging from the back room with the hard drives in evidence bags, and the owner asking when the forensics people would be arriving to dust for prints and hair fibres.

"Sure," Ball said, spotting Murphy and Cleaver. "Because every crime needs treating like murder."

"Sergeant Ball," Murphy said.

"Sir." Ball halted. Glanced at Cleaver. "What's up?"

"In all the excitement, we forgot what wrong-footed us the first time." Murphy had brought with him a copy of the evidence log from that first night. "You signed off on the swab from Karen Krasowski."

"Yeah, but—"

"Is this your signature?"

Ball looked at the sheet in Murphy's hand. "Yes, but—"

"You entered it into evidence," Cleaver said. "But I know you weren't the one handling it."

"Hey, Sarge, is it out of line if we grab a Mars Bar?" The voice came from the back room. When no one responded, Lemmy poked his head out. "Oh, hi there. Umm, I'm just wondering, is it against procedure to accept a comped Mars Bar? Mr. Shah is offering us a couple, but I wanted to check—"

Ball rushed him. "You little shit. You *dumb* little shit." He slammed the junior constable against the wall. "What have you *done?*"

Cleaver raced over and tried to break his mate's grip, choking the youngster. "Leave it. We've got him. We've got all we need."

"It's my signature."

"You didn't know." Murphy was less eager to extricate Lemmy from his mentor's hold, instead dangling the evidence log in Lemmy's face. "You swapped out the DNA swab."

With Ball's forearm pressing on his windpipe, Lemmy choked out, "Just … a journalist. She … wanted a look. A photo of the evidence. Didn't realise she'd … have it in for me…"

Ball released him and turned his back. "Little shit. Stupid little shit."

Lemmy gasped for air. "He assaulted me. You saw it. And it's on camera."

Without turning to him, Ball jangled the hard drives.

"Oh, right. But you saw him."

"I saw naff-all," Murphy said. "How much?"

"A grand." Lemmy slouched to the side. "Okay, you got me. I thought she was a reporter. She wanted a photo for an in-depth piece, but after she transferred the money, she said it was evidence of me taking bribes, and I had to swap out some evidence."

Ball's fists bunched. "You asked me, *begged* me, to let you take that swab."

"We needed a *van*. For the *band*." Again, Lemmy slouched, this time the other side. "She knew we'd be in the area, our turn on rotation, and guessed we'd get the call. I needed a bit of cash, she needed this favour."

Murphy shook his head, disgusted. "All those bloody connections, that complicated bloody plan. But if we'd known that Karen wasn't related to the corpse on day one, it would have pointed us in the right direction. It was the weak point in the plan, even weaker than using Demelza's performance in the Roundhay. If that one, dicy play failed—finding a copper willing to take a backhander—their whole intent would have crumbled."

"Sorry. Look, it won't happen again. I promise."

Ball slowly turned back to him. Murphy and Cleaver readied to fend off another assault. No telling if he'd stop in time.

"What do you think happens next?" Ball asked.

Lemmy glanced at Cleaver, then Murphy, then back to Ball. "I'll understand if you want reassigning. If you want someone else with you. Once the disciplinary hearing's over, I'll go along with whatever."

"You stupid little shit."

"What?" The stupid little shit looked genuinely confused.

Murphy twitched his head. "DI Cleaver, will you do the honours?"

"Constable Leonard Grogan, you are under arrest for the crime of receiving a bribe in public office, contrary to section—"

Lemmy's face reddened. "Arrest! What the hell?"

Ball turned and walked away. Murphy felt sorry for the man. He'd made a mistake in trusting the youngster, left him unsupervised just long enough to switch the samples. Murphy would try to mitigate Ball's part in it, but he wasn't hopeful.

———

"What about Demelza?" the IPCC officer asked. "How did Brenda find her?"

"We're not entirely sure yet," Alicia said. "We'll drill Lemmy, see if he was in deep enough to blab about that as well as swapping out the DNA. I reckon that's the most obvious. It could just be a coincidence too. I mean, she wasn't exactly hiding. A different name, yes, but she was still craving publicity for her big show in Blackpool. All Brenda needed to do was find her new stage name, wait outside one night, and follow her. Could just be a coincidence it was the same night we figured out where she was. But Professional Standards will take that on.

"In the end, it boils down to one thing: with Linda dead and Bobby on the warpath, Dean was in too deep, and wanted to protect Karen. Stopping Bobby, appearing dead himself, and supplying her with a hefty insurance payout. It must have felt like he was making amends somehow."

The officer tapped his bottom lip with a pen. "And Marissa Poole? The homeless man who was murdered?"

"Tomaz probably did it," Alicia said. "But we can't prove that without a retrial. Murphy will push for it, and we'll put some undercovers in the prison Tomaz goes to for the burglaries he's admitted."

"But why did Mrs. Poole kick it out of court?"

"We can't prove any direct corruption. Just a tendency to favour people from families with money." Alicia gathered her things. The interview was over. "Some people are just dicks."

CHAPTER FORTY-TWO

BREACHING certain codes while on maternity leave would mean a slap on the wrists for Alicia, but ignoring the fact she was under investigation for the shooting death of Brenda Williams could bring criminal charges. That was the kind of threat to keep Alicia from presuming her cuteness and track record would carry her through. It wouldn't. Fact.

A visit to Richard Hague's comatose body was not breaching anything.

She stood in silence in the private hospital, outside his door, alone. Stacey was with the Dot-Bot again, the older woman horrified when she learned Alicia had left the girl with Stan, Dot's ex-husband, for almost six hours. He wouldn't know one end of a baby from the other, she'd said.

Although Alicia defended her dad for doing so well, she felt like she was complimenting a child's painting. He'd kept her alive and fed, and only after thirty minutes of tantrum did he send the text message that pulled her out of Sheerton. His only real mistakes were putting a nappy on backward and failing to notice a deposit of spittle that had dried round the back of Stacey's head. Not bad for a first go. A little more training and Alicia would be confident of leaving Stacey with Granddad for longer.

She swore Stacey's biological father would never get close to her again, not after the first time she brought the baby here. She did wonder, since she used to speak openly to the brain-dead killer in the bed, that maybe Katie overheard her that day. Or maybe a nurse did and let something slip to Katie without realising it was a secret.

No matter.

Alicia opened the door but did not enter.

Richard had spread out even more now. His muscles were worked regularly to prevent atrophy but there was only so much a physio could do for him. His brain had been starved of so much oxygen that parts had shut down, with just enough activity to justify keeping him alive. His heart beat unaided, and he was able to fight off illnesses, and occasionally his hand twitched. He still needed a machine to keep his breathing regular, although on the occasions the doctors switched it off he went on for hours under his own steam.

If Katie chose to end Richard's crutch to breathing, he would fade away, slowly, and without pain, into oblivion. For whatever reason, Katie chose to keep milking the trust fund set up for her by the estate partially responsible for her incarceration, and to keep her father breathing.

Alicia left without a word.

She made brief, casual inquiries as to whether anyone heard from Katie, or if they'd received any mysterious mail of late, to which both answers were negative.

Before collecting Stacey and immersing herself in a new mummy routine—yoga, coffee mornings, bounce-and-rhyme at the local library, gym, parent-and-baby swims, et cetera—she had to stop once more by the place she now believed she needed to explore before setting this part of her life to rest.

Richard Hague's house.

Alicia parked directly outside, took a miniature impact drill, hefted a crowbar from the boot, then headed around back via a side passage. The boards out front were steel, and proved the same around back, including the door, which she unscrewed using the powerful electric tool. She carefully removed the metal cover and walked it noisily aside.

She still had her police ID, so if any nosy parkers popped over, she'd be prepared. Likewise, if they called the police. With the gardens not overlooked, and people around these affluent areas making little in the way of active efforts to view their neighbours, she didn't expect much interference.

The crowbar made easy work of the slab of wood over the door, levering it aside. She walked it corner-to-corner beside the metal sheet, then jimmied the door itself.

Inside, she'd expected dust to explode everywhere, and rats to scuttle for cover. What she got was a back utility that was clean and ordered. The washing machine and tumble dryer were still in place, and a basketful of clean clothes sat on the worktop. Richard's clothes. Dusty, from not being touched, but preserved.

Alicia made her way into the kitchen, which was clean except for another fine sheen of dust. The lights didn't work, and the gloom from the covered windows meant Alicia needed the pocket torch she had brought along. Again, no rats, no cockroaches.

If rodents hadn't been able to penetrate it when Richard and Katie lived here, why would they now?

A pile of pizza boxes and other takeout containers filled one corner, stacked neatly, which Alicia investigated, propping one Domino's lid up. Crusts and a little sauce remained.

"No mould," Alicia said aloud.

She headed for the hall, the carpet still intact. Just dark.

Here, the dust motes did plume, swarming in the thin beams of light allowed by the outer coverings.

Alicia called up the stairs, "Katie? It's Alicia. I know you're here. Think we can talk?"

No reply.

"I'm not mad about the letters. I promise I'm alone. I'm not here as a police officer. I want to see Katie. My friend, Katie. My…"

Alicia paused now, wondering if she should give it voice.

"I want to see you. My daughter's sister."

Pause.

Then a creak. A louder footfall. Then the scrape of a door. A torchlight flashed up there, but Alicia held herself still. A police baton sat in her belt, hidden from Katie in case she deemed it a threat, but easy enough to grab and extend it in case Katie posed a danger.

The human figure edged to the top of the staircase and shone the light at Alicia.

Katie's voice: "You're alone?"

"I promise." Alicia held her hand up to the beam, averting her eyes. "Maybe come on down? You've kept the place … neat."

Katie stepped forward, descending two steps. "No power. I can't vacuum. Or cook."

"It's your house, Katie. Not a crime scene. You're not even squatting, not really." She didn't add that social services would need to know about Katie's living arrangements, but that could wait.

Katie came down another four stairs, so she reached halfway. She lowered the beam, so it wasn't dazzling Alicia. This allowed Alicia a better look at the young woman.

Her hair was matted and untended. She wore a long-sleeved top of indeterminate cleanliness, jeans that looked dark, and a pair of slippers in the shape of rugby balls. She kept hold of the flashlight in one hand and gripped a kitchen knife in the other.

"You need that knife?" Alicia asked.

Katie looked at it as if for the first time and set it gently beside her. "Sorry. I didn't know it was you."

"People are worried about you."

"I just needed a bit of alone time."

"We all do."

"You mean ... the baby ... she really is my sister?"

"Yes." Alicia thought direct answers were best.

"I didn't imagine it?"

"No."

"Can I meet her?"

"Soon. Maybe. When you're well."

So much for direct answers.

Katie bowed her head. "It's okay. You're right. I don't feel well."

"You haven't taken your medication?"

"Makes me feel fuzzy."

"Are you taking anything else?"

Katie shook her head. "I stopped drinking when I came home." She gazed around, a blank expression, like someone waking from a dream. "No drugs. Just ... being here. Thinking."

"You sent me some letters."

"I tried a lot of things. Different stuff. Just to try and make the hurting end."

Alicia made a quick assessment and decided now, in an enclosed space, was not the time to broach the subject of a dead girl who looked an awful lot like Katie, a girl not yet identified. This girl needed empathy, not confrontation. Unless Katie brought it up, Alicia would leave it for the time being.

"I made an appointment," Alicia said. "My own therapist. I've been struggling a little myself. Since what happened last year, I've been a bit … reckless. Insubordinate. Taking dumb chances in my job. And now I don't know if I'm just a bit down and tired, or if I'm experiencing full on post-natal depression. I know I'm not myself, but … there are things I shouldn't do. I yelled at Stacey a couple of times. Been crying a lot."

"Think it's like me?"

"I think it's nowhere near what you're feeling. You were forced to kill someone last year. You watched your dad shoot himself to save you, and all the things you learned about him after … I'm surprised you're doing as well as you are. But if my problems mean I'm willing to go to a professional to check them out, maybe you could come too?"

Katie slumped, shoulders high. "I've been to shrinks. They don't help."

"Sure. But if you have a friend to go with you. If you know, at the end of it, you'll be able to visit your sister, isn't it worth it to try?"

"At the end of what?" Now Katie sounded suspicious.

"I know a place. It'll be covered on the trust that keeps your father alive. Voluntary. You check in. They keep you fed, they—"

Katie laughed stiffly. "A funny farm."

"A mental health facility. They treat all sorts, from depression, anxiety, through to full-blown addiction and behavioural disorders. And as I said, it's voluntary. You can stay as long as you like or leave if it isn't doing you any good."

Katie's body relaxed. "I don't know."

"If you complete a series of sessions, I promise I'll come visit. If you show progress, I'll bring Stacey later."

"You can't keep her from me, you know. I'm *family*."

"I can, and I will." Firm now. Not threatening. "If you had a sister, would you want someone seeing her who wasn't fully in control of her actions?"

"I'm in control."

"How long have you been here?"

That caused Katie to fall silent. She frowned in concentration. "That … doesn't mean anything."

"You've lost time. You have blank spots." Alicia just hoped one blank spot didn't include a murder. "Please. Just come with me now. No need to pack. I'll come back for anything you need."

"Now? I could get some pyjamas."

"They'll provide all you need the first couple of nights. Dr. Rasmus will be there."

"He was nice." Katie shifted. Reached for the knife.

"It's okay," Alicia said. "I can tidy that up."

Katie's hand hovered over the kitchen knife's handle, then closed, empty. She stood and took a tentative step down. Then another. And one more, pausing, before descending the remaining stairs into Alicia's arms. Katie was a bit taller, though, so Alicia hopped up on one step to provide the hug she clearly needed.

"Alicia?"

"Yes?"

"I didn't send you any letters. I promise."

"Okay. We'll work all that out soon."

There were no tears, just a long, firm embrace, before the two women walked hand in hand through the hall and into the kitchen. Katie placed her torch on the worktop and did not resist as Alicia led her, shaking with nervous exhaustion, out into the light.

Alicia Friend will return

Either follow A. D. Davies on Bookbub or your preferred retailer, or sign up to the newsletter for updates:

http://addavies.com/newsletter

NOVELS BY A. D. DAVIES

Adam Park Thrillers:

The Dead and the Missing

A Desperate Paradise

The Shadows of Empty men

Night at the George Washington Diner

Master the Flame

Alicia Friend Investigations:

His First His Second

In Black In White

With Courage With Fear

A Friend in Spirit

Standalone:

Three Years Dead

Rite to Justice

The Sublime Freedom

Co-Authored:

Project Return Fire – with Joe Dinicola

The Dead and the Missing

A missing girl. An international underworld. A PI who will not quit…

ADAM PARK IS AN EX-PRIVATE INVESTIGATOR, now too wealthy to need a job. But when his old mentor's niece rips off a local criminal and flees the UK, his life of surfing and travel comes to an abrupt end.

Using cutting-edge technology, Adam tracks the young woman and her violent boyfriend through the Parisian underground where he learns of a brutal criminal enterprise for whom people are just a business commodity.

But when the men who run this enterprise feel threatened by his investigation, Adam is propelled to more dangerously-exotic locales, where he must fight harder than ever before.

To return the girl safely and protect the ones he loves, Adam will need to burn down his concepts of right and wrong; the only path to survival is through the darkest recesses of his soul.

Three Years Dead

When a good man ... becomes a bad cop ... but can't remember why...

Following an attempt on his life, Detective Sergeant Martin Money wakes from a week-long coma with no memory of the previous three years. He quickly learns that corrupt practices got him demoted, violence caused his wife to divorce him, and his vices and anger drove his friends away one by one. On top of this, the West Yorkshire Police do not seem to care who tried to kill him, and he is offered a generous pay-out to retire.

But with a final lifeline offered by a former student of his, Martin takes up the case of a missing male prostitute, an investigation that skirts both their worlds, forcing him back into the run-down estates awash with narcotics, violence, and sex, temptations he must resist if he is to resume his life as the good man he remembers himself to be.

To stay out of jail, to punish whoever tried to kill him, and to earn his redemption, Martin attempts to unravel the circumstances of his assault, and—more importantly—establish why everyone from his past appears to be lying at every turn.

Rite to Justice

A dead cult leader. A federal cover-up. A devout cop will uncover the truth.

In the small town of Hope, Nevada, Detective Roland Recht is a deeply religious man trying to understand his place in the world. And his latest case, the murder of an isolated pastor, hits him harder than usual.

Killed within the Congregation of Saul's compound, the only witness is Lizzie, the Christian cult's newest and youngest follower, and it seems clear that a former member must be responsible.

But when Recht and his girlfriend suffer a personal and terrifying threat, it sends the investigation in a new direction, one that no one, not even his superiors or the FBI, wants him to pursue.

Rite to Justice sees a good man forced to choose between his career as a cop, and following his moral compass, whatever the consequences.

Printed in Great Britain
by Amazon